THE TRAIN
THROUGH THE TUNNEL

Horn punched the spent clip out of the 9 mm and pulled a fresh one from his jacket pocket, then jammed it into the butt of the weapon. Jacking back the slide, he mounted a set of rusting steel rungs leading to the roof of the subway car. It took him two steps before he could peer over the edge. He could see the assassin's bulky form sprawled on its side.

Focusing the red beam of the laser sight on the unmoving body, Horn crawled onto the roof of the lurching train. He moved carefully toward the big man. When he flashed the beam, he spotted the Uzi. The gun was out of the assassin's reach.

Other than a large splotch of blood, Horn could see no indication that he'd hit his target. He eased himself closer and reached out toward the man's neck to look for a pulse. The motionless right hand suddenly came to life and latched on to the barrel of the 9 mm, pushing it up and away. Out of his peripheral vision Horn saw the man's left hand swing up from behind his body with a glinting of steel in the irregular light.

"Have a taste of this, cop!" the killer grated as he drove the blade toward Horn's heart.

HORN
BLOWN DEAD
BEN SLOANE

A GOLD EAGLE BOOK FROM
WORLDWIDE.

TORONTO · NEW YORK · LONDON · PARIS
AMSTERDAM · STOCKHOLM · HAMBURG
ATHENS · MILAN · TOKYO · SYDNEY

First edition October 1990

ISBN 0-373-64002-1

Special thanks and acknowledgment to
Stephen R. Cox for his contribution to this work.

Printed in U.S.A.

BLOWN DEAD

CHAPTER ONE

TONY FRANKLIN TURNED eagerly to close the door and froze in his tracks. The confident, playful expression melted from his face. He stared as the door swung shut and a man with an open trench coat pointed the silenced barrel of a large-caliber handgun at his stomach. When he'd stepped through the threshold of his apartment, he'd felt that something wasn't quite right, but the woman had distracted him. Now the pleasurable anticipation that had been warming his blood turned to frozen slush.

"Hello, Sheila," the gun-wielding man said conspiratorially, looking around Franklin toward the blonde.

Franklin swung his head toward the couch and dazedly noticed that Sheila had sat down and wasn't looking much disturbed. "Hello, Harry. It took you long enough," she said as she stretched languorously.

Franklin turned back to the gunman. "What the hell is going on here?"

Harry smiled benevolently. "Have a seat, Mr. Franklin." He motioned to the leather armchairs flanking a coffee table.

Franklin backed toward the chairs and watched as Harry ambled to the end of the couch and flopped next to Sheila. The middle-aged man allowed his bulk to relax, and his eyes twinkled when he spoke as though he were truly in his element and enjoying himself. With the exception of the gun in his hand, the guy was almost personable.

After clearing his throat Franklin asked, trying to conceal the tremor in his voice. "What's the meaning of this?"

Harry started to say something, but looked sideways as Sheila crossed her long silk-clad legs with a show. Harry observed the length of thigh exposed and chuckled in amusement. "Look at her, will you?" Harry turned toward Franklin, shifting his bulk. He took the gun in his other hand and ran his leather-gloved fingers through his hair. "Here I am figuring a way to kill you in a manner that keeps me out of the loop, and she's making a show of her feminine charms. I never will understand the human animal—especially the female of the species." Harry laughed and shook his head in mock amazement.

Franklin felt his heart drop into a deep well. The spit in his mouth dried up instantly, and he kept clearing his throat in short choking gasps. He watched the man continue to beam at him and imagined this was what it was like to watch your own father hold a gun on you. He glanced at Sheila, who was smiling secretively, not glancing at him at all. He now knew why the blond siren had been so persistent in her recent come-ons. Franklin cursed himself for breaking his own rule: Never go to bed with a woman you work with. Now he was going to pay the price—a price far greater than the original motivation for his rule. His numb brain struggled for a reason why he'd been set up, but came up empty....

FRANKLIN'S LAST DAY on earth had started off normally, at least for a workday. He had pulled his X-Pac series Porsche off Tenth Avenue onto West 207th and gunned the turbocharged machine into the far right lane. At five-thirty in the morning there were already a half-dozen cars lined up at the employee entrance to the New York City Superplex; a three-story, five-square-block sports complex ris-

ing out of the asphalt and concrete like a city unto itself.
Framing the superstructure against the fog-covered darkness of the Hudson River was the Henry Hudson Parkway, already jammed with cars, curving around one end of
the massive horseshoe-shaped stadium like a bejeweled
snake.

Tapping his gloved fingers impatiently on the molded
wheel of the Porsche, Franklin inched his way up to the
guard gate that controlled access to the employee parking
area. After the car ahead finally cleared the gate, he pulled
forward, spun down a tinted window and stuck a coded
plastic card into the control box. A light reading Stand By
flashed in his face, and Franklin knew that sensors
embedded in the asphalt were scanning the sleek black car
from tip to stern. After ten seconds or so, Franklin's card
popped out of the slot and a green light flashed the message to proceed. He watched the spiked tire barrier drop
and entered the parking area, burning across the huge lot
reserved for lower-ranking employees of the state agencies
and contractors operating the Superplex.

Pulling into an opening marked Executive Entrance,
Franklin kept one eye on the digital clock above the radio
controls as he raced the Porsche up the winding switch-
back maze of ramps to the third level. He had punched the
stopwatch function to zero upon entry to the structure and,
as he did every working morning, was trying to break his
record of thirty-three seconds. At the same time, he knew
he was putting on a hell of a show for the security guards
who followed his one-man race on the closed circuit cam
system that left few areas in the gigantic stadium unob-
served.

In a cloud of white tire smoke, the sports car slid to
within inches of the concrete wall on which was stenciled
Franklin. A blue-uniformed security guard holding a huge

Doberman by a chain leash opened the door of the car and Franklin stepped out.

"Good morning, Mr. Franklin."

The guard's voice was impersonal, and Franklin nodded curtly and stepped to one side to watch as the guard let the dog crawl halfway into the roadster, sniffing for explosives or weapons. Pushing his half-tinted aviators up to his hairline, Franklin leaned forward to say, "Are you all done?"

The guard pulled the dog out of the Porsche. "Your car checks out okay, sir."

Franklin leaned into the car. "Look at this—the dog drooled all over the leather." He opened the glove box and flipped a switch, activating the automobile's security system. Muttering disgustedly, Franklin picked up a thin attaché case from the passenger seat and backed out of the machine. He slammed the door and swiveled around, intending to ask the man for the number of his supervisor. But the guard was ten cars down the row of parking spaces, helping a tall redheaded woman out of a new Vitron.

"What a perk," Franklin said aloud as he walked toward a set of steel double doors. Although he had gained what was considered executive status in the MMI—Man Machine Interface—Corporation, Franklin knew he was still on the lower rungs. He figured the guys who arrived for work at the Superplex up on the heliport didn't have dogs sniffing their way through the Aerospatiales and Turbolightnings.

Nevertheless, Franklin had ambitions and played the role of a minor executive in New York City well. He wore expensive Italian-cut suits, hand-stitched leather shoes and red, Wall Street suspenders. Franklin's physical appearance matched his clothes. He had bold features and sported slicked-back dark hair and a closely trimmed mustache. Franklin looked like a would-be gentleman rather than what he was: a 139-IQ computer science engineer from Philadelphia and one of the five personnel accessed to the controlling levels of CYNSYS—the computer bank through which all legalized sports betting was being designed to pass.

Franklin punched a code into the cipher lock on one of the doors and jerked on the handle as soon as he heard the electronic bolts disengage. He walked into what he and the others who worked at WCC—Wager Control Commission—referred to as the "tube." The door automatically closed behind him, and he walked ten yards down a hallway that was bathed in an eerie, soft red light. In the beginning Franklin had thought the light related to an infrared scan, but later he figured it was probably just Security's way of screwing with your mind.

In the center of the tiled floor was a flat, two-square-foot metal pad with yellow shoe prints painted on it. It faced the left wall, in which a window-size mirror had been built. Below the mirror was a telemonitor, and next to it, in the center of a six-inch square of brushed aluminum, was a single hole one inch in diameter. Franklin placed his briefcase on a small shelf and hung his topcoat on a brass hook next to the mirror. He assumed the indicated position. After he'd stared at his weather-beaten face for ten or twenty seconds, the telemonitor flashed on. Franklin looked down and was greeted by the familiar voice and pale, fat face of John Turner, the Security Day Officer.

"Good morning, Mr. Franklin. How are we today?" Turner's voice was a bored monotone. It reminded Franklin of a worn-out synthesizer.

"Fine," Franklin replied dryly, knowing Turner's next question would solicit the day code. "Thanks for asking.'' I'd be better if I didn't have to go through this bullshit, Franklin thought, waiting for Turner to continue.

''Who do you think will win the Super Bowl this year?''

''All I know,'' Franklin answered, wondering how much the person coming up with such junk got paid, ''is that it won't be Cleveland.''

Without waiting for Turner's order, he stuck the middle finger of his right hand into the hole and felt a rubberized clamp lock it into place. There was an irritating prick on the tip of the finger, and he knew his blood was being scanned and compared to the vita in his file.

''Next time,'' Turner said, sounding mildly annoyed, ''wait until I tell you to do that.''

''Sorry.'' Franklin almost laughed. He wanted to give Turner the finger, but figured it would only give the tired security officer an excuse to subject him to more of the same.

''You may proceed.'' Turner cut his video in the middle of the sentence.

Franklin grabbed his coat and briefcase and walked to a door at the end of the tube. He heard the locking mechanism being electronically deactivated as he reached out and pulled the door open. The red-lighted tube gave way to a bright, large room that served as the heart and mind of the CYNSYS Control Center, also referred to as C-cubed by those who worked there.

C-cubed was located in the ''tongue'' of the Superplex—an elevated appendage that stuck out over the playing field from the closed end of the structure. The inside of the tongue was divided into three huge wedge-shaped rooms that looked out over the field through massive curved windows. C-cubed was the center wedge, bordered on either side by VIP suites.

anklin walked to the windows and glanc out a he
d. Workers were everywhere, laying the artificial turf
and putting the finishing touches on the complex that in
two weeks would host the 2026 Super Bowl. Quite an in-
auguration, Franklin thought. He watched two men on an
elevated platform at the far end of the huge stadium test-
flying their RCDs—Remote Camera Drones—small,
camera-carrying Hovercraft that would follow the action
on the field, providing viewers worldwide with what the
World Broadcasting Network called exclusive Omni Angle Vision.

As many times as Franklin had observed the Superplex
during the course of its construction, he never failed to be
impressed by its massive size. The stadium was designed to
seat 215,000 spectators—5000 more than the Mitsubishi
Sportarena in Tokyo—making it the world's largest
sporting complex. It was three stories tall and featured a
self-contained, fully functional hospital, a thousand-man
security force that was heavily trained in riot control and
an elaborate physical security system controlled by one
bank of the CYNSYS system. In emergencies the entire
structure could be locked down in less than thirty seconds. The designers of the security system boasted that the
only way in or out of the structure during a lockdown
would be to fly.

Franklin turned around and looked upon what he lately
came to consider to be his creation: the sleek bank of
LPUs—ten black Lumoplasor Processing Units—light
plasma-based processors capable of handling more data,
and at higher speeds, than any previous configuration of
plasma-based computers. Situated in the center of the ring
of coffin-size LPUs was a dome-shaped device three yards
in diameter. This was the CORBEX memory generator, a
self-programming optical system developed by the Uni-

versity of Zurich. The CORBEX serviced each of the
LPUs and was designed to store all the betting transactions placed through the WCC. The self-programming algorithms licensed by the University of Zurich made the
memory capacity of CORBEX virtually unlimited.

It had been Franklin's idea to place C-cubed in the
tongue of the Superplex. His argument to the WCC was
that it would provide a visual real-time method of checking the game's milestones against the betting line. "Archaic, but effective," he'd stated in his proposal, which
covered several protective devices incorporated into the
design of CYNSYS. The devices were supposed to provide barriers to the electronic thieves who manipulated the
satellite signals in order to gain a margin of anywhere from
ten to thirty seconds—enough time to bet and win mil-
lions.

Franklin had been working sixty and seventy hours a
week to bring the system up and on-line in time for its de-
but, which coincided with the Superplex's inaugural game.
He and the other WCC contractors had checked out all of
the in-house wagering facilities, which consisted of "betting armrests" on each seat in the complex that allowed
spectators to place bets at any time during the game as long
as their electrocash cards scanned solvent. But Franklin
knew the in-house betting was peanuts compared to what
would be funneled in from all over the world through a
complicated mass of satellite dishes and microwave antennae fixed on the top corner of the superstructure, opposite the heliport. It had been estimated that more than three
percent of the nation's gross national product, almost five
billion dollars, would be bet during the three to four hours
it took to play the Super Bowl. The WCC estimated the
added control provided by CYNSYS would increase the
government's profit by ten to twenty percent. While

CYNSYS would eventually control all sports betting in the United States, its first test would be the 2026 Super Bowl.

Franklin spent most of the day bringing up the main system. It was well past dark when he was ready to test the system using simulated satellite feeds and a built-in test program. He turned to a tall bespeckled programmer named Alvin Toppler, who was running a self-test on the IMU—Interactive Membrane Unit—that provided to the operator the interface with the primary controller.

"Listen, Toppler," Franklin said, his tone almost condescending, "are you going to spend all night with that thing? I've got the sim ready."

Without looking at Franklin, Toppler removed the Electro-Optic Imager eyepiece from his glasses and reached to unplug the HI—Hard Input—receptacle from his neck. He dropped the eyepiece and the tiny plug on the table next to the IMU. "There you are, hot shot. Dump your brain," Toppler said, referring to one of the risks of using HI, a fiber optic link plugged directly into the operator's nervous system and tied to the main data bus of CYNSYS.

With HI, the operator's brain functioned as bus controller, directing and controlling the traffic on the data buses that linked the LPUs to the CORBEX. One problem with hard-wiring the operator's nervous system into CYNSYS or any other advanced computer system was that any significant, unplanned drop in bus traffic had a tendency to literally drain the electrical energy from the operator's spine, causing violent, uncontrolled seizures similar to those of epilepsy. In the vernacular of those who HIed, such an incident was a brain dump. Franklin had seen it happen once to a young woman who was HIed into an ancient Compulink system. She had flopped around like a fish out of water for nearly three minutes before someone got up enough nerve to jerk the plug from her neck. Franklin never saw the woman after that, but heard she had been euthanatized by her grieving family.

Franklin slid into the chair Toppler had occupied and plugged the HI into the flesh-colored receptacle on the back of his neck. He opened a drawer next to the control station and pulled out a pair of plastic eyeglasses, without lenses, and affixed the EOI to the right earpiece. Placing his fingertips on the IMU, Franklin bypassed the option for voice activation and called up the simulation program. He punched in a series of codes and watched the high-resolution flat-panel display before him come to life in six series of self-test patterns. Franklin actually experienced the bus traffic pick up as he initiated the simulation program. He leaned back in the padded chair and smiled to himself as a translucent green stripe appeared across the large screen. The first goddamn time, Franklin thought, his ego swelling with pride in his achievement. No one had ever before brought up the green line on the first try, not even the little bastard who designed CYNSYS.

The green line, through which Franklin stared, was five inches wide and ran horizontally across the screen. Within the chloro-colored green, white snow similar to video interference ran through the light at ultrahigh speed. These white flakes represented the electrocash transactions being routed through CYNSYS. By punching a code into the IMU, or by willing it via the HI, Franklin controlled the routing of more than 120 streams of electrocash, which burned through CYNSYS at thousands of dollars per nanosecond.

The majority of the electrocash was funneled into three main banks utilized by the WCC, a simple process. But the operator, Franklin in this case, could direct the stream of electronic dollars to any bank or depository in the world

or in near space that had the capability to effect a satellite
hookup. He went through a series of transfer tests, veri-
fying that his control was 99.6 percent effective.

Franklin went on staring at the green line; its snowstorm was almost hypnotic. He imagined the amount of
money that was screaming across the screen in front of his
face, pictured what it could buy. His thoughts were reflected in the feverish glaze of his eyes. Then he focused on
the EOI with his right eye and noted the favorable read-
ings on the displayed diagnostics. He felt a soft, almost
warm pull on his spine.

"Hey, Tony!" A loud, high-pitched voice broke Franklin's ethereal link with the machine. Jerking his head
around, Franklin was greeted by the perpetual grin of
Chuck, the C-cubed team's gopher.

"What is it?" Franklin asked, displaying an annoyed
scowl. He had been so immersed in the system that the interruption affected him almost like a physical pain.

"Call for you on line Q."

Franklin keyed in the commo mode and accessed Q on
the IMU. He initiated the voice mode and heard the petu-
lant voice of Sheila Walker. "I'm ready. I've been waiting. Did you forget?"

Franklin swore under his breath as he looked at his
platinum Rolex. "I'm sorry. Let's meet at my parking slot
in ten."

"Sure," Sheila answered breathily, and hung up.

Franklin had met Sheila Walker at the Superplex com-
missary. He'd had the impression that she'd picked him
out, but he didn't mind. She was curvy and sexy, and appeared to really want him, and Franklin had loved it. . . .

AS HE STARED into the gaping barrel of a silenced hand-gun, Franklin wondered how he could have been so naive, so stupid.

"You look confused," Harry said almost apologeti-cally, snapping Franklin back from his fear-induced trance to the gut-wrenching reality. "Don't worry about it. I'm a little confused myself."

Franklin wondered what the assassin meant, but he couldn't bring himself to ask for a clarification.

"Hey," Sheila said, startling Franklin. "I've done my share. I don't have to stick around. Have you got the other half of my money?" She started to move toward the door.

"I'll give it to you later," Harry answered. He looked around the apartment and focused on one wall that was stacked from floor to ceiling with the latest in sound and video electronics. Titles like *Mean Man* and a *Man And Three Women*, *Hot Stuff*, vied for space on the shelves. "Look at this junk," he said. He turned toward Franklin. "I may be dating myself, but I've heard that the one who dies with the most toys wins."

"Yeah." Sheila giggled. "He even drives a Porsche."

"Wow!" Harry raised his eyebrows, his eyes sparkling like diamonds.

"Listen, Tony. I have to go now. Sorry about this, but you're really not cut out to be a porn star."

"Hey, what are you doing?" Harry raised his voice in concern as Sheila walked over to Franklin. She bent to plant a goodbye kiss on him, but he immediately grabbed her and shoved her at Harry.

"Goddammit!" Harry jumped up and batted the woman to one side just as Franklin lunged at him. He rapped the side of the pistol behind Franklin's left ear, and the computer wizard fell to the floor like a dead bird.

"Goddamn stupid bitch!" Harry turned his flushed face toward Sheila who was getting to her feet. "Did your brain go south, or what?"

"I'm sorry, Harry! I didn't know he was going to do that." Sheila was yelling her words, pausing between each one as though her mind couldn't handle the entire sentence as a continuum.

Harry's voice dropped to its former soothing level. "That's okay, Sheila," he said, the smile returning to his ruddy face. "You just solved my problem."

"Wh-what do you mean?" Sheila stuttered and looked truly puzzled.

Harry pointed the gun toward Franklin. "I mean with him."

"I don't get it." Sheila crossed her arms and clutched the sides of her sweater.

"Well," Harry continued, turning to Franklin, who was rising to his knees, "I think I figured out how to close the loop on Mr. Franklin's death. You just gave me the idea, sweet knees."

"Oh . . ." Sheila's meek reply said she still didn't understand.

"Listen, friend," Harry leaned over Franklin as if he were talking to a child. "I know Sheila really pissed you off doing...how shall I say...my dirty work. And so—" Harry straightened "—this may be of some consolation to you."

Harry's arm was a blur as he swung the pistol toward Sheila. The silenced handgun emitted a muffled pop, a momentary pressure more than a sound, and Franklin watched in terrified amazement as a thumb-size hole appeared in the middle of Sheila's forehead. A millisecond later the rear of her skull blew out, and she tilted backward as though she were looking at something on the ceiling before dropping to the floor like a rag doll.

"Pretty good shooting for an old fart, huh?" Harry's gentle voice and kindly demeanor didn't miss a beat.

Franklin watched as Harry slowly brought the gun to bear on him. He felt his entire body quivering and fought to control his bowels.

"Take it easy." Franklin mouthed the words through lips that felt as though they'd been dusted with alum. He held up his hands in a gesture that pleaded for mercy. "I— I won't say a word about the girl. Just tell me what you want." It took all of Franklin's effort just to keep his voice from cracking.

"Well," Harry said, an almost jovial look draped across his face, "you're right. You won't say a word about the girl. And, as for what I want, I want this—" he gestured about the room with the pistol without taking his eyes off Franklin "—to look like a murder-suicide, or even a nasty sort of struggle in which you managed to rip Ms. Walker's gun from her grasp and nail her between the eyes. The only problem with this little scenario, at least for you, is that she managed to get off a round during the course of the struggle." Harry lowered the barrel of the weapon toward Franklin's abdomen. "Unfortunately it got you in the old breadbasket."

Franklin saw a flash at the end of the death tube and gasped loudly as the bullet tore into his stomach. He bent forward, clutching his midsection, the gasp changing into a gurgling, low groan.

Harry walked over, grabbed Franklin by his shirt and dragged him to the center of the room. Franklin fell on his side and curled into a fetal position. "You see," Harry said as he turned over a small end table, "there's no forced entry. By the time the cops figure out you two didn't kill each other, my trail will be as cold as you're going to be in another hour or so."

Franklin felt his life draining from the bullet holes in his body. The pain that had twisted through his guts like a red-hot poker was replaced by an almost comfortable sleepiness. He watched as Harry bent over him, smiling and saying something in that fatherly voice of his. It sounded like "Good night, my friend."

Franklin felt gloved fingers on his eyelids and welcomed the darkness.

CHAPTER TWO

HORN STOOD outside the glass doors of the district attorney's offices and watched his boss, Police Captain Dick Kelso, walk up the wide marble hall of the New York City Justice Center. He was rubbing the front of his bald head with one hand. Horn knew that wasn't a good sign. Kelso stopped in front of him and began to speak without looking up. "You know, I feel like I got a hangover and I don't even drink. Why is that, Max?"

Horn looked down at his boss, who was slowly shaking his head. He knew Kelso was going to torture him for several minutes before taking him in and letting the assistant district attorney apply her own brand of sadistic charm to his psyche. Kelso was just softening him up, functioning as the grease band for the main bill.

"Well?" Kelso looked up and over his half glasses. He had moved his hand down from his forehead and was tugging on one end of his brushlike mustache. Horn thought he looked more like a disheveled university professor than a police captain.

"How come I always feel like a kid going to the principal's office when you drag me down here?" Horn turned his head, gazing down the hallway as though he were looking for someone. He ran a gloved hand through his short dark hair and shifted his weight uncomfortably.

"It's good to see that you dressed for the meeting," Kelso remarked sarcastically. He moved back a step and looked nervously toward the doors.

Horn did stand out in the marble-and-glass hallway where men and women in crisp suits hurried along. His thigh-length leather coat, black turtleneck and field pants topping his Gore-Tex street boots were in sharp contrast to the coats and ties that streamed about the little island he and Kelso had formed.

"I'm meeting Winger right after we're through here. There's a homicide on the Upper West we're supposed to handle. You gave us the assignment."

"I know that," Kelso said, waving a hand as though his thoughts were flies buzzing in front of his face. "Speaking of Stu Winger," he added, referring to Horn's partner, "where the hell is he?"

"I told him I'd take care of things," Horn answered.

Kelso looked at his watch, barked, "Let's go," then led the way into the plush offices of the district attorney and his staff. Horn was always amazed at the contrast between the squalor in the streets, just a short distance away, and the clean, controlled environment they'd just entered.

Kelso walked up to a huge stainless-steel-and-glass reception desk where a good-looking woman in her mid-forties was thumbing through a stack of papers. "May I help you?" she asked, not bothering to look up.

"Captain Kelso and Detective Horn from Manhattan South. We have an appointment with Assistant D.A. Service."

"Yes," the woman said, finally giving them a fleeting glance. "Down the hall, third door on your right. Ms. Service is expecting you."

Kelso and Horn moved along the carpet-covered hall, then stopped in front of a smoked-glass door whose gold lettering proclaimed Christina S. Service, Assistant District Attorney. Kelso hesitated, seemingly reluctant to enter.

"Go on," Horn said, nearly grinning. He reached around his boss and pulled open the door. "She won't bite."

Horn followed Kelso into Christina Service's large office. Except for the crowded bookshelves covering the walls, it was sparsely furnished. There were no windows, which made the room look like a secluded library. In the center of the carpeted floor was a huge wooden desk, facing the door. It was covered with legal folders and papers that were stacked neatly along its perimeter, leaving a small work space in front of an empty leather armchair.

Horn noticed there were only two other chairs in the office. If he had brought Winger along, he mused, one of them would have had to stand.

"You think she forgot about us?" Horn asked, after they stood in silence for several seconds, and the two men exchanged a look that acknowledged their understanding that they were being deliberately kept waiting.

Before the captain could respond, the door behind them swung open and Christina Service walked into the room. "Good morning, gentlemen," she said, walking straight to her desk. She stood behind it without sitting and crossed her arms. "I thought there were going to be three of you."

Horn looked at the woman whom the street cops referred to as the Barracuda. She was attractive in a standoffish way. Her blond hair was conservatively styled, barely reaching the collar of her red suit and, combined with her light complexion, offered an interesting contrast to her surroundings. She was somewhat over average height, and her body's lines hinted that her physique could match a long-distance runner's. Her face was character-ized by a lower jaw whose determined set framed her expressions with a tough, independent look. But it was her eyes that Horn found intriguing. They were blue-white, pale but bright. The pupils were intense pinpoints that were strangely beautiful. Horn thought her eyes looked almost alien, exuding a cold but haunting sense of distance that seemed to attract people yet hold them at arm's length.

When Horn realized Kelso hadn't answered Service's question, he spoke up. "Yes, the third should have been my partner, but he's setting up a homicide investigation. I thought it more important that he tend to that." He no-ticed from the corner of his eye that Kelso fairly cringed at his answer.

"Very well, Detective Horn, but be certain you impart what I'm going to say to Detective Winger. Have a seat, please."

Horn was mildly impressed that she remembered their names. He, Winger and Kelso had had a similar audience three months before, when he and Winger had busted two thieves who had stolen five thousand blank electrocash cards. They ended up running the thieves' car off Frank-lin Roosevelt Drive and into the East River. Both men had drowned, and Horn, along with Winger and Kelso, had gotten an intense thirty-six-minute lesson from the assis-tant D.A. that emphasized her intolerance of "archaic police tactics" and "street cops who think they're in the movies." She had turned to Kelso, her cold blue eyes glinting like the edge of an executioner's sword, and de-livered her final words. "The bottom line, Captain, is that I can't prosecute dead men. Now get the hell out of my office."

Captain Kelso didn't seem too comfortable on this occasion, either. Horn watched his boss take his seat uneasily, not even bothering to remove his wrinkled trench coat.

Service sat down, pulled a file from one of the stacks on the desk and opened it. She folded her arms on the desk in front of her and scanned the top sheet in the folder with a calm intensity. ''Your report, Detective Horn, states that on the night of December 15 you and Detective Winger, without requesting backup support, entered a suspected string lab located somewhere on the Lower East Side and forcibly 'dismantled the operation.' Now—'' the assistant D.A. looked up at Horn ''—just what does 'dismantled the operation' mean?''

Horn waited a couple of seconds to see if Service really wanted an answer. Her stare quickly told him that he should be speaking. ''It means,'' Horn said, ''that Dispatch gave me an estimated thirty-nine-minute delay for backup. The, ah—'' Horn hesitated momentarily as though searching for the right term ''—suspects were getting ready to move a load. I made the determination that we couldn't risk losing the bust, and proceeded with the execution of it.''

'''Execution' is right,'' Service said, her eyes boring into Horn's. ''You and Detective Winger managed to 'execute' all eight of the people who were in that warehouse.''

Horn was surprised to hear Kelso interrupt, seizing what he clearly thought an advantageous opening. ''The report also states that the resistance my two detectives encountered included automatic weapons fire.''

Service glanced toward Kelso. ''I know what the report says, Captain.'' She turned her attention back to Horn. ''One of the things you have to understand, Detective, is that my office believes that ninety-eight percent of the string labs in this city are networked. We've been waiting for you people to pick off one that could hopefully provide some living leads into this network. Notice the operative word, Detective Horn, *living*.'' She leaned back in her chair without moving her eyes away from Horn. ''I can't get dead men to roll over.''

''I don't think it would have been any different if we'd had backup,'' Horn said, glancing at Kelso, who seemed to have subsided again.

''We found more than fifty miles of string in the place,'' Horn said, referring to the powerful amphetamine that had become one of the drugs of choice in New York as well as across the country. The drug was called that because it literally was string cooked in a crystal soup of amphetamine, dried, then packaged on spools like dental floss. The user would roll up a moderate length of it into a small ball, then swallow it before coughing up an end of the string through one of the nostrils. The crystal-covered piece of ''speed rope,'' as it was sometimes called, would then be pulled slowly out the nose, supposedly giving the user an unparalleled rushing sensation. The drug, though consumed in an unglamorous manner, was considered to be instantly addictive. Its use had reached epidemic proportions in inner cities across the country.

''Your point?'' Service raised her eyebrows slightly.

''The guys in that lab were holding enough string to qualify each of them for a trip to see the Black Nurse,'' Horn said, using the street term for execution by lethal injection. ''Those guys weren't going to be taken alive. They knew the kind of weight they were carrying.''

''I won't discount your point, Detective, but I want you to understand something.'' Service dropped her voice an octave, apparently to add emphasis to what she was about to say. ''There are two things this office won't tolerate from the police department in this city—corruption and the violation of anyone's civil rights."

She paused to let her words sink in, then raised her voice to its normal speaking pitch. "I'm perfectly aware of the environment you work in, but any use of excessive force by the police is considered by this office as a criminal act itself. Which means, Detective Horn, that I had considered asking for an investigation of this particular bust. There were several indications that you used excessive force in—how did you put it?—dismantling the operation. However, the quantity of the drug and the array of automatic weapons seized does lend credence to your contention that this particular group acted in the manner indicated."

Horn flashed another glance at Kelso, who had straightened up in his chair and was exhibiting an expression of mild relief.

"You were this close to an investigation, Detective Horn." Service held the thumb and index finger of her right hand an inch or so apart.

Horn felt a sudden flash of anger. He held up his gloved right hand and squeezed his thumb and index finger together. "This close," he said, not trying to disguise the anger in his voice.

"What do you mean?" Service asked.

"I mean," Horn went on, consciously keeping his anger in check, "most cops on the street come this close to getting their heads blown off on a weekly basis." Out of the corner of his eye he could see Kelso lean forward in his chair and rub his eyes as though he were enjoying an especially stiff migraine.

Horn had expected Service to fire back one of her withering remarks. But she leaned back in her chair, hands on the padded arms, and to his surprise, just stared at him. Her expression was a mixture of mild shock and something akin to admiration. Horn felt the anger leave as quickly as it had come, and he relaxed.

Finally she looked away. "I'm sure you're right, Detective Horn." Christina Service stood and pushed back her chair. Horn followed suit, tapping Kelso on the shoulder as he got up.

"Huh?" Kelso said, his eyes red from the rubbing he'd been giving them.

"Thank you for coming," Service said simply.

"Oh, yes." Kelso struggled to his feet, seemingly confused by the abrupt end to the meeting. "Are there any, ah, action items or anything we need to do?"

Service ignored Kelso's question and turned to Horn. "Detective Horn, after our first meeting I reviewed your service record. Your career as a police detective has included a number of incidents best described as extreme." Service paused before asking, "What do you get out of this?" She raised her eyebrows slightly, and clarified her question by adding, "Being a cop, I mean."

Horn stared at the woman and realized she most likely knew he wouldn't have an answer to her question. Why did she ask it? An almost nonchalant shrug was his only response, then he stepped around Kelso, walked to the door and pulled it open. "You coming, Dick?"

"Good day, Ms. Service," Kelso said as he walked swiftly to the door.

Horn could feel the blue eyes of the assistant D.A. on the back of his head as he followed Kelso out.

Once they made the main hall, the captain turned and stopped Horn in his tracks. "Horn, you are one lucky son of a bitch." Kelso pushed his chest up toward Horn's, yelling in his face, "She was doing just fine. She was only going through one of her 'police ain't worth a shit' lectures and was nearly at the end, for chrissake. What the hell were you trying to do? She had us by the balls! Were you trying to see if she would yank them off?'' Kelso's voice had gradually become higher and thinner, and suddenly he choked up and started coughing.

Horn grabbed the police captain by the shoulders and firmly patted him on the back. "You okay?" Horn asked the still-sputtering man. "There's a water fountain next to the wall over there. Go get a drink." He gave the captain a gentle shove toward the fountain and followed slowly.

Kelso drank thirstily, then looked up plaintively. "See what you do to me, Horn?"

Horn grinned crookedly. "What do you mean? I didn't do a thing to you. You did it to yourself. Or what's closer to the truth, she did it to you!" Horn pointed a thumb toward the D.A.'s office.

"Bullshit." Kelso glared at Horn before starting down the hall. Horn followed, and as they walked, Kelso turned, shaking his index finger. "Don't get me pulled into her office again. You got that straight?"

They went past the uniformed security guards and through the double doors that led to the street. The sky was gray and the wind was cold as they paused outside the doors. Dirty slush covered the sidewalk, exhaust fog from the traffic in the street rolled up and then disappeared, and people walked hunched over. In the winter everyone in New York City was old.

"There's your partner." Kelso pointed toward a dirty unmarked Chrysler Elint that was parked in a No Parking zone.

Horn could see Winger waving at them from inside the vehicle. Then he half turned toward Kelso, who was turning up the collar of his coat. "Don't worry about Service," Horn said, smiling at his boss encouragingly. "I think she just likes me."

"Yeah," Kelso answered, finally breaking into a grin. 'She sure as hell likes you. I've heard she also likes sleeping with Great Danes—does that tell you anything?"

"Yeah." Horn laughed. "I guess I better learn how to howl at sirens." He patted Kelso on the shoulder then turned and walked quickly to the Elint. As soon as Horn had hopped in and slammed the door, Winger stepped on the gas and wheeled the big machine into traffic.

"How did the meeting with the Barracuda go?" Winger asked as he weaved in and out of the late-afternoon traffic that crawled along Amsterdam Avenue.

"Not bad," Horn answered. "I don't think she's as anticop as everyone seems to believe."

"Yeah?" Winger sounded skeptical as he cut in front of a battered Ford. The driver laid on his horn and flipped Winger the bird. The young cop waved almost casually, smiling in the mirror. "You gotta be shitting me—the blond Barracuda? I think you're ready for the endless bar stool, partner." Winger laughed, still enjoying the term he'd coined for police retirement.

Horn smiled. He liked Winger. The young cop had been his partner for the past six months. At first, understandably, he had been skeptical of taking on a new partner after his partner of more than eight years was killed in a violent shoot-out in the Bronx. Horn had even requested that he not be assigned a partner, but was told the only way to work without one would be to take a desk job. According to the department's personnel director, CSUs—Crime Suppression Units—were two-man operations, with no exceptions.

Winger had been a pleasant surprise for Horn. In the short time they'd worked together, the young cop had gained Horn's respect with his consistency, reliability, innovative methods and guts. Horn had accepted that he could count on Winger, and though he didn't realize it, Winger was the only one he did trust.

Horn thought his partner looked much younger than his twenty-four years. At forty, Horn looked forty, though solid and healthy. Winger, however, stood five-ten, weighed less than 150 and had closely cropped, sandy-colored hair and a boyish face that wore a nearly perpetual grin. He looked like a mischievous teenager. Only one characteristic was inconsistent with that image: Winger had a heavy five o'clock shadow twenty-four hours a day.

Winger was good-natured with a crazy, offbeat sense of humor. Horn was constantly amazed at the insane one-liners and jokes his partner would come up with in even the tightest, most dangerous of situations. But Horn didn't mind, for the younger cop's humor didn't detract from his performance.

While Horn's skills centered around an instinct-driven, no-frills, direct approach to dealing with crime, Winger was more technologically oriented. Most of the time, beneath his thigh-length, black leather topcoat, one could find a wide range of the latest small arms, exotic weaponry and pyrotechnics. These Winger hung from a modified webgear that was strapped in an X-pattern between his shoulders. Winger himself had created a number of the weapons. When Horn commented on the arsenal his partner carried around beneath his coat, Winger tended to laugh and kid him about the "ancient hog leg" he insisted on carrying.

"Tell me about this case," Horn said as Winger pulled off Amsterdam and headed east on 52nd Street.

"Man and a woman. Looks like a struggle occurred and they both wound up dead." Winger stopped at a light and looked over at Horn. "No sign of forced entry. They were discovered around noon by the landlord, who was letting an electrician in to work on the furnace.''

''When did it happen?''

''The bluesuiters checked with their employer, and they were both at work all day yesterday. Therefore—'' Winger held a finger in the air, grinning ''—it happened sometime between six or so yesterday afternoon and noon today.''

''You said 'employer,''' Horn said as Winger accelerated when the light turned green.

''Yeah, they worked at the same place.''

''Were they married? Living together?''

''Not as far as I know. She had her own place near the park. We're going to the guy's apartment—that's where it happened.'' Winger turned onto Third Avenue and drove a block and a half to a section of the street that had been turned into an improvised parking lot for police cars, an ambulance and a crime lab van. He parked the car beside the van.

It had begun to drizzle, and the wet yellow plastic Crime Scene tape that was strung about the entrance to the relatively swank apartment building reminded Horn of forsythia in the spring. He thought it odd that the only bright splash of color he could see on the otherwise gray street was a ribbon flagging the scene of a murder.

''Don't worry,'' Winger said as he reached over and pulled the vehicle's police placard out of the glove box. ''They haven't touched either one of the bodies.'' He placed the plastic card on the dashboard and got out of the car.

Horn followed, and both of them made their way to the apartment. When he saw Police Sergeant Jim Raece firmly installed before an apartment door, Horn knew why Winger was so confident that the bodies hadn't been disturbed. Raece was a tough old bird, and his insistence on following police procedure to the letter was nearly legendary.

"Hello, Jim. Looks like you got a bunch of antsy customers." He looked down the hall toward a group of ambulance attendants and evidence technicians waiting to be admitted to the crime scene.

"Yeah, but don't worry about it." The grizzled, big-nosed cop smiled beneath the bill of his plastic-covered hat. "They get paid by the hour." Raece turned the knob and swung open the door so Horn and Winger could enter.

"Did the landlord touch anything in here?" Winger asked, stepping in front of Raece.

"He says he didn't. You want to talk to him?"

"Later," Winger answered. "Tell the guys there—" he nodded toward the small crowd in the hall "—to go get coffee. Give us about an hour."

"No sweat," Raece answered.

Horn heard Winger close the door as he stood and surveyed the scene. The dead man was curled up on his side next to the couch. A dark, almost black stain spread out from his midsection on the carpet. It framed his stiff body, which formed a rigid curve much like a clenched fist, as though he'd died in extreme pain. Horn knelt next to the outstretched hand and examined the .38 snub-nosed pistol that was still clutched in the dead fingers.

"Look at this," Winger said, standing over the woman, who was stretched out on her back. "She got it square between the eyes."

Horn walked over to look at the second body. "What do you think?" he asked.

"Well," Winger answered, glancing around the room, "the place is a mess. Maybe they had a fight, she shot him in the stomach, he pulled the weapon away form her and plugged her. Could've been some kinky sexual thing that sparked it. Look at this.'' Winger turned and gestured at several rows of video disks on the shelves of the entertainment center that covered a whole wall. "Mostly porno."

Horn rubbed the stubble on his chin. He went back to the man's body and pushed it over slightly with the toe of his boot. The shirt was covered with crusted blood, and Horn could see where the bullet entered the upper abdomen.

"What you say is certainly a possibility," Horn mused aloud as he looked back toward the woman. "But it's eight or ten yards from here to there. The guy was a pretty good shot, especially with a bullet in the guts."

"Yeah," Winger said, "and something else doesn't quite jibe."

"What's that?" Horn asked, kneeling by the woman's coat, looking at the employee badge clipped to the collar. He glanced back at the man and noticed a similar badge clipped to the pocket of his suit coat. Then before Winger could answer his question, he said. "I see how the blue-suiters figured out where these two worked."

"Huh? What did you say?" Winger looked over at his partner.

"They both worked for MMI, the Wager Control Commission specifically. They have the same type badges."

"That's right." Winger leaned against a wall and studied the scene. "Both of them worked out at the new Superplex."

"Now, what were you saying?" Horn looked up. "What doesn't jibe here?"

"This place, these two." Winger gestured toward the two dead bodies. "The gun doesn't fit."

"Go on," Horn said as he walked to the door and examined it for marks of having been forced open or tampered with.

"I'll bet you a cold beer that we're not going to find ammo, cleaning equipment or even a holster... here or at the chick's place." Winger got down on his hands and knees beside the dead man. He stared at the weapon for more than three minutes, cocking his head occasionally. "He's holding the damn thing correctly," he finally said before flopping down on his side directly in front of the pistol. Winger gazed intently into the barrel of the weapon, his eye within two inches of the deadly orifice.

Horn watched his young partner for a couple of seconds before saying, "I hope the guy has finished going through rigor mortis."

Winger peered up at Horn. "Very funny," he said, reaching into his coat. Horn watched him shine the beam of a small flashlight into the gun barrel. Finally Winger stood and put the light back in his coat.

"Well?" Horn asked, raising his eyebrows slightly.

"The gun bothers me," Winger answered, a puzzled look etched on his face.

"Check out the kitchen, I'll do the bedroom," Horn answered. He figured his partner was running the data he'd gathered on the weapon through his brain and would let him know if anything connected.

In the bedroom Horn wasn't surprised at what he found. Given the library of pornographic videos in the living room, he figured the male victim for some type of swinger. There was a mirror over the round bed, and a strange collection of straps and restraining devices hung from hooks in the ceiling. A video camera was mounted on a tripod at what could be considered the foot of the bed. Horn noticed the remote control was on the nightstand next to several bottles of colored oils and a set of old-style handcuffs.

Horn checked out the large walk-in closet, which was filled with expensive suits and shoes. He found a metal file box in one corner of the closet, containing the man's automobile registration, insurance papers and tax records. So far, Winger's right, Horn thought. He hadn't come across anything even related to a firearm.

When Horn walked back into the living room, Winger was once more standing over the dead man, his chin in one hand, staring intently at the gun. "Anything in the kitchen?" Horn asked.

"No." He's got an old 486 computer in there, but it's broken or power-coded. I couldn't get it to come up. Did you check out the bathroom?"

"I'll leave that to the lab," Horn answered. "Don't think we'd find anything anyway. I want to check out the woman's place. Did she live alone?"

"I don't know." Winger was staring at the body again. Horn realized the young cop was lost in his own thoughts. Then Winger added, "I need to T some E."

It was Horn's turn to look puzzled. "What do you mean?" he asked.

"Touch some evidence."

Horn raised his eyebrows in mock surprise. "You got an idea?"

"Yeah," Winger answered. "But I'd prefer to show you instead of telling you about it."

"Go ahead," Horn said casually. "Just don't take it out of his hand."

"What do you mean?"

"The gun," Horn said. "You haven't been able to take your eyes off the thing since we got here."

Winger grinned. "You know what turns me on, don't you?"

Horn watched as Winger walked into the kitchen and reappeared with a clean sheet of paper. He folded it into a four inch square before crouching next to the gun hand. Winger reached into his coat and pulled out the flashlight again. Using the folded paper, he lifted the barrel of the weapon and slipped the flashlight under it so that it was elevated an inch or so. He then placed the tip of his boot on the butt of the weapon, which extended an inch below the pale purple palm of the dead man. Winger took the folded paper and placed it flat against the barrel, turning it carefully as if to get an imprint.

Apparently satisfied that he'd gotten what he wanted, Winger removed the flashlight from beneath the barrel and stood up, stepping back as he did. Horn watched him put the flashlight in his coat then carefully fold the paper so that the portion he'd rubbed against the end of the barrel was on the inside. He tucked the paper into a pocket on one of the upper sleeves of his coat, and buttoned the pocket.

"Aren't you going to show it to me," Horn asked, "whatever the hell it is?"

"Not yet," Winger answered excitedly. "Let's go."

"All right, but get the woman's address before we leave."

"I already have it. Raece gave me the fact sheet."

After turning over the apartment to the crew from the lab, they drove down Third Avenue toward the Lower East Side. Winger kept looking around as he drove, which prompted Horn to ask, "Are you looking for something or just exercising your neck?"

Winger laughed, but didn't answer the question. Instead, he said, "I think the boys in the lab will figure this out, but it'll probably take two or three weeks. By then the trail will be so cold it'll be like trying to track a worm through a plate of pasta."

Before Horn could comment, Winger jerked the Elint into a driveway that accessed a vacant lot next to a burned-out housing project, which was slowly crumbling into the surrounding rubble of the abandoned neighborhood. "This is what I'm looking for," he said, bringing the big sedan to a stop amid the mud and garbage.

"What the hell are you doing?" Horn finally asked as Winger pulled a snub-nosed revolver from inside his coat.

"Okay," Winger answered. "See this?" He held up the handgun, but didn't wait for Horn to answer the obvious. "Don't worry, it's not a throw-down. It's just a, uh, spare."

"What's the point?" Horn was a little taken back by his partner's excitement.

"Well," Winger breathed as he quickly checked the cylinder of the snub-nose, then rolled down the fogged driver's window. "This is a similar weapon to the one the stiff had back there. It's not *exactly* the same, but it's close. The gun in the apartment was an old Smith & Wesson .38 that's been around about five hundred years. This—" he held up the blue steel death handle "—is a German-made replica of the old Police Special .38. It's barrel is about six millimeters longer than the S & W back at the ranch. But it's close." Winger grinned.

"What about the ammunition?"

"Good question. But the weapon used in the crime still had four lead-tipped hollowpoints in its cylinder. I counted them. I have lead hollows in this death-dealing device with the same hexagon-shaped hole that was in the rounds of the murder weapon.''

"Think it matters?" Horn asked.

"Not that much," Winger answered as he pointed the revolver out the window and fired off two quick rounds into a pile of broken bricks and empty wine bottles.

The sound of the two gunshots echoed in the winter air like sonic booms. Horn instinctively looked around and saw three rag-covered men standing around a blackened fifty-five-gallon drum in which a smoky fire was burning. Only one of the trio looked up at the sound of the gunshots. The other two continued staring into the drum as though nothing had happened. Horn looked over at Winger who had removed the piece of paper from the pocket on his coat sleeve.

"Watch this," Horn's partner ordered. He carefully pressed the smoking end of the weapon to the square of paper and turned it for a couple of revolutions against the barrel. When he finished, Winger flipped a switch on the dash, bringing to life the interior lights of the car. Winger stuck the paper in Horn's face. "See?"

"Yeah, I see," Horn answered, looking at a distinct black doughnut shape formed by the carbon his partner had created at the end of the gun barrel.

"Well, look at this shit." Winger unfolded the paper and held it up.

Horn looked at a faint image on the paper that resembled a circle made by a dull pencil and then erased. "Go ahead, partner." Horn smiled, knowing Winger was enjoying the drama he was creating.

Indeed, Winger seemed highly pleased with himself. "What does this tell you?"

"The weapon in the apartment was fired with a silencer on it," Horn answered.

Winger's face turned as black as the paper he was holding. "Yeah," he finally mumbled, no longer so enthusiastic, "it had a silencer."

CHAPTER THREE

"IT'S A DAMN GOOD PROPOSAL, Ashley. The kid is sharp. I mean he's really sharp." John Mayo ran one of his pudgy fingers around the inside of his shirt collar and leaned forward in his chair. "I'm telling you, Ashley," he went on, lowering his voice, "nearly three billion dollars is going to pass through CYNSYS in about three hours. Hoke says we can tap at least one-third of it."

"There's no need to speak as though we're in an alley, John." Ashley Fine looked across the desk at her executive assistant. "Frankly, I'm a little concerned that you're ready to jump into this scheme without sufficient planning."

"It's been planned quite meticulously, I assure you." Mayo nervously folded and unfolded the end of his tie. "That's why I've set it up for Hoke to brief the plan. He calls it the Green Mole Project."

Ashley noticed that tiny beads of sweat had formed on Mayo's forehead. Lately, her overweight assistant's nervous mannerisms and sloppy demeanor had begun to annoy her. Although Mayo wore expensive, fashionable clothing, he always seemed to be on the verge of slipping into a borderline slovenliness.

"Is that name supposed to mean something to me?" Ashley waved her hand as if she were puzzled. "Because if it is, John—" she dropped her hand to the desk and stared at Mayo, her eyes as cold and uncaring as steel hammers "—you've just cornered the market on useless pretense besides wasting my time."

Mayo leaned back slightly and cleared his throat. "I'm sorry, Ashley, I was just trying to present an opportunity that would, ah, be highly profitable for NEXUS." His voice was soft, almost a whisper.

"You sound like a whipped dog, John. Honestly, if you get any more obsequious I'm going to lose my breakfast." Ashley stood and shook back her silver hair. "I don't know what the hell you've got jammed into your head besides paranoia, but it's beginning to affect your productivity as well as get on my nerves."

Ashley walked around to the front of the desk and stood before Mayo, her arms crossed and locked, her legs slightly apart. Although her face and hair correctly pegged her age to be late fifties, her body said she was in her twenties. It was lean and muscular. Even under the conservative gray business suit, her tightly packaged form suggested that she pumped iron as well as pumped cash into the corporate coffers of NEXUS INTERNATIONAL.

"I'll watch the briefing," Ashley said simply, staring down at Mayo as though he were a school kid. "I'll watch it from here on the closed circuit."

Mayo breathed a sigh of relief and looked up at her, avoiding direct contact with her eyes. "What time?" he asked. "I've got him standing by in the conference room on the eightieth floor."

"Five minutes," Ashley answered.

Mayo had to push back his chair in order to stand, for Ashley made no move to get out of his way. He smiled awkwardly. "Thank you. You won't be sorry, I promise." He backed toward the door, stuttering a little as he said, "Five minutes." He paused, his hand on the handle. "Where do you want me?"

"In here," Ashley answered. "Bring coffee."

Mayo looked confused. "Excuse me?"

"Bring coffee, John," Ashley repeated as a small smile played around her lips.

"Okay. Coffee." Mayo's voice was meek and faded with him out the door.

Ashley walked back behind her desk and pressed a button on an inlaid console. A panel on the opposite wall dropped to reveal a large screen. She leaned over and punched the intercom on the televideo. "Mark, what channel is the video for the conference room on eighty?"

"The one by legal?" a youthful male voice came back. "I think so."

"Twenty-seven."

Ashley released the button and punched the indicated number into the closed-circuit controls. Immediately the screen displayed the image of a short, smartly dressed man in his mid-thirties. "This, I assume, is Mr. Hoke," Ashley said as Mayo reentered the office carrying a service tray with coffee.

"Yes," Mayo answered. He walked across the room and set the tray on her desk. "Anderson Hoke. He's set to go on my cue."

Ashley held up a hand and concentrated on observing Hoke, who paced about the conference table, looking more charged with energy than nervous. There was a slight Oriental or Asian cast to his features, and Ashley felt particularly drawn to the man's eyes, which were dark brown to the point of appearing black. They were constantly moving as though seeking a target and lent him an animallike vitality.

"Where does he work now?" Ashley asked without turning toward Mayo.

"MMI," Mayo answered as he poured coffee. "He's the chief systems engineer for that division. He was the one who led the CYNSYS design team."

"I see," Ashley turned to Mayo. "Do they require psy-files at MMI?" she asked.

"Yes. Psychological profiles are part of the background and security check."

"Can he be trusted?"

Mayo suddenly erupted in a nervous titter. "Excuse me," he said, trying to bring himself under control.

"Care to clue me in on the joke?" Ashley felt herself growing irritated.

Mayo cleared his throat. "It's just that we're talking about stealing nearly a billion dollars and...and..." Mayo appeared to sober up as fast as he'd lapsed into laughter. "I'm sorry. He's been tested and approved for access to Level Three data."

"That's better," Ashley stated. "If you expect me to approve this scheme, you'd better start treating the project a little more seriously. I've seen programs with profit potentials of similar magnitude get in trouble because people like you—" Ashley paused to emphasize the *you* "—lost track of the details."

"I understand," Mayo said. "This is Hoke's plan. He first briefed Al Gorman who in turn approached me. I was skeptical at first, just as I'm sure you are...." Mayo chanced a brief smile, but Ashley's face remained expressionless, staring at her executive assistant. "However, Hoke has made it almost foolproof." Mayo clasped his hands and lowered his voice. "He designed the system with a—" Mayo paused to search for the correct words "—*secret window* or *door*, if you will, for this very purpose."

"How do you know he wasn't planning to use the secret window for his own means?" Ashley asked. Then before Mayo could answer she added, "Why didn't he approach us with the plan during the CYNSYS design phase?"

Mayo looked more nervous than puzzled. "That's a good point."

"I'll tell you why," Ashley said as she sat down and picked up her coffee. "I did some checking on Mr. Hoke. While he did lead the design of the system, one of the other engineers on the team was given the assignment of actually implementing CYNSYS. In effect, Mr. Hoke couldn't follow the hardware off the paper." Ashley took a sip of coffee. "He no longer has physical access to the system." Ashley motioned for Mayo to sit in a chair next to the desk.

"I see." Mayo's face suddenly took on a look of concern. "He didn't reveal his plan earlier because he thought he'd get the installation and implementation assignment."

"I think these points are all rather obvious. I also get the feeling you're more intimately involved with the project than you would have me believe. Why is that?"

Mayo shifted his bulk and cleared his throat, but nothing came out of his mouth. "Well?" she asked, raising her eyebrows slightly.

"I, ah, guess I don't understand your question," he replied, rolling his head around as though his neck were stiff.

"You will," Ashley said calmly. "I don't run my operations blindly. Let's proceed." She nodded toward the screen.

Mayo hesitated, then leaned over and punched one of the buttons. "Anderson, this is John. Please proceed with your briefing. The video will be one-way."

Hoke turned and faced the camera. His hyper state vanished and was instantly replaced by a cool confidence.

He looked like a commander on the bridge of a destroyer. "Brief the camera?"

"That is correct. Please begin."

"Very well." Hoke stared at the camera for several seconds before picking up a small device from the conference table. He aimed it toward the wall of the conference room at the far end of the table. A large screen was suddenly illuminated with a view cell displaying the legend Company Classified Project, Level 3. "I assume this audience consists of personnel accessed to this level." Hoke gestured to the screen and looked at the camera.

"Yes, the person I mentioned—" Mayo broke off his sentence when Ashley held up a hand and shook her head firmly. He got the message. "Suffice it to say that all here have the proper clearance."

"Very well." Hoke brought up the next cell. "Please feel free to ask questions as we go along." He turned and gestured toward the first bullet on the screen. "On January 25 it is estimated that 4.8 billion dollars in electrocash will be funneled through the New York Gaming Commission's control center in the Superplex. We refer to this massive betting line as the green line. It nets in all of the continental United States, Canada, Great Britain, the outbound states and most of the near-space colonies, which are too numerous to list here." Hoke waved his hand down the long list of locations on the screen.

"What about the arrangement with China? I thought they were supposed to get netted in this year." At Ashley's question, Mayo glanced at her in mild surprise.

Hoke also appeared surprised, at least for a moment. Ashley watched his expression change, to reflect a subtle enthusiasm. She knew her voice had keyed him in on the fact that he was talking to the one person who could approve his plan.

"That's true," he answered, "but China has fallen into the same bureaucratic mess that Russia did four years ago when they were given the opportunity to participate." He shrugged before continuing, "And believe it or not, not everyone places as much importance on professional football as do the North Americans."

"Please continue," Ashley directed.

Hoke brought up the next slide. "I have developed a program that has the following features:

"It leeches to the controlling program without being detected by the embedded security software. It operates at a speed compatible with the hyperhertz operation of the LPUs. It's controller-initiated via HI. And it's flash-papered out in an emergency, leaving no residuals and is impossible to trace."

Switching to a slide that was titled Timing Sequence, Hoke asked, "Any questions thus far?"

"Ah, yes." Ashley leaned forward, crossing her arms on the desk. "Please go back to the previous view cell."

When her request was accomplished, Ashley remarked, "I may not be formally educated in compuscience, but I know enough to understand your point 'controller-initiated via HI.'"

Hoke turned and looked at the screen. "Yes, what's the question?"

"Who is the controller who will actually implement the tapping of the green line. I understand it has to be accomplished in real time."

"That's correct," Hoke answered. "I was under the impression that Mr. Mayo had already cleared that part of the plan with you."

Ashley turned and fixed her gaze on Mayo. His face had changed from a crimson blush to a deathly white.

"I have a slide that covers the personnel problem a little later in the briefing. Would you like me to go over that now?"

Ashley slowly returned her attention to the screen. "No, please continue with the intended sequence."

Hoke brought back the Timing Sequence slide. "In addition to the postimplementation accessibility of the software, one of the features I managed to get designed into CYNSYS is a little algorithm. It will compress the cash flow at a designated time which will coincide with our tapping of the green line." He traced his finger along a bell-shaped curve. "This shows that over the approximately four-hour period during the Super Bowl when the betting window is open, the heaviest betting will occur in the third hour—which coincides with the last part of the third quarter and the entire fourth quarter of the game. My compression algorithm will lag the betting up to this third hour. Then, when the operator initiates via the HI, it will compress what was lagged into the third hour. It will increase the cash passing through that window by an estimated eighteen percent." Turning toward the camera, Hoke smiled slightly. "I'm rather proud of that feature."

"What does it mean in terms of what we might be expected to net?"

Hoke pointed to a set of figures below the graph. "The plan is to remain in the loop for the entire third hour. Without the compression algorithm we would siphon in the neighborhood of nine hundred to nine-fifty."

"Million," Ashley stated more as a completion of Hoke's sentence than a question or statement.

"Correct." Hoke turned his head slightly and nodded. "*With* the algorithm, however, our figures end up in the range of 1 to 1.2 billion.'' Hoke turned around as though he were expecting someone to applaud.

"Get on with the briefing, Mr. Hoke," Ashley said curtly. "I'm well aware of the magnitude of your proposal."

Hoke appeared slightly disappointed as he brought up a complicated cell that looked like a cross between an intricate schematic and a spiderweb. It was titled Trace Overlay. "This depicts the route the electrocash will take after we extract it from the green line." Hoke swept a hand across the maze of lines and loops. "You can see it's quite elaborate. I used a program generator to split what we tap into six different paths. Each path gets transferred a minimum of twelve times and eventually winds up in these three offshore banks." Hoke pointed to three blocks on the right side of the chart. "The probability of any person or any machine tracing this activity is less than one-one hundredth of one percent. Once we pull out and I initiate the flash paper code, the probability drops to zero in two nanoseconds."

"Please go on to the discussion concerning what you referred to as the 'personnel problem.' " Then Ashley reached over and pressed the mute button on the console. "Do you want to brief this portion, John?" She looked at Mayo, whose face was etched with worry and fear. When Hoke began speaking, Ashley released the button momentarily, telling him to stand by.

Ashley stood up but kept her finger on the mute button. "You see, John, I like initiative in my employees, but not when it comes to murder."

"Wait a minute." Mayo held up his hands, shaking his head. "I can explain—"

"I had a report this morning that two MMI employees were found dead yesterday. One of them happened to be the engineer in charge of CYNSYS operations. Now it's more than just coincidental that Mr. Hoke's plan calls for replacing that engineer with himself."

"I wanted to have everything in place. I was betting you would approve the plan."

"You were betting I would condone murder?"

"We had to take him out," Mayo explained in a voice that was almost pleading. "The state security requirements won't allow changes in personnel accessed to that level unless the circumstances are extreme."

"You're missing the point, John. I'm not discussing *why* you did it, I'm telling you that you overstepped your charter."

Mayo squared his shoulders lightly, as if to give himself some courage. "I figured with stakes this high, the means were justifiable. After all, it's common knowledge what went on when your son ran Titus Steel."

Ashley's tone dropped to the freezing range. "I don't give a good goddamn what you've heard. We're out of the metal business and I don't operate the way my son did."

"Come on, Ashley. You agreed to hear the briefing. In any case, what's the difference crime-wise between killing someone and ripping off a billion dollars?"

"Get out of here," Ashley spit. "Go wait in your office. I'm going to talk to our lawyers and figure out just how much trouble we're really in." She released the mute button. "Mr. Hoke, the briefing is concluded. We'll give you a disposition on your proposal in twenty-four hours." Without waiting for a reply, Ashley punched another button and the screen went dead.

"Does he know that you already had the individual killed?"

"Of course he knows," Mayo answered as he stood. "It's a matter of business. Your response, frankly, bothers me."

"It should," Ashley said flatly. "Now go."

As soon as the door closed, Ashley called, "You may come in now, Mr. Steller."

A side door near the back of the office opened and a man in a black leather trench coat entered. Despite herself Ashley felt a chill run up her spine. Steller was a well-built man whose massive body looked like a piece of olympian sculpture. His short blond hair topped his head like the bristles of a stiff brush. He stood well over six feet, which made his huge chest appear almost normal in size. In contrast to his seemingly perfect body, Steller's face looked as if it had been roughly hewn out of stone. Set in this facial war zone were two eyes that shone like those of a striking cobra.

"Did you hear everything?" Ashley asked as Steller walked to the desk and sat on its edge.

"Word for word." Steller's voice was midrange bass, gravelly. "What are you doing with Mayo, anyway?" He didn't wait for Ashley's answer. "We knew what he was up to from day one. Why did you come down on him so hard?"

Ashley sat in her chair and pushed it away from the desk so she wouldn't have to tilt her head at such an extreme angle in order to look at Steller. "He made the decision to have those two people killed, and it was a decision based on responsibility that I did not delegate to him."

"Not that I care," Steller remarked as he shrugged and held the palms of his gloved hands up in a mock gesture of surrender. "But I'll give Mayo credit for one thing."

"What's that?"

"The hitter he hired did a class job," Steller said with professional admiration. "I shadowed his entire setup and execution. I was impressed." Steller touched his fingertips to his chest.

"Oh?" Ashley raised her eyebrows in true surprise. "*You* were impressed?"

"Yeah," Steller said, clearly at ease with Ashley. "Harry Trower looks like somebody's grandfather. He's out of St. Louis and speaks with that hillbilly sort of accent. I like his style."

"What about Hoke?"

"What do you mean?" Steller seemed caught somewhat off guard by Ashley's question.

"Did you check him out?"

Steller nodded. "Yeah. He's an interesting sort. Seems to be without conscience."

"Did you figure out what they *really* planned to funnel out of CYNSYS?"

"One estimate was more than one and a half billion. I'm certain that Hoke underestimated his figures to Mayo, then Mayo had him cut them even further."

"I expected nothing less," Ashley said. "I don't hold their motivations against them."

"What's the next step?" Steller prompted. "How do we deal with Hoke?"

"I'll take care of that. We're going ahead with the plan."

"And Trower?"

"What do you suggest?"

"Keep him around. He may be useful." Steller smiled crookedly. "I've already tuned him in on who he reports to."

"Very well," Ashley said. "But take care of Mayo."

"No problem," Steller answered matter-of-factly. "He'll be gone by midnight."

CHAPTER FOUR

TWENTY-EIGHT MINUTES after being dismissed in the middle of his briefing, Hoke walked into a steamy, run-down bar on the edge of the Bronx, just across from the long-abandoned Polo Grounds. The sign over the scarred door of the place read Jockey Club, a throwback to the futile attempt almost a decade earlier to bring horse racing back to Colonial Park. Hoke let his eyes adjust to the dim light before heading for a door at the back of the main bar. A huge leather-jacketed man nodded and stepped to one side to allow him to enter.

"Zamora," Hoke said as he stared at the dark young man engrossed by a lap-top computer on a table in the center of the room.

The man looked up briefly through wire-framed glasses, then returned his attention to the backlit LCD screen. "Mr. Hoke, I am happy that you keep your appointments. It makes me less nervous." He punched something into the PC, then pushed the cheap folding chair back from the table and, with a smile, gestured to his guest to take a seat opposite him.

Hoke looked around and noted three other men besides the guard at the door who normally accompanied Zamora. They sat in the shadows around the edge of the room, which was stacked with dust-covered crates, cases of beer and boxes of junk.

"What is this setup, Ruben?" Hoke asked as he walked to the table and took the offered seat. "It's ludicrous." Hoke waved an arm, taking in the whole room and its occupants with a sweeping gesture. "I feel like we're in one of those goddamn ancient gangster movies."

For a minute Zamora's face reflected amusement. In his mid-to-late thirties, he was light-complexioned for a Hispanic. His short black hair was combed straight back and showed touches of gray in the temples. He looked almost distinguished...and quite unlike an heir to the largest South American drug cartel in history.

"This area of the city is violent," Zamora said thoughtfully, his words measured. "Physical. I can control my immediate environment much more easily than if we were in Manhattan."

Hoke almost liked the Colombian, a fact that had surprised him when Gorman introduced them nearly a year before. What Hoke didn't like was the risk that Zamora would let him die like a dog on the Henry Hudson at rush hour. He wasn't afraid of it: he just didn't like it.

When Hoke didn't comment, Zamora went on, "Anyway, how did it go?" He took off his glasses and placed them in the breast pocket of his gray pinstripe.

"I don't know for sure," Hoke answered sincerely. "I think it went okay."

"Tell me about it." Zamora picked up a package of cigarettes from the table and shook one out. He placed it between his thin lips and lit it. "What do you mean you 'think it went okay'?"

"Why don't you fill me in with a little more detail about your plan, Ruben? I've been thinking about my part in the way it's set up now, and frankly, I'm getting a bit nervous." Hoke sat in the chair with his legs apart, his gloved hands clasped together in his lap. He looked anything but nervous.

Zamora laughed softly and sucked smoke from his mouth into his nose. "Anderson, would you like a drink?"

"Sure, vodka straight."

Zamora turned toward a burly shadow. "Leonard, bring Mr. Hoke a vodka, please. I'll have a Scotch."

As Leonard disappeared out the door, Zamora turned back toward Hoke. "I suppose I should have asked him to bring the best in the house, but given the house—" he stopped and looked around the gloomy room, smiling and shrugging his shoulders in an exaggerated manner "—Leonard would probably bring back something with his picture on the bottle!" Zamora laughed aloud and snapped his fingers next to his head in a strange little gesture of self-applause.

"But back to your question." Zamora wiped a corner of one eye with the tip of a finger. "I also must ask you something before I can give you the little more detail that you desire."

Hoke waited until Leonard set the drinks in front of them before saying, "Go ahead."

"Do you really want to know?" There was a hidden meaning in the enigmatic smile Zamora displayed now, and Hoke felt a chill run up his spine. He looked into the South American's black-brown eyes and saw something unfathomable.

"Yes, in my business I need to understand all the risks." Hoke knew his words sounded lame as soon as they escaped his lips. He felt his face flush slightly and picked up the glass of vodka, downing half in one swallow.

"Very well, my friend." Zamora took a small sip of his Scotch and licked his lips. "But I must warn you—to know a little is to know it all." Zamora raised his eyebrows slightly and looked questioningly at Hoke through the smoky light.

Hoke nodded, wondering what the hell Zamora had up his sleeve. "I know you've heard of the South American drug wars that took place in the mid-1990s," Zamora said. "Do you recall the Seven Families?"

"Yes, the ones who literally went to war against the United States when Congress authorized the military to wipe out the source of the drug problems in Colombia." Hoke drained the last of his vodka and motioned to Leonard, pointing at his empty glass. "South America was a primary source for the drug of choice at that time—cocaine, I believe."

Zamora lit another cigarette before taking up the thread of conversation. "The Seven Families were actually one family consisting of my father and his six brothers." He took a deep drag on the cigarette. "Four of my uncles died violently, mainly at the hands of the Colombian authorities, who were out to prove to the United States that we, too, were serious about eradicating the drug problem. In reality, the South American countries were all trying to ensure that the United States would continue to pump money into the economy in the name of the drug war. They needed that money because the United States was trying to destroy the single largest source of income in South America."

"What about your father and the surviving brothers?" Hoke didn't look up as Leonard set a full glass next to the empty. "Are they still alive?"

"Yes, they are still alive. All three are in a maximum security prison near Pittsburgh."

"Ah," Hoke said, finally understanding why Zamora had hired him to scram the Superplex's security system during the Super Bowl. In return Hoke was to get half of what he tapped from the green line plus safe passage to the country or orbiting colony of his choice. "I had wondered why you wanted to lock up two hundred thousand people for an hour or more." Hoke focused on Zamora's face. "You're going to hold them hostage, aren't you?"

"My father has almost ten billion dollars tucked away somewhere. I know at least half of it is in gold." Zamora held up his glass in a mock toast before taking a short drink. "At least it was in 1996."

"Gold?" Hoke's question was more an audible contemplation. "Gold has increased in value during the past ten years more than any other precious metal. If what you say is true," Hoke said as he picked up his fresh glass of vodka and took a quick sip, "then it has to be worth six or seven times what it was in '96."

"My calculations peg it at close to twenty-eight billion."

"Then why are you insisting on half of what I siphon from the green line?" Hoke asked, genuinely curious. "Surely it must be peanuts to you."

"Operating capital," Zamora answered. "The past five years of preparation and planning for this exercise have been rather expensive. I think it's safe to say that I need the money more than you." The Colombian smiled, and Hoke felt another chill race up his spine. He knew he had stepped into the middle of something big and something dangerous. He felt no fear, just a level of excitement that buzzed between his intellect and physical being.

"One thing I don't understand.... Actually, two things." Hoke allowed a smile to creep into his voice and watched Zamora for a reaction, but saw none. "First, what would you have done if you hadn't been, ah, introduced to me? My scheme was totally unrelated to the plan you apparently had already implemented."

"You are correct for the most part. We had two approaches in mind to the problem of locking down the Superplex. We calculated that we would need the complex sealed off for at least an hour in order to effect the release and pickup of my father and uncles. The difficult way would be to rely on force—blow the entrances shut, for example. The preferred manner is to use an insider who has access to and understands the computer system that controls the physical security of the structure. When Mr. Gorman caught wind of our interest, he thought it might be beneficial if we talked. And—'' Zamora smiled widely "—so far, it's been of benefit, don't you think?''

"What did Gorman get out of this?'' Hoke asked, ignoring the Colombian's question. "I'm sure he didn't act as my unauthorized agent out of the kindness of his heart.'' Hoke had divulged only the rudiments of his plan to the minor executive Gorman because the man didn't inspire total trust in him.

"Let's just say he is being compensated in our best interest.'' Zamora flashed the "do you really want to know?'' look at Hoke as though it was a warning flag.

Hoke let it pass without notice or comment. "The second thing about your scheme that I don't understand is how you are going to hold almost two hundred thousand screaming football fans hostage?''

When Zamora looked mildly puzzled, Hoke pressed on. "I mean yes, sure I can lock down the place for at least an hour, but there's really no way down physically. The upper lip of the plex is smooth and curves to a three- or four-story drop. Anyone who makes it over the lip will probably slide to an ugly death on the concrete.''

"I'm well aware of the physical aspects of the Superplex.'' Zamora took off his wire frames and rubbed his eyes with the thumb and index finger of one hand. "So what's your question?"

"What are you going to use?"

"Use?" Zamora put on his glasses and stared at Hoke, his facial expression reflecting either tiredness, or boredom and mild irritation.

Hoke leaned forward. "I mean, what is the danger threatening the spectators that will put leverage on the government to release your relatives?"

"I see what you're asking." Zamora turned toward Leonard and another one of the shadows who were standing near the door and said something in Spanish. All three men burst out laughing. Leonard then made what sounded like a lighthearted remark, and Zamora swiveled around to face Hoke again. "Leonard said that we should threaten them with your speaking." Zamora started laughing again, and immediately Leonard and the shadow followed suit. After ten seconds or so of laughter, the Colombian took off his glasses and wiped the tears from his eyes. "Leonard says that your speaking would put the entire crowd and both teams into—how do you say?—the big sleep."

Calmly Hoke took a drink of vodka and nodded his head slowly as he watched Zamora pull himself together. "That's funny, Ruben, but I didn't show up for this meeting to be the source for your goddamn entertainment." Hoke intentionally allowed his voice to carry an edge that completely snapped Zamora out of his joking mood.

"You are totally correct, Anderson." Zamora's manner was now sober. "I apologize for my irreverent, ah, digression. Would you like another drink?"

"No, thanks." Hoke set his empty glass on the table and waited.

Zamora leaned forward in his chair. The unbuttoned vest of his suit hung open, and his striped tie swung like a pendulum before stopping. The warning look masked his face again. "We have a bomb," he said simply. He stared at Hoke as though expecting a reaction.

Hoke waited a couple of seconds before shrugging his shoulders slightly. "A bomb?" he repeated blankly.

Zamora smiled briefly. "The bomb was built into the structure about a year ago, courtesy of one of Marsh Construction's subcontractors. It's supposed to be small..." Zamora got a pained look on his face as though he were having a hard time explaining. "I don't mean its physical size—" he gestured with his hands to indicate a small object "—because I don't really know how big it is."

Hoke wondered what the Colombian was stumbling toward with his explanation about the bomb. Zamora looked at Hoke and paused. "What I mean by 'small' is the explosion it's supposed to make." When Hoke nodded encouragingly, Zamora delivered his punch line. "It's not big as far as fission devices go."

Hoke ran what he'd heard through his mind a couple of times and stared blankly at Zamora. "Fission device?" he repeated, speaking more to himself than to the Colombian. His eyes focused on Zamora's, and he became aware of a dropping sensation in his stomach, negative gravity. "You have a nuclear weapon hidden in the Superplex?"

Zamora smiled strangely, his thin eyebrows arching up above the round wire frames. "I prefer to call it a bomb, outdated as the term may be."

Hoke had a vision of two hundred thousand screaming humans being vaporized. He felt the flesh on his scalp tighten as he realized what he'd gotten himself into. Hoke picked up his empty vodka glass, looked into it and mechanically set it back on the table. He wondered when his stomach would reach terminal velocity; it felt as though it were still accelerating.

Suddenly Hoke felt calmness wash over his mind like warm rain. Up until then he had thought he understood the risks and all of the implications. He had been warned by Gorman that the Colombians were worse than any of the fanatics of the most extremist groups. "They may not look it on the surface," Gorman had said, "but the bastards have the souls of snakes." Hoke understood now what Gorman had meant. He also realized that he could live with the magnitude of the outcome if the plan didn't work, and that understanding calmed him down. He felt he'd stepped over a threshold of sorts and was no longer burdened by the size of the sword the Colombian carried. Hoke knew he could wield it, too, maybe even better.

"How did you get it?" Hoke forced out the words and felt as though his vocal cords were being commanded by remote control. Although he had consciously stepped through the one-way door into Zamora's world, Hoke's body was resisting. His voice sounded like an unoiled hinge.

"I will tell you and you will not believe me," Zamora answered. Hoke noticed that the Colombian was studying him very carefully. "You might think we would get such a device from India or even Israel, but it was the damnedest thing.... We got it right here in the United States."

"Where?" Hoke was genuinely curious and noticed the nervousness had left his voice.

"It was built by a group of three people in Boulder, Colorado. We checked the design and tested the trigger with a classified piece of software that one of my—" Zamora paused and smiled directly at Hoke "—*compadres* stole from the Pantex plant in Texas."

Hoke sensed a slight change in Zamora. It was as though the Colombian could tell that he had made the psychological adjustment that would facilitate the cocking of such a large gun. "Will it work?"

"Certainly, or we wouldn't have paid two million dollars for it.... It's dirty, but effective."

"How is the trigger commanded?"

"By a scrambled RF code. We have it set up to use the Global Positioning System with a frequency that is virtually unjammable. There wouldn't be a delay as I understand it. Flip the switch and *blammo*; the Super Bowl becomes the worst disaster in the United States since the earthquake of 1996 flushed western Los Angeles into the ocean."

"Which brings me to a question I feel obligated to ask."

"What is that?" Zamora leaned back in his chair with a look on his face that told Hoke he knew what was coming.

"How do I know you're going to pull me out once I initiate the lockdown?"

Zamora put his hands behind his head and tilted his chair back on two legs. "If I don't get you out, then you open the place back up. It ruins my strategy. I have that incentive to make sure the helo is secure and waiting."

"I'm certain you'll understand that, as an added incentive, the offshore account numbers you gave me won't see cash until I am in a location that I'll disclose upon extraction."

Zamora's expression was neutral. He looked as though he were listening to mall music—staring, calm and relaxed.

"I would have been disappointed if you'd stipulated anything less." Zamora's eyes became focused. He directed his attention to Hoke. "I can appreciate your situation, Anderson, and I am impressed by your forethought and planning. I think we have a deal." The Colombian smiled, his nicotine-stained teeth flashing dull in the smoky back-room haze.

"Agreed." Hoke felt the warmth of relief and the fuzzy comfort of the vodka course through his veins. "Are we finished?" he added as an afterthought and straightened in his chair. Something told him it was time to go.

"Almost," Zamora answered, the word rolling off his tongue lazily. He motioned toward the men in the shadows. "Leonard, bring Mr. Gorman in."

Hoke raised his eyebrows and watched Leonard disappear out the door. Seconds later he returned with Al Gorman, who looked as if he'd taken a header down several flights of stairs. His longish hair was matted and crusted with dried blood, and there was a knot under one eye that was spreading shades of purple across the newly bulbous nose. The man's normally well-kept clothes matched his face. His suit was rumpled and covered with dirt, and his tie had been used to bind his arms behind his back.

Zamora motioned to an empty chair, and Leonard shoved down on Gorman's shoulders, forcing him to sit. The hulking Leonard then took an object out of his coat pocket and placed it on the table. Hoke had to stare at the object two or three seconds before he realized what it was—a bar of soap.

"Jesus, Al." Hoke stared at Gorman's face, which looked worse at close range. "What the hell happened?" Hoke shifted his attention to Zamora. "What's he doing here?"

"While Mr. Gorman was kind enough to introduce us, he hasn't been overly selective with whom he discusses your particular talents and means of access. At least—" Zamora glanced at Gorman who was shaking slightly "— that is what one of my associates tells me."

"I don't understand," Hoke said, though he had a pretty good idea of what Zamora was leading up to.

"Well, it's pretty simple." Zamora rocked himself out of his chair and walked around the table behind Gorman. He put his hands in his pockets and spoke matter-of-factly. "Mr. Gorman tried to sell your services to a group of people in the city whom we deal with from time to time. These guys specialize in a *physical* type of work." Zamora walked to the side of Gorman's chair and looked down briefly. "Anyway," he continued, turning his head toward Hoke, "when we discovered your agent here had talked to these guys, I called their leader and he agreed to forget the discussions."

"He's not my goddamn agent," Hoke blurted out, wondering if Gorman had talked to anyone else regarding his plan. He looked at Gorman, who was staring at the bar of soap on the table. "What the hell were you doing, Al? I didn't give you license to peddle my goddamn services."

"Well, I didn't think you had, either," Zamora said. "However, I have to be certain that our relationship remains exclusive as well as totally secret." The Colombian took one of his hands out of his pocket and placed it on Gorman's shoulder. The bound man cowered down in the chair as though shying away from Zamora's touch.

Hoke knew that Zamora was playing out the scene in order to get a message across: he'd better not screw the deal. "I agree," he heard himself say. "I've had my own concerns about his knowledge of my plan." Gorman looked up, his eyes filled with hopeless fear.

"It pleases me to hear you say that," Zamora said with approval. "One of my uncles taught me an old South American custom to be used when someone you had made an arrangement with could no longer be trusted." Zamora picked up the bar of soap. "You would place a bar of soap in front of the person as a symbol that he should come clean." Zamora returned the soap to the table and leaned over so his face was only a few inches from Gorman's. "Now this may seem trite or even stupid, but it's a custom that I choose to carry with me." Zamora looked intently into Gorman's eyes, obviously waiting for a response. When none came, he grabbed the soap and slammed it on the table hard. "Who else besides Waters have you approached?"

Suddenly Zamora straightened. "Get this," he said, turning toward Hoke. "He told Waters that you could access his guys into any area of the Superplex, day or night. He must have thought they wanted to play football or something." Zamora directed his attention back to Gorman. "Just what the hell were you thinking? You could have screwed up this whole operation. Now, who else knows about Mr. Hoke and our plans?"

"No one," Gorman said shakily. "I . . . I swear. I only talked to Waters because I've done business with him before."

Hoke wondered what business Gorman was talking about, but he didn't ask. He knew Gorman had been involved in several questionable relationships and was constantly being briefed on and off the CYNSYS program as a result of his interests outside of NEXUS. Gorman had been, however, his only method of accessing the level of management he needed, in order to try to sell his Green Mole Project.

"Forgive me for soliciting what I hope to be a redundant answer, but are you sure?" Zamora asked as he picked up the bar of soap and tossed it to Leonard.

"Like I said," Gorman said, his voice cracking, "Waters was the only—"

Before Gorman could complete his sentence, Leonard grabbed a handful of hair and jerked his head backward violently. Gorman let out a gasp, and in the same instant Leonard shoved the bar of soap into the gaping mouth with such force that pieces of the white bar broke off and fell to the floor. Leonard ground it in with the palm of his hand as though he were stuffing garbage into a disposal. Hoke could hear Gorman choking and watched as Zamora motioned Leonard to back off. The Colombian then reached into his coat and pulled out a short-barreled pistol with a silencer.

"Here," Zamora said, suddenly turning toward Hoke and holding the weapon. "This is a twenty-two, so shoot him in the temple."

Hoke felt as if his heart had just been dropped into a tank of liquid nitrogen. His breathing froze to a stop as he stared in disbelief at the little death-dealing device. He had pretty much resigned himself to the fact that Gorman was going to die, but he hadn't counted on Zamora wanting him to do the killing. He tried to speak, but all he could do was shake his head.

Zamora was holding the gun by the silencer. He shoved the butt of the weapon into Hoke's chest. "Take it," he said.

Hoke realized the Colombian was going to seal their deal by making him wash his hands in Gorman's blood. He let the air escape from his lungs and took the handle of the pistol into the palm of his gloved hand. Hoke had the distinct feeling that Leonard would be shoving a bar of soap down his throat if he refused. He felt as though he were in a dream as he stood and stepped toward the choking Gorman. His entire body felt weak, washed out.

"Go ahead," Zamora said as he moved out of the way. "This will prove to me that you can be trusted."

Hoke took two steps and placed the barrel of the weapon against Gorman's temple. The gagging man emitted a muffled howl and instantly jerked his head away as though he'd been touched by a red-hot poker. Leonard stepped forward and grabbed Gorman by the neck and hair, holding his head steady. Hoke felt his bowels loosen as he pressed the end of the barrel to the man's head for the second time and tried to will his finger to squeeze the trigger. Nothing happened.

"Go on, get it over with," Zamora said softly as he patted Hoke on the shoulder.

Hoke suddenly seemed to be watching the scene unfold from the far side of the room. He could see himself standing there, holding the gun to the side of the squirming Gorman's head. Something white was coming out of the man's nostrils and Hoke realized it was foamy soap bubbles. He watched Zamora take two small steps backward just as the pistol barked out its death message. For an instant, Hoke felt a soft, barely perceptible pressure fill the room, and found himself with the pistol in his hand, watching Gorman's head jerk in a death spasm as the chunk of lead tore through his brain.

Dropping the gun to the floor, Hoke walked to a waste-basket near the door and heaved up. He felt a hand on his shoulder as the vodka churned from his throat. "There, *compadre*," Zamora said, "that one earned his death."

CHAPTER FIVE

"THIS GUY WE'RE GOING to see is a source of mine that no one knows about except me." Horn looked over at Winger, who was busy gazing into the outside mirror as he wheeled the Elint onto the Henry Hudson, heading toward the Bronx. "And now you."

Winger laid on the horn and forced his way into traffic before glancing at Horn, the perpetual crooked grin spread across his whisker-shadowed face. "No sweat, partner," he said. "I've got a couple of hole cards of my own."

"Oh?" Horn raised his eyebrows. "Hole cards?"

"Yeah," Winger answered, "hole cards." He appeared to ignore Horn's subtle mocking. "One of the cats is literally a hole card. He lives in a hole."

"What do you mean?"

"He's a hopeless, you know, lives in the sewer." Winger glanced at Horn briefly. "His front door is a manhole—Hole card, get it?"

"You mean *homeless*?"

"Huh?" Winger looked puzzled.

"You said he's a *hopeless*. You meant *homeless*, didn't you?"

"Whatever," the young cop said, then added almost enthusiastically, "but no shit, if you ever need to get into a place, you should let me introduce you to Lenny. He's like a key. Especially if there's a sewer near the place you want to access."

"What part of the city?"

"All over Manhattan, but mostly way up on the West Side. I can usually track him down somewhere around Highbridge Park."

"I'll keep him in mind," Horn said dryly.

"Shit," Winger said in the same tone of voice, "he's got to be smarter than this guy of yours. I haven't even met him yet, and I already have doubts about his credibility."

"How's that?" Horn couldn't tell whether Winger was serious or not.

"He lives in the Bronx..." Winger said, as if the answer was obvious. "I mean, Jesus, Horn, you have to be some kind of armor-plated mutant just to go in there, let alone live there. I can tell you this, I sure as hell don't like the idea of you and me going in there tonight, or any night for that matter." The young cop raised his voice as he worked the big sedan through the rush-hour traffic. "I mean night in the Bronx is probably six times worse than the day. And the day is like war. I went in there one time with a bunch of machine-gun-toting bluesuiters from Midtown to rescue some bank president one of the gangs had snatched. It was bad. I'm surprised the firefight didn't make the national news, no shit."

"What's the point?" Horn asked, amused slightly at the way his partner rambled on rather melodramatically.

"The point?" Winger glanced at Horn. "The point is that we are going into the off-limits, what New York City Council declared no-man's-land. On top of that, we are going into the Bronx at night." Winger sounded as though he'd just read his own obituary. "The goddamn zombies crawl out of the sewers at night." He looked at Horn with a mock expression of fear twisted on his face.

It was four-thirty and the winter sun was dropping fast. It pulled a cold gray twilight over the dirty New York City skyline, which hung in the smoky haze like an endless row of steel tombstones. What Winger said was true, Horn thought. More than five years before, the Bronx had been given up, abandoned by New York to function as a city unto itself. A government of sorts had been put together to run the Bronx, but it had proved ineffective and quickly lapsed into a chaotic anarchy where the major players were the gangs and the more violent factions of organized crime. The services usually provided by a city—such as power, water, refuse collection, sewers, police, fire fighters and public transportation—were sporadic and, in some cases, nonexistent. Garbage piled up in the streets, buildings crumbled into dust, and the police force had gone native, being nothing more than a gang extorting and terrorizing those unfortunate citizens who had no choice but to stay. The Bronx was indeed a city wasteland, a crime-ridden war zone in which the desperate were the norm and death danced constantly.

Horn had considered not taking Winger with him to see Dr. August. It wasn't because the Bronx was such a slime hole. Winger ignored danger, which was a requirement for survival on the streets. But Horn knew that the visit would raise more questions from his young partner concerning his past, as well as his capabilities. He was sure that Winger had learned through the same grapevine that links together every police precinct that Horn's right arm and knee were electromechanical prostheses, government replacements for the ones he'd lost in the line of duty. What Horn figured Winger didn't know was that he had junked the government-issue body mods in favor of outlawed, Mil-spec, servo-driven E-mods—enhanced modifications— that had given him a power he was still trying to cope with. At times the power seemed to dance on the edge of control, tempting his mind with thoughts of something akin to an abbreviated immortality. At other times, Horn's E-mods served a more practical purpose—saving his life.

Horn had finally concluded that his partner would find out sooner or later that he didn't possess the usual run-of-the-mill government-issue body modifications. He also figured that he'd let the person who had done his mods explain them. August, Horn knew, liked to talk as much as Winger.

Horn gave directions to get them off the Henry Hudson and onto West 155th Street. "This is the easiest entry point I've found so far," he said as Winger pulled to the curb a block away from the Macombs Dam Bridge, which led over the dead and brackish water of the Harlem River into the Bronx.

"What do you mean, easiest?" Winger asked as he reached in his jacket and pulled out a strange-looking weapon that appeared to be a cross between a long-barreled Magnum and a composite automatic.

"What's that?" Horn couldn't help asking.

"This?" Winger asked as he pulled an odd folding-type of clip from the fat handle of the weapon. He didn't wait for Horn to respond. "It's a hybrid—a .44 Mag with the loading mechanism from a Stoner Close Control machine pistol. Like it?" He held up the sleek weapon and jammed the clip home.

"Yeah," Horn answered. "I hope someone sticks one in my Christmas stocking."

"I bet you do." Winger grinned as he worked the weapon back into its holster. "You wouldn't give up that ancient red-eye for love or money."

Horn instinctively squeezed his left arm against his side and felt the bulk of his laser-sighted 9 mm automatic hanging in its holster. "It's dependable."

"Hey," Winger called, raising his voice, "what did you mean by this being the easiest way in?" He nodded toward the bridge.

"You always have the toll takers," Horn remarked, referring to the lowlife who hung around, often blocking the entrances to the Bronx, frequently extracting tolls violently from those forced to stop or stupid enough to stop of their own volition. "But there never seems to be too many of them here. Less traffic."

"You speak from experience, I assume." Winger revved the turbocharged engine and dropped the Elint into gear.

"Once we get across the bridge we will likely encounter a barrier—burning tires, junk cars. Whatever was handy." Horn spoke with a degree of seriousness in his voice, and he noticed that Winger had sobered and was listening intently. "The best approach is to hit the sidewalk and keep your head down." He hesitated a moment before adding, "Maybe I should drive."

Winger peered into the darkness on the other side of the bridge for a couple of seconds, then without speaking he unfastened his shoulder harness, opened the door and got out. He walked around the car and opened the passenger door. Horn slid across the seat and beneath the wheel and strapped himself in. He watched Winger do the same, then reach beneath the dash and remove a pistol-gripped 12-gauge riot gun. It was an ugly black automatic and sported a square magazine that held twenty rounds of caseless ammunition. Winger popped open the end cap of the magazine, checked to ensure it was full, then snapped it shut. He pulled back the slide and jacked one of the deadly flesh-eating cylinders into the chamber.

"Think we're going to need that?" Horn asked.

"This is one of the few weapons NYPD's got that're worth a shit," Winger said, ignoring the question. "It's crude, but effective."

Then Horn jammed the car into gear and gunned the engine. He aimed the big machine toward the dark hole of the Bronx, leaving a rooster tail of dirty slush as the car picked up speed. Halfway across the bridge, the scenery changed dramatically. The streets and skyways of Manhattan had been likened to a bombing range; when compared to what Horn and Winger hit as they crossed into the Bronx, however, they were closer to the ice-slick robot highways of United Germany. A battered sign hung over the bridge with the legend: No New York City Emergency Services Available in the Bronx. Enter at Your Own Risk.

Horn rounded the gradual curve that turned into Jerome Avenue, weaving around the larger pieces of junk scattered across the wide street. Off to the right he could see a couple of fires burning in the old Macombs Dam Park, around which several rag-covered figures were huddled to fend off the cold. Out of every dozen streetlights only one or two worked, and their weak yellow light bled across the street like dirty smoke.

"This place is worse than I remember," Winger said. "Is this the upper- or lower-class neighborhood?"

"For the Bronx or for hell?" Horn answered as he swerved to avoid the burned-out hulk of a step van.

Winger grinned. "Is there a difference?"

"Want to ask these guys?" Horn jerked his thumb toward a line of overturned vehicles stretched across Jerome Avenue. Standing around several burning barrels set in front of the junk barricade were a dozen or more men. Hulking, dark figures in ragged coats and shredded garb that looked almost like fur, they appeared fantastically prehistoric.

In contrast to their Stone Age demeanor, however, Horn noticed they weren't carrying clubs or spears. Each man had an automatic weapon or shotgun, many equipped with night-vision scopes.

Bringing the Elint to a stop in the center of the street about two hundred yards from the welcoming party, Horn squinted into the distance. "Does the sidewalk on the right look clear?"

"Why don't you turn around and try a side street?" Winger asked, staring at the armed hulks who were pointing at the car and checking their weapons. "Who are these guys, anyway?"

"To answer your first question," Horn said calmly, "there is a routine to follow when you come in here. The side streets may be open, but more than likely they're cabled, or if they have—"

"What do you mean 'cabled'?" Winger interrupted.

"They string a steel cable across the street where it just clears the hood." Horn ran a gloved hand in a slicing motion across his throat. "Gets you right about here."

"Shit," Winger muttered and swallowed in the manner of a man whose spit had just run dry.

"As for your second question, these creatures who look like a cross between humans and buffalo are what pass for the police of this particular section of the Bronx. They're paid by the residents to control who comes and goes. It's like one of those exclusive, closed neighborhoods. You can't get in unless you're on the list." Horn grinned. "And I don't think we're on the list."

"Why the hell didn't you have this guy we're visiting call us in?" Winger asked.

"I don't know," Horn answered, before craning his neck around in an exaggerated manner as though he were looking for something. "I think he's got an unlisted number."

"Asshole." Winger reached into the back seat and grabbed a set of old night-vision glasses. He peered into them for several seconds, scanning the area around the blockade. "I think you might have a chance over on the left," he said, lowering the gogglelike glasses and handing them to Horn. "There's a stack of garbage, but it doesn't look solid."

"Yeah, I see what you mean." Horn handed the glasses back to his partner. "You've got smoke, don't you?"

"Sure," Winger answered. "I've got a couple of handhelds." Once again he leaned into the back seat. This time he pulled out a tubelike device about a foot long with a rounded object the size of a fist on one end.

"I want you to put that down about twenty yards in front of them. Once we clear the smoke, I'll head for the sidewalk." Horn looked over at his partner, who was rolling down the window. "If they start shooting, try firing a couple of rounds over their heads with your shotgun."

"Over their heads?" Winger's voice reflected anything but enthusiasm.

"Yeah," Horn answered. "Sometime they bluff shooting at you. We don't want to shoot anyone unless they're really trying to take us out. Right?"

"Ah, right," Winger muttered as he leaned out the window and twisted the bottom part of the tube. "Whenever you say," he yelled.

"Go ahead," Horn ordered. He watched Winger slap the bottom of the tube with the palm of his right hand. There was a loud bang as the ball blew off the end of the cylinder and shot into the haze. It trailed an arch of white smoke and landed thirty or so yards in front of the barricade, spewing out crazy circles of thick fog as it spun and bounced on the pitted asphalt.

All the men who had been standing around watching the unmarked police car as though they were lions watching a distant prey suddenly crouched or took cover behind the drums or whatever junk happened to be available. Most raised their weapons, taking aim in the car's direction. "Shit, here it comes," Winger yelled, dropping the tube. He grabbed the riot gun and held it in a left-handed grip, resting the barrel across the edge of the open window.

Horn watched the smoke billow in front and noticed that two of the men had moved away from the others to head toward the car. "Keep your head down," he said, dropping the Elint into gear and flooring it. The turbocharger whined like a banshee as the tires broke traction, making the big machine fishtail wildly. Horn aimed the nose toward the two on-comers, who were approaching through the smoke, their outlines blurry and distorted.

The two men froze in their tracks as they realized the car had cranked up and was now bearing straight toward them. They took running leaps and rolled to safety behind the burned-out hulk of a taxicab that rested on its frame in the median. There was a loud explosion as Horn blew past the junker, and he heard pellets splatter the passenger side of the cop car.

"That sure as hell doesn't sound like bluffing to me!" Winger yelled above the din.

Horn cranked the wheel over hard as they broke through the smoke and slid the straining machine sideways, flanking the wall of junk. He started to yell for Winger to fire, but his partner had already opened up with the autoloader, blasting several rounds above the heads of the toll takers, who dived for whatever cover they could find. Huge bursts of sparks exploded as the fleshette rounds collided with the wall of junk, creating a crazy pattern across the rusting barricade.

"Holy shit!" Winger screamed as one of the men managed to return fire, driving a round through the open window, inches above the detective's head. The supersonic chunk of lead slammed into the doorpost directly behind Horn's head, creating a sound inside the car like a thunderbolt.

Horn cranked the wheel around and managed to get the sedan into a slide. He aimed the hood ornament for the sidewalk opening and stood on the accelerator. Winger's shotgun bounced up and slammed into the top of the window opening as the car hit the curb and rammed into the pile of trash. Splintered wood and assorted junk blew across the windshield like matchsticks.

Once on the sidewalk, Horn kept the foot feed down as the machine plowed through a seemingly endless wall of garbage cans, junk and several unidentifiable objects that thudded ominously against the car. Horn had fleeting thoughts of bodies rolling beneath the vehicle. Out of the corner of one eye he watched Winger pop the second smoke canister and dump it out the window.

"That'll slow 'em down," Winger yelled as Horn sent a final garbage can spinning into a doorway. The Elint bounced off the sidewalk and back into the trash-filled street, sliding into a tire-smoking semicircle before coming to a rocking stop.

The smell of burning rubber wafted into the car through the open window as Horn straightened the wheel and gunned the engine, heading down Jerome. "Once you make it in," he said as Winger cranked the window closed, "they seem to leave you alone. At least the *police* do." Horn smiled at Winger who returned a halfhearted grin. "I guess they figure if you want to get in here badly enough to crash their roadblock, then you must have legitimate business.''

"Sure, partner.'' Winger appeared to have regained his composure. ''You're so full of it, your eyes are turning brown.''

Horn slowed the machine, turned off Jerome onto 172nd Street and wound through a neighborhood that looked as if it had been firebombed. Surprisingly enough, lights shone here and there where people had fashioned places to live, dim lights of habitation in the crumbling darkness.

"Where the hell are we going?'' Winger asked as Horn pulled around the skeleton of an overturned bus and drove up the side of a dirt embankment onto what was left of the Mount Eden Parkway.

''To Dr. August's favorite watering hole,'' Horn answered as he watched a battered Aeriel sedan drive by on Webster Avenue. It looked like a ghost car in the smoky haze, leaving a trail of vapor as its exhaust polluted the cold night.

It was strange, Horn thought. Once they made it past the barricade, things were normal. Sort of. Normal for the suburbs of hell, maybe. Horn had made several trips into this restricted section of the Bronx, which was known as Death Row, not necessarily because one could meet an easy death within its desolate boundaries, but because so many convicted murderers and hardened criminals had escaped across the junk-strewn borders into the safe harbor of its lawless confines.

Horn turned onto the next street, drove a block to the Bronx Expressway and pulled into a litter-filled parking lot beneath the abandoned freeway's rusting steel and cracked concrete superstructure. Several battered cars and motorcycles were parked around a crude building that leaned against one of the expressway's massive concrete supports. Hung over the dented steel door was a red neon sign sporting a three-foot squiggly shape, below which the glass tubes spelled out Red Worm.

"Red Worm?" Winger said as Horn pulled into an unmarked slot next to a Honda Speedwing. "How did you come up with this place? Before Horn could answer, Winger returned the shotgun to its place beneath the dash, and got out of the car.

Suddenly he held up his hand and whispered, "Hold it." Then he quickly reached into his jacket and extracted the machine pistol. Two huge men had walked around the crooked line of vehicles and were headed their way. One carried an ancient pump shotgun while the other held an automatic with a banana clip by its pistol grip.

"Take it easy, partner," Horn said quickly as the two men pulled up and aimed their weapons at Winger. "These guys work here. They're the bouncers."

"You should warn me about this kind of shit," Winger muttered as he stuck the weapon back in its holster.

Horn next spoke to the two bouncers. "It's okay, guys, he's a newcomer," he said, indicating Winger. "We're here to meet someone and have a beer." Horn spread his hands to show he wasn't palming a weapon and watched the two men slowly lower theirs. When one of them nodded toward the door, Horn skirted the front of the car, grabbed Winger by the arm and led him to the entrance. "I hope they don't check your ID in here," Horn said as he shoved the door open, letting Winger enter first.

"Screw you," Winger responded, stepping sideways into the smoky den.

The inside of the Red Worm wasn't much different from the outside. It was crude, rough-hewn and suggested that the furnishings had been culled straight out of a shipwreck. The bar, which ran the length of the long room, consisted of one lane of a bowling alley. It was elevated from the asphalt floor by six massive hydraulic jacks of the kind used to lift houses. Several sets of mismatched tables and chairs were scattered around the room and a couple of worn booths had been stuck against one wall.

Horn took the lead and headed for the bar, winding his way through the crowd. There were bikers, leather-clad throwbacks to the street gangs, down-looking shadow dwellers with trench coats and wide-brimmed fedoras and a number of tough-looking people with coarse features who didn't fit any particular category other than hard.

At the bar, Horn and Winger were greeted by a behemoth of a Spaniard who wiped a rag across the wood and smiled, revealing a mouth full of gold teeth. His dark eyes glittered in the dim light. "Señor Horn, good to see you again," he said with a heavy accent.

"Hello, Manny," Horn replied. "Meet a friend of mine, Winger." He casually pointed a thumb toward his partner, who had bellied up next to him.

Manny wiped the top of his sweating bald head with the rag and nodded at Winger. "What'll it be?" But before they could answer, Manny jerked his head toward the shelf behind him on which sat several dozen bottles of clear liquid. "How about a bottle of the good stuff?"

"I'll just have a beer," Horn answered. "Maybe you can talk Winger into trying it."

Winger squinted his eyes and peered across the bar at the bottles, which were plastered with colorful labels all printed in Spanish. "Hey," he said, "what the hell is that in the bottles?"

"Huh?" Manny said, turning slightly without really looking around. He ran one of his fat hands down his face and over his short goatee. There was an amused expression on his acne-scarred face. "You mean this?" he said, reaching behind and retrieving a bottle, which he slammed on the bar in front of the young cop. "It's mescal, I make it myself."

Winger stared incredulously at the bottle, focusing in on the object that floated near the bottom. "I thought mescal was made from some kind of plant in Mexico. And the worm—" he picked up the bottle and held it up "—I thought the worm was, well, smaller than this." He gave the bottle a shake and watched the reddish-colored worm move slowly in the liquid. It was more than three inches long.

"That's true," Manny answered, taking the bottle from Winger. "But it doesn't like shaking—it disturbs the sediment." A cloud of gunk floated up from the bottom, shrouding the pickled worm in its mysterious flotsam. "My brother sends me the cactus up from Oaxaca and I distill it right here, out back. As for the worm, my brother could not get worms, so I improvised." To Horn it looked like a big earthworm.

Manny unscrewed the cap and held out the bottle to Winger, who shook his head. "No?" Manny tilted his head back and chugged nearly half the bottle, his Adam's apple bobbing as the worm heaved around in the liquor, threatening to slide down the neck of the bottle and into Manny's gurgling throat. He slammed the bottle down on the bar and burped loudly. Sweat ran down his neck and soaked into the top half of his shirt.

"Hey, Louie!" Manny yelled to a skinny, stringy-haired man who was working farther down the bar. "Slide me a glass."

"How 'bout just a beer," Winger said.

"Don't worry, gringo." The fat bartender laughed as he stopped the cocktail-size glass that Louie had rocketed down the smooth wood. "I don't make you drink the mescal. Perhaps you couldn't handle it, anyway."

Horn watched Manny pour the mescal until the glass was overflowing. Finally the worm drained out and fell into the glass with a little splash, one end of it hanging an inch over the lip.

"It is said that the mescal worm can give you wisdom, even cause you to have visions," Manny said, picking up the drink and sloshing the booze over his hand. He placed the rim of the glass to his glistening lips, then suddenly tilted it and his head back as though he were downing a shot. The mescal drained down the corners of his mouth and straight into his ears. He set the glass back on the table and smiled madly at Winger. One end of the worm was sticking out from between his gold teeth.

Horn watched Winger recoil slightly as Manny loudly sucked the worm completely into his mouth, then swallowed in an exaggerated fashion.

"I, eee, ya!" Manny suddenly gasped, his eyes bulging. He grabbed his ears and started shaking his head violently, all the while screaming something in Spanish.

"What the hell!" Winger backed away from the bar as Manny swung around, knocking the empty bottle off the bar. The huge man dashed for a door near the back of the bar, looking like a rogue elephant run amok.

Louie came over, wiping up the spilled mescal as though nothing had happened. "You want a beer?" he asked Winger.

"Yeah," the detective replied. "What was his problem? Did the worm do that to him?"

Louie uncapped a bottle and placed it on the bar. He stared at Winger a couple of seconds as though he were waiting for him to start laughing. "You're kidding, right?" he finally said.

"Kidding?" Winger picked up the beer. "I wasn't kidding. What the hell was wrong with the guy?"

"Shit," Louie breathed before braking into a fit of high-pitched laugher. The scrawny bartender bent over, clutching the edge of the bar with one hand. He held the other across his midsection as his laughter turned into a choking sound.

"Is this some kind of private joke?" Winger directed his question to Horn.

"Sort of," Horn answered, grinning crookedly. He took a long pull on the beer bottle before explaining. "It wasn't the worm that got to Manny, it was the mescal. It ran into his ears." Horn chuckled. "He was screaming that his ears were on fire."

"Sí, sí. His ears, they burned like fire!" Louie added, finally bringing himself under control.

"You speak Spanish?" Winger asked.

"A little," Horn answered, taking a credit wafer out of his pocket and tossing it on the bar.

Horn suddenly stiffened as someone walked up behind him and placed a hand on his shoulder. "Your money's no good here, friend." He turned and looked down into the eaglelike face of Dr. August, who picked up the wafer and stuck it into one of the pockets on Horn's jacket.

August stood at no more than five feet five inches. He was wearing military-style camouflage pants stuffed into the tops of leather jump boots. Stretched across his broad shoulders was a cracked and worn leather flight jacket. It bore a round Space Pioneers patch on the left side that had an ancient-looking logo Horn had never seen before. August's shoulder-length thinning white hair was pulled back and tied in a ponytail with a strip of leather cord. Beneath the jacket Horn could see a shoulder holster with a large-caliber handgun.

"You look good, August," Horn said, holding out his left hand.

"So do you," August answered, his crystal-blue eyes flashing beneath the arched shrouds of his eyebrows, which were the same silver-white as his hair. Instead of taking the proffered left hand, August grabbed Horn's right wrist and pulled it up to his chest, running his hands up its length, squeezing and slapping it in a manner that made Winger take particular notice.

"You always shake hands like that?" Winger asked, peering over August's shoulder.

"Who's the Leroy?" August asked.

"That's my partner, Stu Winger," Horn said, then directed his attention to his partner. "This is Dr. August, an old friend."

August released his grip and turned deliberately toward Winger, who placed his beer on the bar and held out a hand. "So, you're Horn's new partner...." August grabbed the young cop's hand and pumped it firmly.

"Yeah," Winger answered, lowering his voice, "but keep the 'partner' nomenclature down."

"Huh?" August looked momentarily dumbfounded, then realized what Winger was talking about. "Oh, I see," he whispered, tilting his head toward the young cop. "You don't want any of these desperadoes in here to know you and Horn, here, are cops." August had raised his voice when he said the word *cops*, which caused Winger to grimace noticeably. The short man picked up on the reaction and smiled strangely. "These folks in here don't care if you guys are cops!" he yelled. Leaning over, August tapped a burly, bearded man on the shoulder. He was busy pulling a length of string out of his nose. "This guy's a cop," August said, pointing a thumb toward Winger, who shrank against the bar.

"I don't give a fuck if he's a goddamn yak," the hulking man said. "Bother someone else, pal." He turned away from them and continued pulling out the string.

"See," August said, smiling, "you're invisible here." He looked at Horn. "You wanted to talk. Let's find a table."

The leather-jacketed fireplug of a man led Horn and Winger through a maze of crowded tables to an empty booth near the door through which Manny had fled. Horn and Winger took a seat opposite August and ordered beer from a jolly fat woman, who leaned over and gave the doctor a big hug.

"Hi, sweetie," she said, squeezing August's face against her ample breasts. "What'll you have?"

"I know what I'd like to have," August answered, winking at the waitress, who blew a string of hair away from the front of her flushed round face. He took a credit wafer from a pocket on the belt line of his trousers and tossed it on her tray. "But I probably can't afford it, can I?" August laughed loudly, slapping the tabletop.

"You probably wouldn't live through it," the waitress said with a cackle. "It would be a case of too much saddle for the horse."

August smiled. "No doubt. Bring me a shot and a beer."

As soon as the big woman walked away, August removed a worn pipe and tobacco pouch from the inside of his jacket. "How about the Giants?" he said. "I didn't think the assholes would make it to the play-offs, let alone the Super Bowl."

"No shit," Winger piped up, surprising Horn, who hadn't realized his partner knew or cared anything about football. "If they beat Denver, I'll make some money."

"Whose odds are you tied to?" August asked, his interest apparent.

"Oh no," Winger answered, holding up a hand. "I'm not into that kind of betting. It's just a small pool back at the precinct. It covers the whole season."

"I see," August said, taking his beer and a shot glass full of amber liquid off the tray the waitress had placed on the table. "Ever since they legalized football betting, the country's gone nuts." August quaffed down half the whiskey in the shot glass, then poured the rest into his beer. "It's worse than the lottery craze of the nineties."

"You bet on the games?" Horn asked.

"Hell, yeah." August grinned, lighting his pipe. "If New York wins by twenty-three points, I'll pick up close to seventy thou. If I remember correctly, that's about what I charged you to do this." August leaned over and rapped his knuckles on Horn's right arm, which rested on the table. A dull metallic sound emanated from beneath the sleeve.

"Hey, watch what the hell you're doing!" Winger growled as a biker fell against him, knocking over his beer. The young cop shoved the man back in the direction of his own table where a hard-looking woman stood, her hands on her leather-clad hips. She was wearing a skintight T-shirt with the inscription Biker Chick. She smiled, exposing sharp predator's teeth.

"Why, you asshole!" The biker swung toward Winger. He leaned over and reached into one of his boots, extracting a pearl-handled knife with a long carved blade. "You made me look bad in front of my chick."

Horn quickly reached around and grabbed Winger's arm to stop him from withdrawing the machine pistol. "You don't need that," he said. Just then, the biker lunged forward with the knife and swung it down in an arc. Horn raised his right arm and met the knife with the palm of his hand, snapping the blade like a matchstick. Closing his grip, Horn crushed the handle of the knife along with a couple of the biker's fingers. The man pulled his hand away, cursing loudly.

"You son of a bitch!" he gasped, reaching into the front of his oily pants with his left hand. He yanked out an ancient snub-nosed revolver. "You're gonna die now!"

Horn lifted himself slightly in his seat so he could clear Winger's head, and backhanded the biker across the mouth. Although the blow didn't appear that hard, the man's head snapped back with the force of a slap-shot puck. As several of his teeth flew into the air, he staggered backward into the Biker Chick and they both went over a table, crashing to the beer-stained floor amid broken bottles and overturned chairs. The crowd around them erupted in applause and catcalls as the woman struggled to crawl out from under her boyfriend, who was out cold.

Suddenly Manny appeared, holding a short club in one hand. Horn noticed there were wads of tissue sticking out of his ears. He looked at the couple sprawled on the floor then looked questioningly at Horn, a scowl on his face. Horn shrugged.

"Get 'em out of here," Manny ordered a couple of goons, who had followed him to the scene of the disturbance.

"Sorry, Manny," Horn said, taking a ten-credit wafer from a jacket pocket. He held it out to the fat bartender whose scowl turned instantly into a grin.

Manny took the wafer, and waved the club over his head. "Any more give you trouble, just yell."

Horn sat back down while Manny and his two bouncers started to drag the unconscious biker and the swearing woman toward the door.

"Now, that was convenient," August said, reaching over and grabbing Horn's right hand. He attempted to peel off the black leather glove, but Horn shrugged him off. "Come on, I saw what you did, but let me see 'em, anyway. After all, I am your goddamn doctor!"

"Doctor?" Winger said, apparently very interested in what was going on.

"He doesn't know?" August tilted his head inquiringly toward Winger.

Horn shook his head and reluctantly allowed August to remove his glove and roll up his right sleeve. He glanced at Winger, who was staring at his hand and forearm as though they were photographs of naked women. August picked up the smooth, titanium-covered hand and turned it over, examining it closely. The original combat-green color of the hard metal had been worn down to a polished silver hue that shone dully in the dim light of the bar.

"How's it been working?" August asked as he moved his hands along Horn's arm.

"Fine," Horn answered. "Still have that problem whenever I get shocked."

"You always will," August replied. "The things are multiplexed directly into your spine, which feeds off electricity. Any time you get a shock, your mods are going to glitch. Learn to live with it." August's pipe had gone out; now he leaned back and relit it, blowing the smoke up at the ceiling. "How's the knee?"

"Fine," Horn answered. "Aren't you going to crawl under the table and check it out?"

"Still have that guttersnipe sense of humor, don't you, Horn?" August chuckled and waved at the waitress for one more round. "The hand—" August nodded as Horn rolled down his sleeve "—looks like it's been *used* quite a bit."

"How's your business?" Horn asked, intending to get the conversation diverted from his E-mods.

"You need to drop by my place sometime," August said, ignoring Horn's question. "I've got a new bus analyzer that lets me check out the signal lags. I'd like to see what yours are."

"Listen," Horn said, pulling on his glove and leaning across the table, "I didn't ask you to meet me to discuss my mods. I need a lead on two murders we're investigating on the West Side."

"Why come to me?"

Horn was mildly surprised and somewhat pleased when Winger chimed in. "They both worked for a company called Man Machine Interface."

"MMI, yeah, I'm familiar with them." August drew on his pipe. "They make a pretty good EOI. Go on."

"One of the people who bought it was an engineer heading up the implementation of a computerized betting system for the Wager Control Commission. The other worked on the tech pubs for the system. It's called UNI-SYS or something."

"CYNSYS," August corrected. "Read your notes. There was an article about it in *Electronic News* last month."

Winger looked a little irritated at having been set straight by August. "Anyway, the guy was key in getting the CYNSYS thing going. It's supposed to be operational in time to handle the betting on the Super Bowl."

"How did they die?"

"Shot in the man's apartment," Winger said. "It was made to look like a murder-suicide following a brief struggle."

"Sounds to me like you should be out looking for tracks instead of dicking with an old man." August took a long pull on his beer.

Horn leaned forward. "We want to talk to an insider who's got a line on what's going down in the world of computers. I've got a feeling that the murders are connected to the victims' jobs."

"You mean," August said, smiling, "you want someone who's in the know about the *underworld* of computers." He waited for Horn's nod, then went on. "I may know someone who can help you." August took a small notebook and pen from a pocket in his jacket and scribbled on a page. He tore it out and tossed it across the table. "There you go. If there's anything on the street, Sarah is aware of it. Tell her I sent you."

Horn looked at the paper, which bore the name Sarah Weed along with a Manhattan address. "Anything in particular you want to tell me about her?"

"She will know the answers to your questions, or at least where to get them." August smiled between puffs on his pipe. "But whether she will give the answers to you...well, that's another story."

CHAPTER SIX

ANDERSON HOKE PARKED his BMW in the slot once occupied by Franklin's Porsche. He had no trouble gaining access to the tongue and CYNSYS. He knew Mayo had greased his track into Franklin's old spot. Hoke was glad about that, at least. With less than two weeks to go before CYNSYS was scheduled to be on-line, he knew he was going to have to bust ass to make it. The less hassle he had with security and administrative bullshit, the better chance he'd have of setting up everything in time for the Super Bowl. The real question in his mind was how much damage had Franklin done in his attempt to integrate the system. Hoke's opinion of Franklin's technical acumen had never been too high.

As soon as he walked into the Control Center, Hoke was greeted by a conservatively dressed woman in her midthirties. Her hair was pulled back into a severe bun, and she wore large horn-rimmed glasses. Her body looked stiff and thin, and she introduced herself to Hoke as Alexa Burton, his administrative assistant.

"I didn't ask for an assistant," Hoke said calmly as he unbuttoned his coat and hung it on a rack near the door. The woman shrugged and crossed her arms defensively. "Were you Franklin's assistant?" Hoke asked.

"Yes."

"Then you may be of help," he said. "However, until I call on you, stay out of my way." He pulled a white lab coat off a hook and donned it as Alexa left without saying another word.

Hoke went straightaway to one of the main terminals and queried up the current configuration of the system. He studied the long list of routines that made up the CYNSYS operating software until his eyes locked onto one particular module that was labeled GRASP EXE Rev B. Hoke breathed a short sigh of relief. At least Franklin didn't screw with this, he thought, noting that the rev letter hadn't been changed. Although Hoke hadn't disclosed it during the briefing Mayo had arranged, he'd been worried that Franklin may have tampered with the CYNSYS software in a manner that would have delayed or even precluded the execution of Project Green Mole.

Picking up the thin fibre optic cable that was attached to a special fixture next to the terminal's monitor, Hoke examined the gold-plated HI connector that stuck from the end of the cable like the stub of a hypodermic needle. He removed the sterile cover, then, out of superstition, placed the golden tip in his mouth and bathed it with his saliva. Holding the connector between his thumb and forefinger, he reached around to the back of his neck and felt for the receptacle with his middle finger. He found it just below his collar line, nestled in the short hair on his neck. Hoke licked his lips and plugged it in. A mild electrical jolt coursed through his spine as the computer adjusted the speed of its bus traffic to match the pulse synchronization of Hoke's nervous system.

Hoke pulled up the diagnostics program and watched the software trip through the routines that were supposedly designed to protect his brain from surges, whiteouts and other hardware and software anomalies.

The diagnostics checked out, and Hoke punched in the access codes that gave him command over CYNSYS. He initialized the command and felt his scalp crawl with electricity as the classified executive came up on the monitor. A flashing message at the top of the screen announced: YOU ARE CYNSYS—HI IN EFFECT. At the bottom of the screen, in red, the message F1 TO ABORT was displayed. "I am CYNSYS," he whispered to himself as he pulled the leather swivel chair away from the console and eased himself into it.

Hoke spent nearly four hours plexed into the machine, running through a random shakedown, before he was satisfied. Franklin hadn't managed to botch the integration or introduce any incompatible subroutines that could interfere with his tapping or flash paper programs.

After putting the executive into a standby and locked mode, Hoke unplugged the HI and got up from the chair to stretch his legs. He walked over to the huge, curved glass window that looked out over the playing field, and watched a crew of workers operating a machine that was embedding the yard markers into the synthetic green turf. Hoke stared, and a nagging doubt crept into his mind, asking him if he really knew what he'd gotten himself into. He gazed around the massive complex that would soon be transformed into an acre of screaming humanity and wondered where Zamora had hidden his bomb. The possibilities were almost infinite, given the Colombian's information that it was built into the structure during its construction. Hoke shook his head and wondered if there really was a bomb; it all seemed nearly unreal. He felt a mild numbness sweep over him as the scene with Gorman replayed itself in his mind: the muffled report, the head twitching violently, the blood. Zamora had grinned like the devil receiving another soul, another blood-anointed ransom.

Hoke forced the scene out of his mind and walked back to the console. He licked the HI connector, plugged it into his neck again and brought up the executive that managed the green line, forgoing the built-in test routines. Activating a program that was designed to simulate the flow of electrocash, Hoke punched up the commo center on the intercom and was told that satellite feed would be initiated on his command. He ordered it activated.

It was Hoke's intent to bring up the green line with the simulated flow of electrocash and inject his program into the CYNSYS operating software via the GRASP EXE, which he had originally designed to function as an unlocked door into the mind of the machine. He watched, unaware of the smile that had spread across his face as the green line manifested itself across the screen, the blizzard of electrocash blowing through the emerald hue like a billion shooting stars. A pleasant electrical sensation ran through his neck and down his spine. He felt his legs twitch strangely, involuntarily, and interpreted the reaction as a side effect of his talking not only *to*, but *with* the machine.

Hoke felt warmth sweep over his body as he controlled the diamond-white flow of electrocash merely by willing it. The HI had given him the link with CYNSYS that was almost a new consciousness. Hoke knew he pushed it further than others who used it. He went deeper into the machine-ordered world of CYNSYS than what its tech orders and operator's manuals outlined; they restricted HI access to the executive level only. On several occasions Hoke had slipped his mind past that upper level line of demarcation and into the partition of the machine, whose universe functioned at a speed not relative to flesh and bone. Hoke found his excursions into the machine world to be euphoric, almost druglike. Even manipulating the stream of electrocash—splitting it up, routing it to various locations—gave him a sense of power and a feeling that bordered on being sensual.

Hoke ran the green line through all of its scenarios and functions, manipulating the simulated electrocash flow to test the line's ability to handle surges and radical changes in the flow's profile. He was pleased that it didn't hang up or drop its operating speed during any of the tests. Hoke decided it was time to test-run his tapping program. He disengaged the data recording subroutine that monitored the performance of the testing and started to pull out the thin wafer disk in his shirt pocket that held what he privately called his pilot-fish program. He suddenly froze, aware that someone was standing behind him. Wondering how long they'd been there, Hoke swiveled around, feeling his face flush as anger pumped up his blood pressure.

"What the hell are you doing?" he barked, staring into Alexa Burton's frowning face.

"I was in the lab and saw on the monitor that you were in the green line," she answered matter-of-factly.

"So?" Hoke let the tone of his voice tell her he was quite annoyed.

"So, it's the two-person rule," Alexa said in an aggrieved tone as though Hoke should know what she was talking about.

"Huh?" Hoke focused on the woman's face, trying to understand what she was saying.

"The two-person rule," Alexa repeated. "It's a security procedure. I'm surprised you're not familiar with it." She stood with her arms crossed and raised her eyebrows. Hoke noticed she was gazing at his shirt pocket and moved his hand away as casually as he could. "You are accessed to Level Three, aren't you?"

Hoke gave her a look to convey that he saw her as nothing more than an irritating pain in the ass. He didn't answer her question, but turned and activated the audiovisual intercom. "Get me John Mayo."

Seconds later, Mayo's administrative assistant came on. "May I help you?"

"John Mayo, please. This is Anderson Hoke." He sensed Burton still standing behind him and figured she was probably smirking.

"I'm sorry," the woman answered, "but Mr. Mayo is in a meeting. May I have your—"

"Interrupt him," Hoke ordered. "Now."

The woman hesitated for a moment, staring at the screen with a blank expression plastered like another layer of makeup across her face. "Very well," she finally said. The screen immediately came up with Stand By Please written across it.

"What is it?" Mayo's voice came out of the speakers a second before his chubby face appeared.

"I'm in the process of running the routing tests on the green line." Hoke noticed out of the corner of his eye that Alexa had stiffened when Mayo's image appeared on the screen. "It seems someone has invoked the two-person rule whenever the line is accessed." Hoke turned and nodded at Alexa. "At least according to Ms. Burton, here."

"Shit," Mayo muttered, obviously annoyed. "Ms. Burton, wait in the lab. I'll have Security call you and let you know the two-person rule is waived. Anything else?"

Hoke looked at Alexa, holding out his hand as if to give her the floor. She turned and strolled toward the door without speaking. "That's all," Hoke said, punching Mayo off the intercom.

"Not that it would have done you any good," Hoke said as the door closed behind Alexa. He reached over to a button on the console and disconnected all outside monitoring. Then he reached into his pocket and pulled out the wafer disk. He inserted it into one of the auxiliary drive slots on the console and pulled up the executive. It took less than ten seconds to transfer his tapping program through the GRASP EXE doorway. He removed the wafer and placed it in another slot on the console that instantly erased the program it had contained. Opening a drawer at the bottom of the console which was filled with blank wafers and other miscellaneous junk, Hoke dropped the disk into it, smiling to himself.

With the minor exception of one checksum routine, which Hoke fixed on-line, the tapping program ran flawlessly. He spent about fifteen minutes going through a simulated bleeding of the electrocash before he was totally satisfied that it could be initiated and run in a manner that was virtually invisible to anyone who happened to view the monitor during the operation, especially those who were not intimate with the functional concept of the green line. Hoke then tested the initiating sequence for his flash paper routine using a dummy program he'd set up parallel to the tapping software. It worked perfectly, erasing the test file in the wink of an eye.

Hoke shut down the green line, watching the snowstorm of electrocash fade from the screen. Once again he pulled up the executive and accessed the Superplex's physical security controls, noting with a grin that the two-person rule was applicable to the security modules. The requirement was plastered across the screen in large red letters.

It didn't take long to find what he was looking for—the emergency lockdown controls. Several warnings were flashed on the screen as he ran a simulated test on the software mechanism that would close and lock every entrance in and out of the gigantic structure within five seconds of being tripped. One warning stated that bodily injury or death were likely should personnel become trapped in the doorways once the lockdown was effected. Hoke knew that was an understatement. He'd seen one of the twelve-foot-wide, six-inch-thick steel alloy doors slam shut during a demonstration. It reminded him of the jaws of a shark snapping closed during a feeding frenzy.

Hoke pulled up the code listing for the lockdown software and studied it carefully, noting the commands for the release, or unlocking sequence. He filed the code away in his head, figuring it would be a simple matter to write an override command that would freeze the release sequence for however long he dictated. According to his calculations, it would take less than half a minute to effect the lockdown and scram the release mechanism. This, he knew, even negated the emergency manual system by cutting off the electricity that operated the doors. After that, it would take a two-ton battering ram or the equivalent to break out or in.

As Hoke was exiting the security controls, the light on the console began blinking, indicating a call on the intercom. He went ahead and cleared the program module before punching on the call. It was Alexa.

"You have an outside call," she said, her voice cool. "It's Mr. Mayo."

"Put him on," Hoke said and watched Mayo once again appear on the video. He had a sickly smile on his face.

"It looks like management's going to drop the green flag...." Mayo ran a finger around the inside of his collar and appeared to be thinking about something else. "At least, I don't know why else she'd want to see you."

Hoke noticed Mayo's dark eyes were shifting about nervously and a bead of sweat ran across his forehead. It wasn't hard to see that Mayo was being tortured by the demon paranoia. "I assume when you say 'she,' you mean Ashley Fine," Hoke said, wondering himself how he rated a personal audience with the head of NEXUS.

"I certainly don't mean the goddamn bag woman who cleans out the rest rooms," Mayo answered. The perspiring executive held up his wrist and glanced at his watch. "As a matter of fact, she wants you over here in forty-five minutes."

"Are you going to be in this meeting?"

Mayo looked pained. "No."

"What does she want? Do I need to bring anything or prepare in any manner?" Hoke shrugged his shoulders and watched Mayo, who played nervously with his tie.

"I don't know what the hell she wants!" Mayo snapped. "She just said to have you in her office at three o'clock."

Hoke understood now what was eating Mayo alive; Ashley Fine was cutting her executive assistant out of the loop. Hoke didn't mind; he thought Mayo was almost as flaky as Gorman. "Hell," he blurted out unexpectedly, wondering if the meeting was *about* Gorman. If NEXUS found out about his connection with Zamora, he'd be in deep trouble without a plausible explanation. He felt a sharp stab of fear himself and wondered what the Colombians had done with Gorman's body.

"Excuse me?" Mayo asked, looking at Hoke in a strange way. He seemed interested in Hoke's inadvertent outburst.

"Nothing," Hoke answered, regaining his composure. "I just remembered I had another appointment at three."

"Cancel it," Mayo said. "I'll want a full report of your meeting with Ms. Fine as soon as it's over. As a matter of fact, come by my office afterward."

"It might be late," he said flatly.

"I don't give a shit. I'll wait for you."

Hoke's thoughts sobered and he ran several scenarios through his mind that might have disclosed his connection with Zamora. None seemed likely; however, he couldn't rule out the probability that his parallel scheme with the Colombians had been discovered. If it had been, he knew his statement to Mayo would likely come true; it would be late when he got out of his meeting with Ashley Fine—real late.

In forty-five minutes Hoke was occupying a leather couch in the large reception area of Ashley Fine's plush office. He was glad when minutes later the secretary told him Ms. Fine was ready to see him—glad that he didn't have to spend any more time thinking about whether or not he was going to wind up with a bullet in his head.

Hoke had never met Ashley Fine. He had guessed she was the one asking most of the questions when he gave his abbreviated one-way video briefing, but he'd had only his imagination to tell him what she looked like. As he walked into her large office, Hoke was struck by her muted beauty. Her silver-white hair made her look rather like a steel angel. Hoke felt her eyes bore in on him as he crossed the room to her desk. He was mildly surprised when she stood and held out a hand. Although she was wearing a conservative, high-cut suit, Hoke could tell her body was well-built and in excellent condition. He took her hand and knew by her smile that his pact with Zamora was safe.

"I am glad that I've finally gotten to meet you, Mr. Hoke," Ashley said, her eyes never leaving his.

"I am pleased to meet you, Ms. Fine," he replied, feeling a strange chill run up his spine as Ashley's eyes seemed to tell him he was about to step over another boundary of darkness.

"This is Mr. Steller, an associate of mine on this project." Ashley gestured toward a chair that was set somewhat aside from the rest of the furniture groupings.

Hoke turned; he'd been unaware that there was anyone else in the room. He gazed at a man of massive size who sat slightly slouched in the overstuffed chair with his elbows resting on the arms and gloved hands clasped and serving as a rest for his huge, square chin. He merely nodded slightly at Hoke by way of a greeting, but there was no response at all on the roughly chiseled face. Hoke shivered involuntarily as their eyes met. The blond giant had an air of leashed violence about him. Returning the nod, Hoke turned back to face Ashley. She had sat down and motioned for him to take a seat in the only chair in front of the desk.

"Would you like coffee, a drink perhaps?" Ashley asked as she leaned back in her chair.

"No, thanks," Hoke answered. Something akin to fear made itself known in the pit of his stomach. The woman was still staring at him, and he figured Steller was doing the same. The skin on the back of his neck began to feel cold and bumpy.

"I thought it was time we met face-to-face." Ashley spoke through a continuous half smile that exuded a restrained sensuality. "We've decided, after all, to proceed with your project."

Hoke breathed a short and highly tentative sigh of relief. "I'm glad to hear that," he said, then decided to make sure Mayo's initiatives weren't attributed to him. "But to be honest, I was under the impression we had been given the go-ahead, at least on a limited basis."

"That isn't totally correct. Mr. Mayo has a propensity to stretch his charter."

Hoke's suspicions had been just confirmed by Ashley's answer; Mayo had been sticking his neck out all along. "I want to assure you—"

Ashley waved a hand. "Don't be concerned, Mr. Hoke. From now on you'll know your instruction is legitimate because you'll be getting it directly from me." The strange smile suddenly vanished from her face. "Unfortunately, we were somewhat forced into going ahead with the project as a result of Mr. Mayo's zealousness."

"I'm afraid I don't understand," Hoke said, though he knew perfectly well what she was implying. He'd known all along that Mayo had been acting on his own and had even encouraged him. He figured no one in their right minds would go along with the Green Mole, especially if it involved killing two of your own employees. That had been Mayo's idea. Hoke had merely helped the executive see it as an expedient means to a quick promotion to a VP or general manager's slot. Mayo, Hoke had discovered, was one of the most amoral, power-hungry, little big men he'd ever met. In Mayo's mind, murder was to be avoided only if it could not be made foolproof. And murder, in Hoke's mind, wasn't really murder as long as he didn't pull the trigger. The Colombian, however, had rendered that distinction meaningless.

"Instead of following procedure, or clearing it through the proper channels, Mr. Mayo proceeded with the unauthorized murder of Franklin and the Walker woman." Ashley raised the silver lightning bolts above her eyes slightly, as if to elicit a response.

Hoke wondered what kind of procedure NEXUS had for *authorized* murder. He almost found her statement humorous. "I see," he responded, feeling his own eyebrows rise involuntarily as if they were following Ashley's lead.

The enigmatic smile had returned to Ashley's face. "Now, you still need to understand a couple of things that are integral to the execution of your project."

"Go on," Hoke said.

"You are an accessory to murder, I'm afraid. Does that bother you?"

Once again Hoke found her statement to be grimly humorous, and it made him want to laugh. If only she'd seen him plugging old Gorman, Hoke thought. He nodded and felt something flash into his eyes. It was a *look*, the same look he'd seen in Zamora's eyes, and just a few minutes before in Steller's. Ashley saw the look and recognized it. Hoke knew because her face froze and her mouth hung open ever so slightly.

"Should it?" Hoke realized at that moment he was madly confident.

Ashley didn't answer right away. Hoke noticed that she glanced over his shoulder at Steller before returning her attention to him. The sirenlike smile had returned to her face. "Not in this business," she said. "We do, however, have a problem with one particular cog in this machine you've dubbed Project Green Mole."

Hoke felt his heart jerk out of its temporary state of calm, but he forced himself not to fly out of the roller coaster.

"John Mayo not only overstepped his bounds," Ashley said, apparently not noticing that Hoke's face had taken on a sickly cast, "but he has become rather useless in terms of executing the operation. Right now he is more of a risk than an asset."

"I agree," Hoke said, clearing his throat even as a grim possibility gripped his mind. He wondered if Ashley was going to make him kill Mayo, to seal his deal in blood as Zamora had required.

"You understand, of course," Ashley continued calmly as Hoke wondered if he'd gone mad, "that we're going to have to get rid of him."

"I understand," Hoke said.

"I'm glad you agree," Ashley said, flashing a set of perfect teeth. "It confirms to me your commitment."

Though Hoke wanted to point out that *understand* wasn't synonymous with *agree*, he kept his mouth shut and waited for her to tell him he was going to be granted the pleasure of punching a hole through Mayo's thick skull.

"We're going to use the very same assassin Mayo hired to dispose of Franklin and his girlfriend." Ashley spoke as though she were selecting someone to manage a project instead of discussing the plans for a murder.

Hoke stared at Ashley with strange fascination. She reminded him of the dark women in his dreams; he would resist them and then curse himself after he awoke for having done so.

"Mr. Hoke—" Ashley smiled and leaned forward "—are you there?"

Once again Hoke felt his attention snap back. "Excuse me," he said. "I was hardlined into CYNSYS all morning. It gets to be quite a drain." He realized that he was off the hook regarding Mayo and was surprised that he didn't experience relief. Instead he was filled with an odd indifference, a dull pang of nothing.

"I understand," Ashley said, as she got out of her chair and walked around the desk. Simultaneously the door had closed behind Hoke, and he realized that Steller had left the room. "You'll have to tell me what it's like to be wired into a machine as powerful as CYNSYS."

Hoke felt the skin covering his entire body instantly turn into gooseflesh as Ashley strolled behind his chair and put her hands on his shoulders. He felt her fingers trace their way to his neck and locate the HI receptacle. She ran one of her fingers around its small, stainless-steel collar.

"Is this where you plug it in?" Ashley asked, her voice carrying a provocative tone.

"I guess you could say that." Hoke noticed his mouth had gone dry. He also noticed that Ashley was lightly running her fingers along his shoulders. Then she moved around to stand before him with a come-and-get-me expression on her face. When Hoke stood, she didn't move back but leaned forward and covered Hoke's mouth with her own. A liquid heat rammed through him, and he had a mild vision that he'd just gone Hard Input with CYN-SYS.

Maybe she thinks she's swapping spit with the machine, Hoke thought as he lost himself in Ashley's seduction. It was a dream, and this time Hoke knew he wouldn't curse himself when he awoke.

CHAPTER SEVEN

As HE STARED through the windshield, Horn thought that the financial section of Manhattan was an illusion, though not in the sense that it didn't exist. The monolithic super-structures had remained real enough; steel and glass megaspires protruded from the earth's crust like some crazy form of acupuncture. The business-suited Wall Streeters were real; the workaholic financial bees who crowded the skyline hives and gray Manhattan sidewalks were flesh and bone, born into the consciousness of the dollar. It all existed and had flourished, albeit in a cyclical manner of extremes, throughout the latter part of the twentieth century and the first quarter of the twenty-first. It was an institution that was seemingly self-perpetuating, immune to everything but a direct hit by a nuclear-tipped cruise missile. It was real all right.

Just as real were the junkies, the string addicts, the needle racers, the prostitutes, the six New York City Housing Authority's classifications of the homeless, the zap children, the winos and the many-collared criminal element who had long ago migrated out of the darker areas of the city into the dubious light of the financial district. This secondary fungus, however, had become invisible af-ter having been ignored for so long. They were always a strata below the regular worker bees—a concrete form of mud level.

The illusion had evolved from the way the financial district was viewed. It was a matter of perspective. From an illusory viewpoint there was only the upscale business madness of Wall Street in all its pin-striped glory. But a realistic look revealed a desolation-row survival school for the rejects of humanity. It was the difference between Eldorado and Purgatory. Where that scenario left people like Winger and himself, Horn knew, was dealing with all the aftermath of greed and corruption—an endless sludge of misery.

Winger had to park the Elint on Cedar Street, which was two blocks away from the Hanover Street address August had given them. It was midmorning, cold and gray. As they walked down the sidewalk, Horn thought it smelled like snow in the air and mentioned it to Winger, who laughed and asked him when snow started smelling like sulfur. The two detectives had just come from the Justice Center where Horn had had another meeting with assistant district attorney Christina Service.

"I think the Barracuda likes you," Winger said, turning up the collar of his coat. His breath came out in a fog, then disappeared as the wind whipped it away.

"I think you are, as usual, full of shit." Horn grinned and gave his partner a playful shove, knowing nothing he said could prevent Winger's razzing.

"She actually smiled at you!" Winger raised his voice in mock surprise. "Yessir, Horn-man, I think she may even have an inclination to jump your bones."

Horn had to admit that the woman had been civil, even friendly. He had been further surprised at the reason Service had called the meeting. It wasn't for another lecture on the relationship between cops and society. Based on his previous experience, Horn had half expected something to that effect. Kelso had said the meeting had to do with the case they were working. Horn had wondered if she'd somehow found out about their excursion into the Bronx, knowing they would certainly catch holy hell for entering the highly restricted area without authorization. Instead, she had information related to the case, though she'd warned him that it was a long shot.

Two high-priced and highly effective hitters had been reported to be *back* in New York City, back in the sense that they hadn't been on the scene for more than a year. One of the murder-for-hire specialists, a man from St. Louis named Harry Trower, had been spotted in Manhattan the week of Franklin's and the Walker woman's death. Horn had pointed out that the crime lab's preliminary findings indicated that the two probably killed each other in a "self-consuming, sexually-based incident." The assistant D.A. had smiled and said, "But I read *your* preliminary report, Detective Horn. You stated that homicide by a professional was the most likely cause of death. Although the evidence didn't support your conjecture, I had a strange feeling that you might be on to something. I'm sure you're aware that Franklin had a rather sensitive job with one of the WCC's major contractors." Horn had told her he was aware of Franklin's position, but didn't tell her about the in-advance analyses he and Winger had done for the evidence techs. He wondered when, if ever, the lab would get around to checking the barrel of the weapon.

Horn had asked her where she'd gotten her information, figuring it had been published in some police briefing he hadn't seen. She had laughed, and said, "Cops aren't the only ones who have sources on the street."

As he and Winger walked toward the Citibank Building, which shot into the winter sky like some kind of alien surveyor's stake, Horn realized that to a certain degree he was intrigued by the icy-eyed assistant D.A. The feeling was a mixture of respect for her ideals and an admiration of the gutsy, yet intelligent manner in which she carried herself. He also had to admit that he found her physically attractive. Her body, despite her normally conservative clothes, revealed lean but feminine lines like a swimmer's.

"You can say whatever you want to about the woman," Horn remarked as he and Winger crossed Wall Street, "but she seems to be one of the few people in the D.A.'s office who have their head together."

"Uh-huh," Winger grunted, in an exaggerated "yeah, sure, I believe in Santa Claus, too" voice. He pulled a piece of paper out of his coat pocket and stared at it a couple of seconds before pointing across Hanover Street to the run-down Wall Street Building. "That's the address. This Sarah Weed's operation, whatever the hell it is, is supposed to be in the basement."

"August said we would figure out how to get in once we got here," Horn remarked as they crossed the street.

The once proud Wall Street Building was in a sad state of repair with several windows boarded up and the lower portion of its skirt teeming with graffiti. The structure was on its way to becoming invisible and already served as a mere backdrop, a condemned and dirty curtain for the legions of homeless. Horn knew they were waiting for the building to begin its evolution toward abandonment during which they would fill the voids, existing in the powered-down shell until the demolition technicians moved in to sweep it away. A part of Horn acknowledged a certain respect for the adaptability of these street people who were surviving in a world that ignored their very existence.

Horn and Winger had to walk around to an alleyway entrance off Beaver Street to find what they were looking for. The alley, which was actually a barricaded two-lane street that ran between the Wall Street Building and what had been broken off as its annex, was a trashed-out, junk-filled stretch of pitted asphalt. Several overturned Dumpsters, their contents spilled haphazardly, lined the gray strip between the two buildings. The burned-out hulk of a 2020 Lincoln was resting on its crushed nose, leaning against a grease-smeared wall. Someone had spray-painted ART across the dead machine's hood.

"That must be the door to Sarah's place," Winger said, nodding toward a couple of men who were pacing before a short series of steps leading down to a battered steel door. "August didn't mention that her place was in hell, did he?"

When Horn and Winger approached, one of the men was in the process of lighting a cigarette with the butt of another. He immediately dropped the butt and reached into his coat. "This is a private entrance," he snarled. Horn noticed his buddy had followed suit and also had his hand in his coat.

"We're looking for someone," Horn responded, as he watched the two men. He was slightly amused at the way the two thugs were dressed. They looked as though they'd been dragged straight out of an old-fashioned gangster movie, complete with dirty fedoras. But Horn wasn't taking any chances, even if some people liked to play roles, and he was pleased to notice Winger moving casually off to one side. Winger had his hands in the pockets of his trench coat, and Horn knew that his partner's right hand was through a slot in the pocket, gripping the handle of the deadly small machine pistol. Winger had shown Horn the modification he'd made to his coat that would allow him to fire through it if necessary.

"Who da hell are youse lookin' for?" the spokesman asked, puffing on his cigarette and blowing the smoke out of his nose.

"Yeah, who da hell are youse lookin' for?" the second thug joined in. He was standing a couple of steps behind his fellow guard, and was no smaller than him. Both men were huge—fat by most standards—but their more than six-foot height disguised their bulk.

"We're looking for Sarah Weed," Horn answered.

"Yeah?" The lead man spit the cigarette out of his mouth and it landed on his chest. He bounced his hand around inside his coat, in order to knock the smoldering butt off the ratty fabric. "Well, who da hell sent youse dickless wonders here?"

Winger pointed at an old voice-only, hand-held phone that hung next to the door. "Why don't you just pick up that piece of plastic and call her?"

"Huh?" the first man jerked his head around and stared at Winger for a couple of seconds. "Who are youse guys anyways, cops?"

"What if we were?" Horn asked. "Would it make a difference?"

Horn's questions seemed to truly puzzle the man, whose mouth hung open slightly. "I don't know," he answered. "Cops don't normally come around heres fuckin' wid us."

"Then let's just say we're here for a social visit. So just call Ms. Weed."

"I think youse are cops," the man hissed, as he pulled a large automatic out of his coat.

Horn took two quick steps up the short stairway, yelling for Winger to hold his fire. He swung his modified hand down on the automatic just as the muzzle swung toward him. Horn felt the gun kick even as he wrapped his hand over the end of the barrel, causing it to blow apart. The slide blew straight back as other pieces of the weapon flew out from Horn's grip like shrapnel. The sharp end of the cocking mechanism struck its owner in his right shoulder and planted itself a good two inches into the flesh. The man screamed in pain and staggered backward, knocking number two, who had managed to pull a big Magnum halfway out of his coat, against the door.

Horn brought his right knee up and into number two's midsection. He tried to check the force of the blow, but the momentum drove his plated kneecap deep into number two's massive belly. The man doubled up, and Horn grabbed the back of his head. He stepped to one side and flung the hulking form down the steps as though it were a rag doll.

"Goddammit!" Winger yelped and he jumped to one side, then followed up and planted his boot on the man's back. "Want me to cuff these guys?"

"No, don't cuff them," Horn said. "We didn't come here to bust a couple of throwbacks."

"Help me," the first attacker cried weakly as Horn turned back around. "Get it outta me, I'm dyin'."

Without hesitating, Horn reached down and grabbed the end of the slide with his right hand. He jerked it out of the flesh in a blur. The man sucked in his breath, and his eyes rolled backward in his head. He slumped over, out cold.

Horn picked up the phone and punched a single, dirty button on its handle that was labeled Call. A rough voice came on the line. "What is it?"

"We're here to see Sarah Weed," Horn said. "Tell her August sent us."

"Who the hell is this?" asked the person at the other end. "Where're Sal and Flick? Let me talk to one of those guys."

"They don't feel much like talking right now, so just give Ms. Weed my message."

"Hold on," came the response. Though there was a discussion taking place in the background at the other end,

Horn couldn't make anything out. The exception was whomever he'd just been talking to, who yelled, "I told you we shouldn't put those two assholes on the door."

"Who is this, please?" A woman's voice was suddenly emitted by the earpiece.

"My name is Max Horn . . . is this Sarah?"

"Yes, it is, but I don't know you. What do you want?"

Horn chose his words carefully. "I'm looking for some pieces to a puzzle that I don't have much time to put together. Dr. August said you could help me out."

"August? Doc August?" Sarah's voice suddenly sounded cheerful. "I haven't seen him for— Are you a cop?"

Horn hesitated a moment before he answered, "Yeah, but it's just me and my partner."

"I know," Sarah said. "I was wondering if you would lie. Dr. August called me this morning."

"You should have told your doormen here to expect us," Horn said.

"I did," she answered. "What can I say? I'll send someone up."

The line went dead, and fifteen seconds later Horn heard someone fumbling with a locking device on the other side of the door. It finally swung open, revealing a short, balding man who took one look at the doorman and said, "Shit." He looked at Horn and nodded toward the inside of the building. "You guys go on down. I'll clean up this friggin' mess."

Horn motioned for Winger to follow and led the way down a narrow, steep stairway that was lit by wire-mesh-covered bulbs hanging from the concrete ceiling. Signs painted in the shape of hands provided direction on the walls. Their fading fingers pointed down. There was one written sign stating, Fallout Shelter—Capacity: 200 Persons. At the bottom of the stairs, Horn pushed open a door and walked into a dimly lit room roughly the size of a large hotel suite. However, the size of the place was the only way it resembled a hotel suite. Horn stopped, allowing his eyes to adjust to the gloom.

"What is this place?" Winger asked as he stepped beside Horn. The room looked like a hackers' rummage sale. Every wall was covered from floor to ceiling with computer and electronic equipment. The gear was stacked randomly and haphazardly as though little or no thought had gone into its configuration. Six CRT monitors were lined up along one of the walls, and endless streams of numbers were scrolling down the phosphor glow of their ancient screens. Two men were busily bent over old-style keyboards on folding tables directly below the monitors.

"Haven't you ever seen a skim house?" A female voice directly behind them answered Winger's question.

Both men jerked around, startled that the woman had gotten so close without their noticing.

"Sarah Weed," she said, holding out her hand. "Which one of you is Horn?"

"He is," Winger answered, shaking her hand and nodding at Horn. "My name is Winger, Stu Winger."

Horn couldn't help noticing that his young partner seemed to be instantly enamored of Sarah Weed and was obviously reluctant to release her hand. Horn took in the young woman, who appeared to be in her mid-to-late twenties. She was dressed in baggy men's trousers, a loose-fitting blouse that revealed a good rift of cleavage and a ratty, olive-drab cardigan sweater that was as baggy as her pants. Her short, blond hair stuck straight up in a haphazard manner that seemed appropriate in the skim house.

What Horn found striking about Sarah was her eyes and skin, which highlighted each other in a beautiful contrast.

Her eyes were bright blue, set in her high-cheekboned face like gems or burning stars. Forming an almost striking backdrop to the light dancing in them was the pale white color of her skin. It looked like snow in moonlight. Horn figured it was from working too long in that pit of electronics. But in spite of her skin color, he could tell the woman was healthy. Sarah Weed blushed slightly as she pulled her hand away from Winger, seemingly embarrassed that she had to initiate the action.

"You, Mr. Horn," Sarah said as he held out her hand, "are held in rather high regard by old Doc August, in spite of being a cop." She smiled warmly, revealing perfect teeth.

Horn held out his hand and realized, too late, that his glove had nearly been torn off during the scuffle. He watched Sarah for a reaction, wondering what she would do when she felt hard metal instead of warm flesh pressed against her milk-white palm. Horn figured that if she knew August, then she also knew his line of business. He gripped her hand firmly and watched her freeze momentarily. Her reaction was brief, however, and she released his grip without further indication that anything was amiss.

"Exactly what is a skim house?" Winger asked, keeping his eyes on the woman. "I think I've heard the term, but don't really know what it means."

"Skimming," Sarah said, gesturing about the room, "is just about the lowest form of computer-based crime that I'm aware of." She turned and spoke directly to Horn, locking her eyes with his. "August says you're looking for information about someone who may be involved in some type of scam. He said I could trust you. Can I?"

"Yes, you can," Horn answered, figuring that Sarah had to be at least mildly concerned about opening her doors to a couple of cops she'd never met. "We're investigating a homicide. I can assure you that my partner's question was asked strictly out of curiosity."

Winger suddenly caught the gist of the conversation and chimed in awkwardly. "Oh, yeah, I wasn't trying to... I mean..." The young cop held his hands out, palms up, stuttering until Sarah let him off the hook.

"For your information, Mr. Winger—" Sarah flashed a smile "—this operation is designed to pick off the sixth and seventh decimal places of a random sampling of electronic transactions running through the bank across the street."

"You mean Citibank?" Winger asked.

"Yes. If you went up to one of the vacant offices on the ninth floor of this building, you'd find a camouflaged cluster of directional antennae aimed at those microwave dishes on top of Citi." Sarah addressed her words to Horn again, who noticed that it made Winger look mildly forlorn. "We keep our skimming, if you will, down in the noise level. Hopefully, it gets written off on their profit-and-loss statements as interference expense, or some such crap." She laughed. "That's what we are, interference. Running a skim house is like dirt-farming the median of a twelve-lane freeway. Not much money, but it's a living."

Horn returned the woman's smile. "It's interesting," he said, "but what August told you about us looking for information is correct. If you have time..."

"Let's go in my office." Sarah led the way to a door set between two banks of uninterruptible power supplies.

Horn and Winger walked into the tiny office. Sarah had affixed herself behind a battered government-issue steel desk that was littered with stacks of software listings, manuals and several books on microwave signal processing. Two folding chairs were situated in front of the desk, and Sarah gestured toward them. "Close the door, please,'' she said to Winger, who pulled it shut before taking a seat. ''Now, what can I help you with?''

Horn caught a whiff of her perfume, which seemed out of place in the strange electronic vault. He noticed that Sarah had once again focused her attention on him. ''We're investigating a double murder,'' Horn began, glancing at Winger, who was staring at the woman with a look on his face like that of a dog waiting to be petted. ''One of the victims was leading the integration of CYN-SYS, a computer system designed to—''

''I know what it is,'' Sarah said, cutting him off. She leaned back in her chair, staring at a spot on the wall next to the door. After several long seconds she tuned in on Horn again. ''I didn't read about Hoke being murdered in any of the papers.''

''Who?'' Horn asked, puzzled by her statement.

''Hoke, Anderson Hoke,'' she answered. ''I took a class with him at the City College of New York once. He's considered the father, more or less, of CYNSYS.''

''No,'' Winger said, pulling a small notebook from inside his trench coat. ''The guy's name was Franklin, Tony Franklin.'' Winger thumbed through the pages until he found what he wanted. ''He was like the chief systems engineer for a company called MMI—''

''Man Machine Interface,'' Sarah said, defining the acronym. ''But what happened to Hoke?''

''What do you mean, 'what happened to Hoke?' This is the first time we've heard his name,'' Horn responded.

''I'm surprised,'' Sarah said, crossing her legs Indian-fashion in the seat of the worn swivel chair. ''Anyone plexed into the fabulous world of confusers knows who the hell Anderson Hoke is. Are you guys detectives or what?'' She laughed and rocked back and forth in the chair.

Horn smiled at her teasing. "Why don't you tell us about him? We're sort of naive when it comes to anything more complicated than an ST model lap-top."

"If Hoke didn't get tapped to do the actual integration of CYNSYS," Sarah said thoughtfully, "he had to be one ticked-off cowboy."

"Why's that?" Horn asked, enjoying the nearly theatrical way in which Sarah spoke.

"CYNSYS was his invention. He conceived it, designed it from scratch." Sarah paused as if considering whether she should say any more. After several seconds, she continued. "He used to allude to some rule-the-world scheme he had, using CYNSYS. It was just bar talk, I'm sure."

"I'd like to hear more," Horn said.

Sarah smiled politely. "Not today, I'm afraid."

Horn didn't want to push the woman. "Okay. When should we come back?"

"Not today and not here," said Sarah, sounding playful. "Why don't you meet me at the Edge tomorrow, after work?"

Horn felt a mild yet pleasant shock as he realized that she was directing her invitation only to him. A glance revealed that Winger looked like someone who has just gotten a bucket of ice water dumped down his shorts. "Sure," Horn answered. "How about six?"

"Six it is," Sarah said, standing. "I'll look forward to it."

The balding, short man let them out into the alleyway. As soon as the door slammed shut, Winger grabbed Horn around the shoulders. "Partner, I fell in love with that woman and she doesn't want anything to do with me. Just promise me one thing," he said, his voice filled with mock pleading.

"What's that?" Horn let his partner carry out his theatrics.

"Promise me that you'll make a video!" Winger slapped Horn on the back and broke into laughter.

Horn didn't respond. His mind was busy with what Hoke's takeoff on Hemingway could mean, and with the green line. He recalled what August had said and wondered if Sarah Weed would tell him.

CHAPTER EIGHT

"SEND IN MR. STELLER," Ashley said, then punched off the intercom. Something was bothering her about the Green Mole Project, but she couldn't put her finger on it. It was a feeling in the pit of her stomach, a nagging manifestation of the voice in her head that kept asking, *Are your tracks covered?* What bothered Ashley the most was that this was the first time in her career that she'd felt as though she should be looking over her shoulder.

The door opened, and she watched Steller enter the office and walk straight to her desk. Without waiting to be asked, he took a seat. "Good morning," he said. "Why the unscheduled meeting?"

"I want an update on Hoke's project. I was going over the revenue projections with Strach, and making Mr. Hoke's scheme work is critical to our health."

Steller crossed his legs and rested his elbows on the arms of the chair. "Strach, he's one of your bean counters, isn't he?"

"He's the corporate controller," Ashley answered.

"Does he know about the project?" Steller asked, rubbing one of his gloved hands across his scarred chin.

"He does now," Ashley admitted. "But don't worry. He was involved in the New Pittsburgh disaster and managed to cover our tracks pretty well. We even made money when I thought we would end up losing our asses."

Steller nodded his head calmly. "What do you want to know?"

"Give me a rundown on everything," Ashley said, as she tensely fiddled with a pen on her desk.

"Very well." Steller's voice was deep and resonant, but it sounded mechanical in cadence and void of emotion. "A couple of things have come into play that could make the operation somewhat complicated."

Ashley sensed the movement in the shadows and felt her stomach drop a couple of stories as though she were in a high-speed elevator. "What do you mean? Why wasn't I told about these complications earlier?" She kept her voice under control, but could feel anger well up in her chest. An ever-so-faint taste of fear caused her to lick her lips involuntarily. She saw that Steller had noticed.

"I don't think they're anything you should be overly alarmed about," he said, staring straight at Ashley. "I was going to brief you during our regular meeting tomorrow morning. If I'd thought they posed any significant risk, I would have made the report sooner." Steller paused before adding, "I'll be glad to go through them with you now."

"That's why you're here."

"I talked to Hoke last night," Steller began. "He ran the program on CYNSYS using simulated satellite feeds and—"

"Dammit!" Ashley snapped. She held up the pen and shook it in time with her voice, which sounded like a band saw cutting through metal. "I want to know about the problems—the 'things that could make the operation somewhat complicated.' I believe those were your words."

Steller stared at Ashley, whose face had flushed red. "Everything checks out," he said slowly, finishing the sentence she'd interrupted.

Ashley stared back at Steller and felt her blood turn cold. His eyes were like twin chunks of ice. She knew that Steller had killed more people than she was aware of, and there were many she knew of. It was what he did, it was *all* that he did. He was an assassin and he was smart. Ashley figured she had best not get Steller out of her loop; having him in her corner gave her a sense of power and security that was like a second ego.

"Pardon me, Mr. Steller," she immediately said, lowering the tone of her voice but being careful not to sound apologetic. "I've had an uneasy feeling about this project that I can't explain."

Steller waited a long five seconds before he opened his mouth again. "Two pieces of information have surfaced that weren't planned in or accounted for." He spoke slowly, methodically, as though his brain had gone into an automatic retrieval of the information from his memory. "The first is the guy, Alfred Gorman."

"Who?" Ashley raised her eyebrows, a puzzled look spreading across her face.

"Gorman. He was a midlevel manager in marketing whom Hoke had originally approached with his mole scheme."

"I remember the name—what about him?" Ashley's puzzled look changed to one of concern.

"He was found in the trunk of a rental car at La Guardia. He had a hole in his temple the size of a pencil." Steller's reptilian eyes glinted with the slightest degree of concern. "I have no idea who killed him, or why."

Ashley was taken aback. "That's strange," she said, more to herself than to Steller.

"Right now the police are running a check on him through our security department. I don't think they'll turn anything up that could link him to our project, but I don't

like them nosing around this close to the Super Bowl.''
Steller uncrossed his legs as though he were programmed
to do it at that particular time.

"It's certainly not good timing, given we've already had
two of our employees turn up as homicide victims,'' Ashley responded. "Are they still going by the murder/sui-
cide scenario?''

"That brings up the other odd thing about all of this,''
Steller answered.

"What's that?'' Ashley asked, getting a strange feeling
that the real source of her unknown anxiety was about to
be revealed.

"One of the cops investigating Franklin's murder is Max
Horn.'' For the first time since he'd been speaking, Steller's voice showed a trace of emotion.

Ashley felt as though she'd just been slammed across the
chest with a big paddle. "Horn,'' she barely whispered as
a mixture of disbelief and fear pumped through her heart
like ice water. "I thought he was dead.'' Ashley focused
dazedly on Steller, who ran one of his gloved fingers
around the collar of his black turtleneck.

"I never told you the full story. He'd shut down all the
escape routes on the asteroid, except for one. But I had
managed to catch up with him and hid out in the cargo
hold of the Lear Business Needle. I was in no condition to
tackle him at that time, and as you know, I had been in the
specialty clinics getting my body parts in order.'' Steller
stopped to flex one of his huge hands in the black leather
glove, then stripped the gloves from them and held up his
smooth titanium appendages for her shivering admiration. "I still have a score to settle, and I mean to do it
right—and soon.''

"He has to go.'' Ashley's voice was suddenly flat and
businesslike. "We have to get rid of him as soon as possi-

ble. He has a way, if you recall, of playing the spoiler role.''

''I'll take care of him,'' Steller said, his voice returning to its normal machinelike quality. ''I'd already planned on it.''

''Do you think we should call off having Mayo eliminated?'' Ashley asked. ''It might draw even more attention to NEXUS.''

Steller raised his arm and looked at a silver Rolex strapped around the cuff of his turtleneck. ''It may be too late,'' he said. ''Mayo is taking today off, and Trower was going to take care of him at his house. Anyway, officially his transfer to Panama has him leaving tomorrow. I don't think it's a problem.''

''I want Trower to take out Horn,'' Ashley said, still tight-lipped. She had been shaken, but her confidence had returned in some measure when she'd realized what was lurking in the shadows. To be sure, Horn was a danger, but now that she was aware of his presence, she could deal with it.

''I don't think he's up to handling Horn,'' Steller remarked. ''Trower is good, but not that good.''

''He might get lucky. And if he doesn't, well, we won't have to worry about paying or disposing of Mr. Trower, will we?

''Anyway,'' Ashley went on, wanting to make sure that Steller wasn't overconfident in his presumed ability to defeat Horn, ''what makes you so sure you can get the job done?'' She was careful to keep her voice free of sarcasm. ''You tried before.''

''It was a fluke,'' Steller answered.

''Of course.''

''I'll talk to Trower tonight.''

"Tell him we want Horn serviced tomorrow." Ashley looked at a calendar on her desk. "The Super Bowl is less than a week away. The sooner Horn is eliminated from the picture, the better."

"I agree." Steller stood up, "Anything else?"

"Let me know the outcome with Mayo," Ashley said, and after nodding, Steller walked out of the office without saying another word.

HARRY TROWER STOOD in the shadows watching John Mayo walk into the workshop area of his three-car garage. Harry had been there nearly an hour, leaning against one of the Mercedes, waiting patiently. It was his style to let his victims come to him. He knew he could have approached Mayo in his house. The man lived alone; his wife had left him two years earlier, and his children were grown and out on their own. Harry figured Mayo probably would have allowed him into the house, even though he would have wondered how Harry had gotten his home address and why he was paying him a visit. But it wasn't Harry's style. He preferred to be waiting when his prey showed up. That way, he controlled the situation from beginning to end . . . an end that Harry always made sure was literal.

Harry didn't expose himself right away. He watched Mayo turn up the thermostat before pulling out a tall stool and sitting down in front of a bench that was stacked with shortwave radio equipment. Silently Harry moved around the Mercedes and walked up behind Mayo, feeling for the grip of the Glock automatic in the pocket of his tentlike trench coat.

"Hello, John," Harry said with warmth.

"What the—" Mayo screeched and jerked around, his eyes wide with fear. "Jesus Christ!" he gasped, eyeballing Trower. "How'd you get in here?"

"Surprised to see me, are you?" Harry smiled, his eyes sparkling like diamonds.

"Goddamn, Harry." Mayo couldn't disguise his fear. His fat face was the color of chalk and he was shaking visibly. "What the hell is going on?"

"I just thought I'd drop by and see how the packing was going." Harry maintained a benevolent expression as his eyelids drooped slightly, giving him the appearance of being extremely relaxed.

"Packing?" The fear on Mayo's face was now mixed with confusion. "What are you talking about?"

"I understand you're getting transferred to Costa Rica or one of those countries down there." Harry walked slowly to another stool and pulled it away from the bench until it was situated in front of Mayo, just out of his reach. "I just wanted to stop and say 'so long.'" He hiked his left leg up on the stool.

"What is this bullshit?" Mayo looked around the garage, his eyes shifting wildly. "I don't know what the fuck you're talking about," he said in a voice that was edged with desperation.

"Then I guess you just haven't gotten the word yet," Harry said, enjoying Mayo's discomfort. He liked this part of his job the best—watching his victims suffer like animals in a trap before he inflicted any actual pain.

"What are you really doing here?" Mayo demanded, having managed to get his voice enough under control that it wasn't cracking.

"Who do you think will win the Super Bowl?" Harry asked, ignoring Mayo's question. He raised his eyebrows independently of his eyelids, which were at a sleepy-looking half-mast. "You know I never thought the goddamn Giants would make it in this year. To tell you the truth, John, if it weren't for Manson, the quarterback, I doubt if they'd have made it to the play-offs. Now if they beat Denver, I'll probably shit my pants.'' Harry chattered away as though he were in a neighborhood bar talking to one of his buddies instead of the man he'd been hired to kill.

Mayo stared at Harry in disbelief as the man went on. ''But you know what I don't like.... I don't like that goddamn aluminum ball. Sure it's got a gyro in it that makes it spin straight—'' Harry made a spiraling motion with his left hand and whistled through his teeth ''—but I saw a guy during one of the play-off games get his jaw broken trying to catch a pass. Give me the old leather....''

''What the hell is going on?'' Mayo screamed. He stood up from the stool.

Harry was on his feet before Mayo had straightened. ''Sit down, John,'' he said calmly. ''I'll tell you what's going on.''

''You better,'' Mayo said, pointing a finger at Harry's chest. ''You won't get any more work out of NEXUS pulling this kind of shit.''

''Come on, John,'' Harry said as Mayo eased himself nervously back on the stool. ''Your boss hired me to kill your fat ass.'' He watched his victim cringe. ''Don't act surprised, either. I thought you'd be smart enough to see it coming, for chrissake. I know that you didn't think I've been waiting around in this garage to have a conversation with you—''

Harry's speech was suddenly cut short as Mayo lunged unexpectedly and struck him full force in the midsection. The two huge men sprawled on the concrete, wrestling wildly. Harry was surprised at Mayo's quickness and cursed himself for allowing the man to get a jump on him. He tried to pull the Glock out of his pocket, but Mayo had him pinned. Harry reached out and grabbed the leg of the stool and rammed it as hard as he could against the side of Mayo's head. It wasn't much, but it was enough to make Mayo roll to one side slightly. Harry took advantage of the movement and heaved his body upward, unseating Mayo from his perch on his gut.

"You son of a bitch," Harry grunted as he pulled out the automatic, ripping his pocket in the process. He rose to his knees and slapped the weapon across the side of Mayo's face. The blow knocked Mayo into semiconsciousness, and Harry stopped himself from putting one of the soft-tipped 9 mm slugs into the man's brain. "No," he said, rising to his feet. He grabbed Mayo by the back of his shirt and dragged him toward the end of the workbench. "You're not getting off that easy."

Harry let Mayo's bulk drop to the floor as he spun open the jaws of a large vise that was bolted to the steel bench top. "Come on, you son of a bitch," he said, reaching down and grabbing Mayo by the shirt again. "I'll teach you to take a jump at me." He pulled up as hard as he could and heard the sound of ripping cloth. Against his better judgment, Harry placed the Glock on the bench and grabbed Mayo under the arms. He managed to get him into a sloppy sitting position after two awkward tries. "Wake up!" Harry slapped Mayo's cheek twice, hard. "Now, stand up!"

Mayo started moaning loudly and struggled to raise himself from the floor. Harry picked up the gun, and as Mayo got closer to the level of the vise, he guided the man's head square into the steel jaws. Harry spun the handle with his left hand and tightened the jaws just enough to lock Mayo's head in solidly.

The pressure seemed to bring Mayo totally out of his unconscious state. His eyes suddenly fluttered open and frantically searched from side to side in an attempt to see what had his head in such an ironlike grip. Mayo's mouth dropped open, and a mournful, wailing scream erupted from somewhere deep inside his guts.

"Shut the fuck up!" Harry yelled, then gave his prisoner a sharp kick in the stomach.

"You see," Harry said, bending over so he was face-to-face with Mayo. "I have a slight problem." He looked at Mayo, whose eyes were beginning to roll up into his head. "I forgot to bring the silencer for my old Glock pistol here." He held up the gun in front of Mayo's face. "That means I'm going to have to improvise."

"Go to hell!" Mayo choked out the words.

Harry straightened up and looked around on the bench. "I'm sure I will," he said, finally resting his eyes on what he'd been looking for. "But you're going to get there first." Harry laid the Glock on the bench and picked up a cordless three-eighths-inch variable-speed drill. "Yeah, John," he said, squeezing the trigger and watching the bit turn, "you're going to get there first, and in style."

CHAPTER NINE

HORN WAS SIPPING a draft, his back to the bar, when Sarah walked into the Edge. Once she got inside the door and removed her gloves, she looked around until she spotted Horn. She smiled and Horn waved to her. He watched her get halfway across the crowded pub before a tall, skinny guy wearing a black beret stopped her. They spoke for a couple of seconds, then Sarah pointed toward Horn. The guy turned his head and stared at him briefly before shrugging and holding his palms up in a gesture that reminded Horn of an Italian gigolo who'd just lost a sale.

"Surprised I showed up?" Sarah asked as she took off her scarf and shoved it into the pocket of the leather flight jacket she was wearing.

"Should I be?" Horn helped her out of the heavy jacket and draped it across a bar stool. Before she could answer, he asked another question. "What are you drinking?"

"I think I'll have an Irish coffee. It's cold out."

Horn turned and motioned to the bartender. He put a ten-dollar disposable credit wafer on the bar and ordered her drink. Turning back to her, he asked, "You didn't shake that guy by telling him I was a cop, did you?"

"Who, Terry?" Sarah turned her head slightly toward the door, then back to Horn, zeroing in on his eyes with her blue marbles. She laughed lightly, and the sound reminded Horn of water rolling down a rocky streambed. "I told him you were my father."

"Your father?" Horn responded, surprised enough that he could think of nothing else to say. He broke out laughing and figured she probably did tell the man he was her father. "Do I look that old?" he asked, retrieving the mug of Irish coffee from the bar and handing it to her.

"Sure you do," Sarah answered. She took the mug in her left hand, then reached up and ran the tips of her fingers through the hair on the left side of Horn's head. "You're getting quite a few gray hairs in there, Dad."

"Let's find a table," Horn suggested, picking up his change and Sarah's jacket. He led the way to a corner table that was next to a small stage. There was a stool and an old-fashioned microphone on a stand in the center of the slightly raised wooden structure that looked more like a farmhouse porch than a stage. "They have entertainment here?" Horn asked, nodding toward the stage. They took a seat around the proverbial postage-stamp-sized table, in the center of which was a wine bottle containing a burning candle.

"Sure." Sarah answered as though surprised that Horn wasn't aware of what went on in the smoky club. "This is amateur night."

"Amateur night for what?" Horn asked. "Is this a comedy club?"

Sarah chuckled tentatively. "You mean you've never heard of the Edge?"

"It's a bar, right?" Horn couldn't tell if Sarah was serious or not.

"It's probably one of *the* places for tapping into the literary vein of the city," Sarah answered, sipping her coffee.

Horn looked around the bar and figured it was also probably one of *the* places for tapping into a number of other things—mostly illegal and mostly in a form meant to run through the nose or into the arm. The good thing about the place was that the people seemed pretty much laid-back, not keyed to the violent side as were most of the crowds in the deadfalls Horn usually found himself in. "Looks like it," he finally said, draining his beer.

When Sarah excused herself to go to the rest room, Horn ordered another beer and Irish coffee from a waitress whose black hair hung almost to her knees. She was wearing a black skirt that covered her shoes and a blouse of the same color that was buttoned as high as it could be buttoned. Horn wondered what she was hiding, but he didn't wonder too long. She introduced herself as Felicia and made Horn laugh aloud when she asked him if he was a writer. "You look just like Joshua Pentecost," she said, her eyes crossing slightly.

"Never heard of him, I'm afraid. I'm about the farthest thing from a writer that you can get." Then, on a whim he said, "I'm a taxidermist."

"Huh?" Felicia looked puzzled for a moment. "You mean you stuff animals?" she asked, a disgusted look spreading across her face.

Horn laughed to himself. "You got it," he said, thinking that being a cop really wasn't that different from being a taxidermist. A cop stuffs animals—the ones that walk on two legs.

Felicia wrote down Horn's order, shaking her head, and walked back toward the bar without saying another word. As soon as she had left, Sarah returned and sat down. "Who is Joshua Pentecost?" Horn asked.

"Joshua Pentecost is a songwriter here in the city who's become somewhat of a cult figure. He only writes material that deals with death and oppression. Why do you ask? Is he here?" Sarah looked around the bar, craning her neck. "I've heard he comes every now and then."

"I don't think he's here," Horn answered. "The waitress thought I might be him, though. She said I looked just like him."

Sarah laughed as though it were one of the funniest things she'd ever heard. "You?" she said between peals of laughter. "That's a howl. Joshua Pentecost shaves his head and wears pancake makeup. He looks like a dead mime."

"I'll have to thank Felicia for the compliment," Horn said, enjoying Sarah's company. It was a long time since he'd been with a woman and had a good time simply by carrying on a conversation and feeling comfortable. Horn suddenly found himself wondering how it would be, *right then*, if his wife and daughter were still alive. Would he be looking at this strangely beautiful woman and feeling the same if Sharon and Julie were at home waiting? The thoughts brought pain... and an abiding, burning hatred for the blond assassin... Horn felt his mods glitch as though pulsed by a stray electrical charge. He forced the thoughts from his mind and wondered if Sarah had noticed the spasmodic jerking of his arm and knee.

"Felicia? Who's Felicia?" Sarah asked, her laughter fading, yet remaining in her eyes. If she noticed his jerking motion, she wasn't letting on that she did. Horn was glad she was talking. It helped him pull his mind out of the shadows.

"The waitress," Horn answered. "By the way, I ordered you another coffee."

"Thanks," Sarah said. "Old Doc August said I would find you interesting. He was right." She reached out and tried to touch Horn's right hand, but he moved it off the table. "Come on, Detective Horn," she said, smiling strangely, "what are you hiding with the glove? Ashamed of your manicure?"

"Call me Max," he answered, thinking it was time to change the subject. "Let's talk about Anderson Hoke for a minute before Joshua Pentecost or some other cult figure takes the stage."

"If you insist." Sarah had a look on her face that told Horn she must have felt the cold, hard metal of his mod when they'd shaken hands the day before.

They were interrupted briefly as Felicia brought their drinks. Horn paid with a credit wafer and told her to keep the change. She half nodded and scurried away as though Horn had a communicable disease.

"She's certainly enamored of you," Sarah said, picking up her coffee and taking a small sip.

"She thinks I'm Joshua Pentecost," Horn answered.

"What is it you want to know about Hoke?" Sarah asked, surprising Horn by the way she was jumping to the reason for their meeting. "Don't worry," she added, obviously noticing his look of mild surprise. "I just want to get this police crap out of the way so I can enjoy the evening."

Sarah's smile made Horn wish it were strictly a social meeting they were having. "Very well," he said, returning her smile, "let's start with how and when you knew him."

"I met him at City College. Like I said yesterday, we took some classes together." Horn remembered that she had said they had taken *a* class together, but let it pass. "Anyway," she continued, "the thing that struck me about Andy initially was that he cheated."

"You mean academically?" Horn asked.

"Yes," Sarah said. "But cheating when you're studying computer engineering, especially at CCNY, generally requires more brains than it takes to learn the crap to begin with. Andy just liked to cheat. He could come up with some of the most ingenious ways to beat the system. One time he used a self-programming routine he'd written to completely restructure the real time hardware-software problem we were supposed to solve. In effect, he wound up giving himself his own test.''

"Did he ever get in trouble with the law?"

"Yes, he did," Sarah answered. "He and another grad student devised a way to access the earthbound airline reservation center and had a little business going where they would upgrade a person's ticket class for a small fee. They called it—''

"I assume they got caught," Horn interjected.

"They did," Sarah continued. "Since they couldn't really advertise, most of their market was developed through word of mouth. Unfortunately for Andy, the Federal Aviation people heard about the scheme and sent an undercover agent to get his ticket upgraded.''

"Did Hoke go to prison?"

"No. He got probation, though. It was his first offense. At least—" Sarah smiled humorlessly "—the first one where he got caught.''

"Did you know that Anderson Hoke took Tony Franklin's slot at MMI?" Horn asked, having checked out that morning who had replaced the dead man.

"Tony Franklin?"

"Yes, remember I told you Franklin was the murder victim who had been integrating CYNSYS for the Wager Control Commission." Horn watched Sarah for a reaction.

"I remember now," she said, then paused as though contemplating something. "He's got to have some connections or they must have had a real schedule problem for him to get that position so quickly.''

"What do you mean?" Horn asked.

"I'm not sure how MMI does it, but most of the big firms segregate the hardware designers and the systems integrators, or implementers, if you will."

"How come?"

"They don't want to give the designers an opportunity to create sleepers that they can wake up later, for their own gain, of course. Follow?" Sarah raised her eyebrows before taking a sip of her coffee.

"I think so," Horn answered. "I take it by sleepers you mean a program or scheme that could be effected at some later date."

"Yeah," Sarah answered enthusiastically, obviously enjoying the subject matter. "It's like squirreling away the key to a lock you designed, but can't have access to. If you do the integration, however, you have the opportunity to expose the keyhole. The separation of the designers and the integrators has been defense policy for decades. It's especially critical for computer-based security systems."

"And now, computer-based financial systems," Horn added.

"True.... If you could design some sleepers into a system like CYNSYS, there's no telling..." Sarah's voice suddenly trailed off to nothing and she stared blankly at Horn for several seconds. "I see what you're saying," she finally said. "If Andy is setting himself up to use CYNSYS for the obvious reason, then he has to have had something to do with...the...murder."

"Maybe not directly. If he got the slot so easily, then the company may have some involvement. At least certain people in the company."

"What are you going to do?" Sarah asked.

"Check it out. The motivation is certainly there."

Sarah allowed a slight whistle to escape her lips. "I'll say. If you could skim the one-hundredth decimal point from what the WCC runs through its processors in an hour, it would make my scheme look just like what it is..." Sarah laughed before completing her description "—a little leech of an operation."

"If I weren't a cop," Horn said with a good-natured look, "I'd consider your operation to be almost admirable. Sort of like a pioneering type of venture."

"More like an exercise in eyestrain, which is what I've been getting lately instead of profit." Sarah returned Horn's smile, but lowered her voice to a serious note. "I did hear one thing about Andy that doesn't quite fit in your thinking."

"How so?" Horn asked.

"Well, it doesn't jibe with Andy having inside help from the company to get Franklin's slot. Actually, it may not fit with anything, it's just sort of...noteworthy." Sarah shrugged.

"What did you hear?"

"A friend of mine, who's in one of my nets, said he saw Andy at an uptown bar with a couple of shady types." Sarah laughed slightly apologetically. "I hope that doesn't sound too dumb."

"No, it doesn't. Go on," Horn said, interested in what she had to say.

"He said they were South American, Mexican or something. Like the old Mafia, only worse." Sarah took a drink of her coffee. "They were like, you know, criminals. Big-time."

"What was he doing with them?" Horn asked.

"I don't know. Allie just said they probably weren't talking about who was going to win the Super Bowl."

Horn rubbed his chin, his glove making a scratching sound across the stubble. This is a new twist, he thought. "Does Hoke use drugs?" he asked.

"He has an affinity for Russian vodka, but that's about it. Unless you consider being addicted to scheming the same thing as being addicted to drugs."

"You seem to know Hoke a great deal better than you originally led me to believe," Horn remarked without the slightest degree of emotion in his voice. "Do you still see him?"

"Not hardly," Sarah said, and a trace of bitterness flashed in her eyes. "Let's just say that Hoke treats the women he knows the same way he approaches his studies."

Their attention was suddenly diverted to a bespectacled, gray-haired man in a shabby pin-striped suit who chose that moment to mount the one step to the stage and switch on the antique microphone. "Good evening, friends," he said. "Eddie Mayfield here." He held a hand over his eyes as though the lights were too bright.

Horn chuckled. "Is this guy a comedian?"

"Shh," Sarah hissed, holding a finger up to her pale lips. Horn noticed a crazy sort of smile emanating from her eyes and couldn't tell if she was serious about what Eddie was about to unleash or just leading Horn down some joke-lined trail to the fool-of-the-month award. He did notice that the crowd had grown funeral quiet.

"I can see some of you out there, and it looks like we have a full house." Eddie dropped his hand and stared at the floor of the stage as if he were watching something crawl across the worn wood. "Tonight," he said, raising his head, "we are fortunate to have one of the most widely recognized, albeit unpublished poets in New York City, reading from his draft manuscript, *Lower Ground*. I am pleased to introduce from right here in the Village, Mr. Derek Chesterfield."

Horn watched Eddie stumble off the stage, then leaned across the table and whispered to Sarah, "Who is this guy? I've never heard of him."

"You're a trip, Max," Sarah said out of the corner of her mouth.

The crowd began to snap their fingers in unison. It sounded like crickets on a summer's night. A slender man in his mid-thirties, wearing parachute pants and a gray sweatshirt with black lettering spelling Down made his way through the crowd. Horn wasn't sure, but he thought the man had been behind the bar when he and Sarah entered the place.

Derek Chesterfield took the stage. He wore wrap-around sunglasses that gave his bent-nosed and acne-scarred face a look that suggested he'd been living in a supersonic wind tunnel most of his life. His jet-black hair widow-peaked on his forehead and was combed straight back.

Horn almost choked when Chesterfield held up a hand as though he was imitating Eddie and gazed at the tightly packed crowd. "Thank you," he said, in a vaguely Midwestern drawl, "thank you very much."

Chesterfield sat on the stool, grabbed the microphone and pulled it toward him until the stand was between his legs. "That's better," he said. "Tonight I'd be honored to read from my last work, which Eddie correctly IDed as *Lower Ground*. Thank you, Eddie." Chesterfield solemnly passed his hand over his eyes again and pointed to somewhere near the back of the bar. He snapped his fingers a couple of times.

"I'd like to begin my reading with an untitled selection." Chesterfield lit a long thin cigarette and let it dangle from his lips as he spoke. The smoke curled up around his head, giving him a halo-effect.

"Wait a minute—" Chesterfield patted his numerous pockets until he found what he was looking for. He pulled out a bent sheaf of papers and thumbed through the pages. He leaned to one side and let the cigarette drop from between his lips to the floor. He didn't bother stepping on the butt with his pointed-toed boot, instead he stared at it for a couple of seconds before looking out at the audience and clearing his throat.

"Is he really going to read something or is he just putting us on?" Horn whispered, leaning toward Sarah.

"Shh . . ." she hissed again, and a look of mock anger flashed across her face followed by an amused smile.

"Lights, please," Chesterfield intoned in his gravelly voice, and the houselights immediately dimmed. A single weak spotlight illuminated Chesterfield on the tiny stage. "Untitled, from *Lower Ground*," he said, then started reading.

There among the summer women
the young, the mystic, come down
from the Motherhead of the Nile,
there among the summer women
am I.

In high tide with wind the same
on the beach,
in the summer of some crazy delta,
me.

There among that wild perfume
of women and nature's madness,
there among the traffic on that haunted freeway,
there I was holding your photo,
shifting into the fast lane.

After a pause of perhaps twenty seconds, the first ten-tative snapping of fingers occurred. Chesterfield stared somewhere out into space as the members of the audience realized the poem was over, and the finger snapping in-creased to cricket level. A couple of people even whistled.

Horn picked up his beer and took a sip. The poem wasn't what he'd expected to come out of Chesterfield's mouth. It struck him as odd, as though he'd just heard something on the border that separates a joke from some-thing real. It fit, he thought. The whole scene existed on that tenuous border.

"Did you like it?" Sarah asked as she picked up her coffee.

"It wasn't what I expected," he answered honestly. "Why don't we get away from here and have dinner?"

Sarah locked her eyes onto Horn's. "Let's listen to one more," she said. "This guy is supposed to be on the verge of getting his stuff published. Then—" Sarah smiled se-ductively "—I'll take you back to my place and fix you something to eat. Deal?"

"Sure," Horn agreed, relaxing against his chair. He felt a warm excitement stir inside him like a pleasant memory.

Someone stepped out of the shadow of the audience and handed Chesterfield a short glass filled with amber liquid. "Thank you. Thank you very much," he said, tipping the glass back and downing half the drink in one swallow. He wiped his mouth with the back of his shirtsleeve, then leaned down. When his hand got fairly close to the hard-wood, he stopped as though he could bend no farther and released his grip. The glass banged to the floor next to the still smoldering cigarette and splashed its contents across the stage.

Chesterfield again examined the floor for several sec-onds before he continued. "Now, on a grimmer note, I'd

ike to read a poem I wrote during a rather bleak period of
ny existence. It's called—'' He squinted at the paper.
'Ah, okay,'' he said, ''this is also untitled.''

The sun rises in the city
where smoke crawls across the river
inside the green line,
by **the** steel tombstone,
pul**ling** that filthy blanket away
from the face I had almost forgotten.

There were memory pages
blown down those gray streets;
the winter wind edging
into every abandoned doorway,
erasing that vein of light
like chaff ejected from my mind

Chesterfield paused and looked down to the floor as if
he wanted another drink, or maybe a smoke, before raising his head and jamming his lips against the chrome
ridges of the microphone.

Her voice echoed
among the burned-out buildings;
a siren for the heartless
who followed to the edge
and pulled gallows leaps
into the manic darkness of her past.

I thought a dream
on that hazy December afternoon
of the back-street ghost she had become
who would haunt me with a futureless kiss
and leave the taste of yesterday
on my tongue.

The crowd seemed to be more tuned in to Chesterfield's finish this time and broke out in finger snapping almost as soon as he'd recited the last word. Someone in the back of the crowd shouted, "Yo, Derek!" Chesterfield nodded a couple of times, his nose banging into the microphone, making the sound of a stone dropped into a well.

"Ready?" Sarah asked as she stood. Horn helped her with her jacket before putting on his own. He allowed her to lead the way out of the bar, winding through the crowded tables.

"Do we need a cab?" Horn asked as they stepped into the cold night air. It was spitting snow, and the wind was beginning to kick up, blowing in across the ice-covered Hudson, carrying the faint smell of sulfur.

"No, come on." Sarah reached out and grabbed Horn's arm, pulling him beside her as she took off briskly down the dirty sidewalk. "I love the city," she said, holding the top of her jacket closed with one hand. Horn wondered how she could love something that seemed to be dying, feeding on itself in a mad frenzy of annihilation. Chesterfield's line about the "steel tombstone" stuck in his mind, but Horn checked his thoughts, knowing his eyes were biased by his job. He had cop's eyes; they saw only bad things. It was their job to look for them.

Sarah led Horn across the Avenue of the Americas and up to West Tenth, finally guiding him to a doorway situated next to a used bookstore. "You live here?" he asked.

Sarah punched a code into the security panel that was welded to the steel doorframe. "That flat over the store," she told him as a buzzing click sounded and the door popped open a couple of inches.

Horn reached around her and pulled the door open, allowing her to enter the narrow stairway first. He followed her up to the landing where she activated the mechanism on the door of her apartment. The lights inside came on automatically as the door swung open.

Horn was surprised at the size of the place and looked around as Sarah secured the door. The unusually large single room had been divided into four distinct areas. One quadrant of the hardwood-floored room contained a queen-size bed and a mismatched chest of drawers. Affixed to the wall was a long coatrack affair from which hung Sarah's sparse wardrobe. Horn noticed there weren't any dresses. Next to the bed was the only other door in the apartment besides the one they'd entered through.

"That's the bathroom," Sarah said, holding out her hand, motioning for Horn to take off his jacket.

"Nice place," he complimented, peeling off the jacket and handing it to her. "It's bigger than you might think from looking at the front of the store."

"I know," she said. "It costs a fortune to heat in the winter."

Horn noticed the kitchen was in the corner opposite the bedroom area. It was a simple setup: stove and refrigerator, built-in cabinets and an L-shaped counter covering the sink and dishwasher. An old, round wooden table with two worn chairs demarcated the area.

Next to the kitchen was a comfortable-looking sofa facing the only window in the apartment, which looked out across West Tenth to a row of brownstones. A padded rocking chair sat next to a reading lamp surrounded by books stacked several feet high. Horn assumed they were from the shelves that covered the entire wall next to the window.

"Why don't you come over to the kitchen, and I'll pour you a glass of wine." Sarah tugged on the sleeve of Horn's turtleneck, and he followed her across the room.

"Is that your playpen?" he asked, indicating the space next to the door. It was covered with a large, maroon-colored carpet. Sitting in its center was a jet-black Mini Mac Nine personal computing system. Horn recognized it from a recent police bulletin that pegged it, along with the latest Mercedes models, as one of the hottest items targeted by thieves. A number of electronic devices that he didn't recognize were lined up on the carpet next to the sleek Mini Mac. One particular item looked like a strange helmet with large protruding bubbles where the openings for the eyes should have been.

"I guess you could call it that." Sarah laughed. She took a gallon jug of white wine out of the refrigerator and poured two glasses. "Here's to an interesting evening," she said, holding up her glass, her eyes sparkling.

Horn returned the gesture and took a drink of the wine. "Thanks," he said.

"Have a seat." Sarah motioned to one of the chairs at the table. "I'm going to fix some pasta and a salad. It'll take less than twenty minutes."

Horn turned the chair toward the kitchen counter and sat down. He watched her prepare the meal and listened as she named several established writers who had gotten their start at the Edge. Horn didn't tell her that he hadn't heard of any of them. He couldn't resist asking, "Do you think old Chesterfield will make it?"

Sarah paused in the middle of tearing up half a head of lettuce and carefully considered the question, making Horn almost sorry he'd asked. "I don't really know," she answered. "His stuff is pretty, well, you know..."

"Morose," Horn completed the sentence for her.

"Yeah," she said and resumed making the salad. "People can only take so much of that manic-depressive stuff."

"You want a hand?" Horn asked. "Let me set the table."

Sarah told him where he would find the silverware, plates and napkins. He poured them both more wine as she broke a loaf of crusty French bread in half. Horn didn't realize how hungry he was until he started eating. It seemed as though he hadn't had a decent meal in years, at least nothing to measure up to Sarah's home-cooked fare, as simple as it was.

"This is outstanding," Horn said as he buttered a piece of bread, then used it to soak up the sauce on his plate.

"Glad you like it." Sarah leaned forward as she went on to say, "But do all cops have manners as bad as yours?"

"Huh?" Horn stopped chewing and looked up at her questioningly.

Instead of responding verbally, Sarah slowly moved her eyes down to the table and focused on the thin, black leather gloves on his hands. She had a half smile on her face that said, I've got you now; so what have you been hiding?

Horn chuckled lightly. "You really want to see what one looks like, don't you?"

Sarah nodded, looking up at Horn's face. "I really want to see August's work," she said. "He told me your mods were some of the best he'd ever done."

"Why didn't you ask earlier?" Horn was surprised that he didn't feel uncomfortable with their discussion.

"They're illegal, aren't they? And that's why you keep them covered up, isn't it?" She suddenly burst into laughter.

"What's so funny?" Horn demanded as he poured them both more wine.

"You're a cop and part of your body is illegal!" Sarah howled.

"Yeah, I guess you're right. Think I should give myself a ticket or something?"

Sarah laughed even harder. "Come on, big boy," she said, finally recovering. Tears were streaming down her dove-white cheeks. "Let me see the arm, and we'll save the knee for later."

Without saying anything, Horn unfastened the Velcro on his right glove and pulled it off. The combat-green titanium skin covering his electromechanical hand had been worn to the point that it gleamed. Horn heard Sarah draw in her breath as he flexed it a couple of times, causing a faint mechanical sound like the working of a shock absorber.

"The other reason I wear the glove is to deaden the sound," Horn said, figuring the little show-and-tell would be all right as long as she didn't ask about the history of his body parts.

"May I?" Sarah tentatively reached out toward his hand.

Horn nodded and watched as she ran her fingers over the enhanced mod as though it were a religious relic, and as carefully as though it were alive. She looked up at him and started to say something, but stopped before words crossed her lips. She had a look on her face that could have been mistaken for fright.

"Is it as you imagined?" Horn asked, not wanting to give her a chance to change her mind and ask or say whatever it was that seemed to hang her up momentarily.

"Sort of," she answered, returning to her old self. "I felt it the first time we shook hands and I called August that night. He said it was your arm and your..."

"Knee, right knee," Horn said.

"Come on," Sarah said, suddenly getting up. She grabbed his arm and pulled him up. "It's my turn. I have something to show you."

"What is this—" Horn grinned "—show me yours and I'll show you mine?"

"Something like that," Sarah said as she led him to the maroon carpet. "Sit here," she ordered, grabbing a pillow from next to the wall and placing it about five feet in front of the black form of the Mini Mac.

Horn plopped down on the pillow, wondering what Sarah was up to. He watched her trip a bus switch. Three sharp clicks followed, and a whirring sound belched out from somewhere inside the Mini Mac's composite case. The backlit LCD high-resolution monitor came on-line an instant later, staring at Horn as if it had been awakened unexpectedly and were trying to get its bearings. A Ready prompt flashed on the screen, indicating that the computer's operating software was up and ready to run.

"You ever do VR?" Sarah asked as she knelt next to Horn.

"I've never even heard of it," Horn answered honestly. "I hope you're not going to ask me to smoke something or abuse my nasal passages, because I—"

Horn's statement was cut short as Sarah brought her hand around and slapped him lightly on the back of the head.

"Knock it off!" she chided. "What's the matter with you? Can't you get your brain out of its cop mode?"

Horn thought the question was probably the most legitimate one he'd been asked in a long time. "Doesn't seem that I can," he answered.

"No," she said finally. "VR isn't a drug—" she hesitated before adding "—it's better."

Horn looked at her and shrugged to indicate Okay, what's next? with his body.

"VR is a form of computer cybernetics that was developed more than forty years ago, but no one ever really paid that much attention to it."

"What does VR stand for?" Horn asked.

"Virtual Reality." Sarah flashed him a teasing look. "And don't worry, you don't smoke it."

"I assume this has something to do with it." Horn gestured toward the helmet and other gear next to the computer.

"Correct. It's a way of creating a completely interactive environment that's like another dimension. A different form of consciousness."

"How come I've never heard of it?"

"It never really caught on, I guess." Sarah held up her hands and shrugged. "I know there's an underground cult, almost a religion, that's based on VR. They did a lot in terms of developing the sensory inputs and software. That's how I got my copy of the program and the interface equipment."

"You were a member of this church, or whatever it is?"

"Are you kidding? The Brethren of Zone are hard-core. They don't do anything but VR. I heard they all weigh about eighty pounds because they don't eat or sleep. They base their whole lives on VR and try to stay in Zone, as they call it, most of their breathing time. I never really made contact with them firsthand. I got my package, you know, through a friend of a friend." Sarah made a stepping sort of gesture with her hand. "It wasn't cheap, either. Those bastards charged me twenty thousand in nontraceable scrip, and that was before my agent tacked on his handling fee."

"That's pretty steep. Is VR legal? I mean, it sounds addictive."

"I don't think it's illegal, but, yes, it's addictive. At least, for some people it seems to be. VR is so far out of the mainstream, however, that the government probably doesn't want to take the time to screw with it. After all, it's not like tone or string or junk. It doesn't spin off a lot of violent side effects, if you know what I mean."

"I guess not," Horn said, picking up the helmet, which was surprisingly light for its size. "You just put this on and fade away."

"As long as you've got at least a quad-X-based machine with five megabytes of RAM and a constant power source." She glanced at him coquettishly. "Want to try it?" She leaned close to Horn. "I'll make it worth your while," she almost whispered, and Horn felt her warm breath wash over the side of his face, sending a tickling shiver up his spine.

"Sure," he said. He had to admit he was intrigued, but he couldn't tell what was intriguing him more—the woman or her claim that he could enter a new dimension.

"Good," Sarah said, as though she'd just chalked up a sale. "Let me get another headgear and the gloves. I'm going with you." She stood and walked to an antique steamer trunk next to the door.

"What do I need to do?" Horn asked.

Sarah came back with another odd-looking helmet, several coils of thin, fiber optic cable and two right-handed gauntletlike gloves made out of Nomex, with a metallic thread woven through the material. "For now, just relax.'' She laid the equipment on the carpet and plugged two of the longer fiber optic cables into a switching box on the back of the Mini Mac. She then plugged the free ends into the backs of the two helmets. ''It'll just take a second to hook this up,'' she said, connecting the helmets to a carbon fiber receptacle on each of the gloves.

''Now I need to load the program.'' Sarah punched in the code Open Zone and the color screen immediately came to life with flashing red letters on a pale blue background: Warning: This software contains an overlay program to prevent tampering or reproduction. Any attempt to penetrate the overlay or reproduce the code will result in the total erasure of Zone. Copyright 2023, Brethren of the Zone, Burbank, California.

Horn almost laughed when he read the warning. The Brethren sure seemed to have their stuff together when it came to protecting their software, he thought. Horn imagined a skinny bunch of baldheaded, robe-clad monks in an abandoned movie studio in Southern California writing the code that sustained their own spiritual existence as well as making them twenty grand a pop when they were able to win a new convert.

After several seconds the warning light left the screen and was replaced by the message:

Welcome to

ZONE

A Doorway to Nonexistence

Press ESC to Exit

Horn heard strange music and realized it was coming from the helmet Sarah had placed in his lap. It sounded like a chorus of sirens, beautiful and ethereal. He turned the helmet over and was nearly blinded by the light emanating from the inside of the flat black fiberglass shell.

"Don't turn it over until you're ready to put it on," Sarah instructed, pulling on the glove attached to her helmet. "It'll screw your eyes up. Put on the glove first."

Horn couldn't ignore the music floating out of the helmet. It was like nothing he'd ever heard. "If you like it now," Sarah said with a knowing smile, "wait until you put the helmet on." He listened and tried to identify an instrument, but couldn't. It was as though female voices had fused with harps or some other stringed instruments. The music seemed to have plugged itself into a portion of his mind that he'd previously been unaware of. It was almost haunting. He wondered if the sailors of Greek mythology heard such luring sounds as they drove their ships into the rocks.

Horn had a sudden pang of anxiety as he pulled the glove on over his mod. "Who's going to shut this down if both of us are in there?" he asked.

Sarah laughed. "I will," she said. "I've done this several times alone."

"Ever do it with someone else?" Horn felt his head almost being drawn into the helmet by the music, which he now seemed to sense in his very flesh and blood as well as hear.

"No, but I've read about it. Don't worry." Sarah reached over and touched the side of Horn's face with her gloved hand, "I'm not going to leave you in there."

"Will we be able to talk?" he asked, feeling a lump in his throat as Sarah turned her helmet over, bathing the entire room in a blue-white light.

"In a way," she answered, raising the glowing helmet over her head. "Now put it on. I want to see you inside."

Horn watched her head seem to dissolve into the light, which disappeared when a foam rubber sealing mechanism closed in below her eyes and across the bridge of her nose. He thought she looked strangely alien and held that image of her as he lifted the helmet, allowing himself to be absorbed into the light and music.

At first, Horn thought he'd stepped through a door into a room whose walls were blue sky. He'd imagined the experience would be a carnival ride type of light show, like a Disney World. It was nothing like that. He could see, but it was more than seeing. Horn felt a totally weird sensation sweep over his body. It reminded him of something he'd read somewhere about a dog being placed on a mirror and what it does the first time it looks down and sees only sky.

Five feet across the room Horn saw a glove floating in the beautiful blue and realized it was Sarah. At least it was her glove, which was glowing as though it were outlined in soft neon. The rest of her body was invisible, nonexistent. He looked down and was mildly shocked to find his body was gone, vanished save his glove. The dog-over-the-mirror sensation increased exponentially as he raised the glove in front of his face and flexed his hand—it was all that was there. Out beyond was only blue sky, stretching to infinity.

"Max." Sarah's voice came from somewhere inside his head, and he looked in her direction, toward her glove. It was waving at him. "You like it?"

Horn tried to say, I don't know. Where are we? But he got no feedback that his lips were moving and that his vocal cords were working.

"I can hear you fine, Max." Sarah's voice was calm, soothing. "Just think what you want to say."

"Where are we?" he said.

"We're here, in this place," she answered. "This is Zone." Horn watched Sarah's glove turn palm up. "Watch," she said. Moments later one of the brightest, reddest apples he'd ever seen appeared in her hand and moved toward him. "Here," Sarah said, placing the fruit in his glove, "take a bite. I promise it's not poisoned." Horn heard Sarah's laughter blend in with the music, which was literally soaring inside his head.

Raising the apple to where he hoped his lips were, Horn took a bite. There was no sensation of his teeth breaking the shining red skin, but the sweetest apple taste Horn had ever experienced seemed to absorb him. It was as though his entire being were involved in tasting, each cell individually flooding with the flavor. He pulled the fruit away, and sure enough, a mouth-sized chunk was missing from its succulent flesh.

Sarah's hand reached out and took the apple. Horn watched it being raised to where her mouth should have been had she been visible. Amazingly, another bite disappeared from its form. "That was good," she said. Horn watched her hand dip slightly, then toss the apple over the area where her shoulder should have been. As soon as it left her hand, it faded out, vanished into the blue. "You try it," Sarah said.

"What do you mean?" Horn found the situation to be so bizarre that he wondered if he hadn't gone insane. Strangely enough, he also felt a sense of comfort. It was as though his existence had been suddenly redefined as a concentration of his senses.

"Just think of something," Sarah answered. "It can be an object in your hand or in front of you, wherever you focus."

Horn thought of a burning candle and focused on a spot between himself and Sarah's floating appendage. A flickering light instantly appeared, followed by the floating form of a white candle. He was elated. He started to speak, and the image disappeared as suddenly as it had come.

Sarah's laughter floated through Horn's mind like the music. "It takes a little practice." Horn watched her glove float up, near the source of his sight. He felt the tips of her fingers on his cheek just as he'd felt them before he'd donned the helmet. "However—" Sarah's voice was somewhere close, near his ear "—I didn't bring you here to practice."

Horn felt the soft sensation of lips being pressed over his and felt Sarah's tongue glide in between his teeth. He caught his breath and felt his entire body become absorbed in the kiss. It was as though he were kissing the woman with his entire being. "This is good," he heard her breathe into his ear, her warm, moist breath causing the skin on the back of his neck to ripple lightly. He felt her hands moving on his body and looked down. The gloved hand was all he could see, but he could feel her other hand pressing the small of his back.

"I've always wanted to do this," Sarah whispered, kissing him again, drawing his tongue into her mouth. Horn felt her hands pull off his shoulder holster, then drop quickly down to his belt. She had the buckle undone, and then his pants were down at his feet so quickly that he uttered a true gasp of surprise when she took him in her gloved hand.

Horn reached out and pulled Sarah toward him. He closed his eyes and ran his invisible hand down her back. A mild sense of wonder hit him when he felt only naked flesh. He moved his fingers farther down to the smooth skin of her buttocks and pressed firmly. Sarah moaned and Horn felt the silky tendrils press willingly against his hardness. He had a floating, weightless feeling as he moved arah's warm body up against his own until he felt her reasts softly move against his face. His lips found one of er nipples, and he ran his tongue slowly around it, feeling it grow taut. Horn took his time, and in turn nearly ainted each time Sarah ran the gloved hand over his hard nd ready body. He heard her moaning blend in with the usic and take off like wind blowing through bare trees.

"I need you now," Sarah said simply. She moved down, rapping her legs around Horn's waist and guided him to her secret place. The pleasure was so intense that Horn hought for a moment his head was going to fly off. He lanted tiny, tasting kisses along Sarah's neck, and the alty taste of her sweat threatened to overload his senses. Iorn felt Sarah begin rotating her hips in an agonizingly low but exceedingly pleasurable manner. She had vrapped her arms around his head and was breathing hard nto his ear.

Horn knew things couldn't be prolonged much longer nd sensed Sarah was also near. She had increased her hythm to the point that told Horn her body had taken the ead away from her mind. He felt the peaking begin somevhere near his toes like the first tremors of a massive arthquake.

Horn hooked his chin over Sarah's sweat-slick shoulder nd opened his eyes, expecting to see the infinite blue. Vhat he saw caused his heart to hang suspended midbeat n awe. His mind blinked off and on several times, as he ried to comprehend what he was viewing. Stretched out or as far as he could see was a raging ocean. The sky was ray, hanging above the infinite whitecapped waves like the kirts of winter.

Horn felt something ominous, almost primal, stir deep vithin his bowels. A sense of something two or three steps eyond wonder filled his mind as his entire body con-

vulsed with a pleasure he'd never thought possible. Just a
the powerful sensation swept over him, the largest iceber
Horn had ever seen broke through the surface of the wa
ter and rose several hundred feet in the air like a giant whit
whale. It seemed to float suspended there in the gray sk
while his body shook madly against the woman's.

Horn didn't know how long he hovered there. There wa
no sense of time. Finally, the vision began to fade, slip
ping back into the infinite blue the Brethren had created
Horn closed his eyes and leaned backward. There was
cushioned sense of falling and he felt himself drift into
comfortable darkness.

CHAPTER TEN

JUST PAST the boarded-up carcass that used to be St. Vincent's Hospital, Horn stopped beneath the yellow haze of a working street lamp and looked at his watch. It was 3:00 a.m. He had awakened less than fifteen minutes earlier, flat on his back, with Sarah's naked form curled in the crook of his modified arm. The VR helmets and gloves were scattered on the carpet like empty wine bottles. Horn, however, felt no ill aftereffects from his excursion into Zone. He had expected a hung-over feeling, given what his mind had been through, but there was none. Actually, he had been surprised when he awoke. He felt good, refreshed, and wondered if it was the woman or the VR that made him feel that way. Sarah had gotten up as he dressed and let him out with a cheery kiss after making him promise they would get together again, soon.

Turning up his collar against the chill, Horn headed toward Fourteenth Street, where he'd pick up the old Purple Line, cursing himself for not taking Winger up on his offer to use the Elint. He'd thought about calling a cab, but at that hour cabdrivers were at a premium.

Horn wasn't a stranger to New York City's subway system. He'd spent the better part of his teenage years riding through the underground snakes. But over the past ten years or so, he'd shunned the subway, which had turned into a rolling showcase for violent crime. The Transit Authority had attempted several times to make the system

safe. All their so-called upgrades succeeded in making it
safe for exactly one person per train: the engineer. In 2015
and 2016, the Transit Authority had automated more than
ninety-five percent of the trains and christened them Nullo
Trains, meaning unmanned trains. The engineer no longer
had to wheel the iron beast through the subterranean concrete tubes.

Horn reached the station in less than ten minutes and
ducked down the stairs, glad to be out of the cold. It had
begun to rain fine slivers of ice. He stepped into the dirty
chute that led to the gates and thought he'd just walked
into the opposite dimension of Zone. Graffiti covered
every square inch of the walls and ceilings. Horn couldn't
tell what color the place had originally been; graffiti had
long been painted over graffiti, the multicolored maze of
spray-painted designs, words and symbols made the place
look like a futuristic cave covered with the hieroglyphics of
a race that burned out short of making the history books.

The station was deserted except for a handful of street
people who had made a shelter out of several garbage cans
stacked across a stairwell. They peered out from between
the dirty metal drums like frightened rats, staring at Horn
as though he were an alien. He wondered if they ever slept.

Horn stuck a credit wafer into one of the Transit Authority's jam-proof token slots and was mildly surprised
that it worked. He squeezed through the Plexiglas turn-
stile and strolled out onto the Purple Line's concrete platform. Horn looked around and saw no one. The place was
dead, a cold concrete tomb. He walked to a schedule bolted
to one of the walls behind a piece of thick Plexiglas. The
rumbling sound of the train reached his ears before he had
time to check his watch, and he turned just as the battered
machine rolled noisily out of the black hole. It's single
headlight shone with a dim yellow glow through the vapor

clouds that billowed from beneath its dirty metal skirt. Horn wondered why it had a light if it didn't have a driver, guessing the reason might be to let deaf people see the beast coming. The city government thought of things like that.

As soon as Horn walked through the grime-covered sliding doors, he heard laughter. At a bench at one end of the car two seamy characters were hunkered over a spool of string. One of the men looked up as Horn got on and gave him the finger. Horn ignored it, but chuckled when he noticed the man's hair. It was long and stringy on the sides with the tips dyed orange. The top was cut flat, which gave his head the look of a landing zone cut out of a crazy orange jungle. He noticed he was getting more than a cursory glance.

"Hey, asshole," the man suddenly barked. "You like my hair? Wild, ain't it?" He ran his hand up the back of his head and slid it across the LZ, then gave Horn the finger again. "Get a load of the asshole," he said, slapping his buddy, who had a dirty New York Knicks stocking cap pulled down over his ears. "I think he likes my hair something hot."

"Maybe he's got the hots for you," the second punk answered, laughing in a short, choppy series of duhs-duhs-duhs. The effect was the staccato sound of a toy machine gun.

Horn took a seat at the opposite end of the car and was glad when the two men turned their attention back to the large spool of string. As the doors closed and the train moved out, Wild Hair unwound a section of the amphetamine and broke it off with his teeth. He rolled it into a ball and popped it into his mouth. After coughing a couple of times, Wild Hair blew through his nose until the end of the string appeared from one nostril. He grabbed it with the tips of his dirty fingers and pulled it out slowly.

"Ahhh, that's sweet," Wild Hair said, tossing the spent string to the floor. He wiped his fingers on the front of a down parka, which was covered with grease stains that nearly obliterated its original orange color. Horn figured it had to have previously belonged to a diesel mechanic.

Feeling himself gag slightly, Horn turned away, but it wasn't soon enough. "You still lookin' at me, dink?" Wild Hair's voice came across the car as though it had been blown from a cracked speaker.

Horn shrugged. It was one more idiot angling for a showdown. He watched impassively as Wild Hair stuffed the spool in one of his jacket pockets and stood. His buddy followed suit. Horn got up from his seat when the two approached him, holding on to the overhead rings as the train rocked.

"You two don't want to screw with me," he said calmly.

"Why not, chief?" Wild Hair asked, placing a fingerless gloved hand into his nylon coat as though he were going to pull out a weapon. "You afraid to shit your pants in front of old Dog Work and me?" Wild Hair pulled his empty hand out of coat and slapped it against Dog Work's chest, a smile breaking across his face like dirty ice cracking.

"Yeah," Dog Work agreed, his speed-drenched eyes staring at a point somewhere above and to the right of Horn's head.

"Because I'm a cop." Horn locked his eyes onto Wild Hair's, hoping the man would realize he was treading on uncertain ground.

"Yeah?" Wild Hair raised his voice. "Well, I'm a fucking priest, whaddaya make of that?"

"I make it that you and your friend are fools," Horn said, resisting a sudden, almost overwhelming urge to bring his right arm around and wipe the punk's face right off his dirt-covered body.

It was Horn's turn to reach inside his jacket. "Whoa," Wild Hair said, holding up his hands. "The cop here is gonna show us his badge."

"Not hardly," Horn said, pulling out the 9 mm and squeezing the trigger just enough to activate the laser sight. He allowed its pencil-thin red beam to focus on the tip of Wild Hair's nose.

"She-e-e-it," the grease stain of a man gasped. An expression flooded his face that reminded Horn of someone who'd just had his body drenched with ice water. He stared at the end of the weapon's barrel, his eyes crossing crazily.

"Why don't you and your pal here—" Horn paused and nodded toward Dog Work "—back off before I show you my badge."

Wild Hair held up his hands, his face like unmolded cheese, sweating slightly and glistening like melted wax. He stuttered something Horn couldn't understand and backed away, grabbing Dog Work by one arm.

Horn stuck the big automatic back in its holster and watched the two string heads retreat to the far end of the car. He felt the train slow suddenly as though someone had tossed out an anchor and saw a sign flash by through one of the cracked windows: Penn Station. He sat down again and watched a hulking, gray-haired man in an oversize trench coat walk by the windows and enter the car. Horn had an odd sort of feeling, because he was pretty sure he'd just seen the same guy get out of the car in front of his.

The man stopped and looked around as soon as he'd cleared the sliding metal doors. He appeared to be in his late fifties, and his silver hair hung down over his collar. Horn saw him stare toward Wild Hair and Dog Work for several seconds before turning deliberately and walking toward him. A copy of the *Times* was draped over his right hand.

"This seat taken?" he asked, easing into the seat across from Horn. He smiled at his lame attempt at humor.

Horn felt his eyes drawn to the newspaper, thinking there was more than the big man's arm hidden beneath the folds of newsprint.

"Well, well, well," the man said good-naturedly, shifting his weight on the stained fiberglass bench. His eyes twinkled in the dirty light as the train surged forward, causing his head to rock to one side. "You must be the indestructible Mr. Horn."

Horn froze, his stare shifting up and fixing on the man's face. Several long seconds went by as he ran the face through his memory. Nothing. "Who are you?" he finally asked, his lips barely moving.

"Harry. Harry Trower." He held out his left hand.

Horn didn't move, but now his memory clicked over only once before the man's name hit the jackpot. Harry Trower. Christina Service had said he was in town. For what? For the only reason he ever was anywhere: to carry out a hit. Horn's mind raced up several dead ends trying to find out why he deserved to be sitting across from a hired killer.

"Franklin's murder," Horn said, the obvious finally coming to him.

"Well, that poor boy and his girlfriend had, you know, a sexual problem." Harry chatted on, smiling and shaking his head in mock pity. "And now, since you more or less got stiffed with the case, well, you've got a longevity problem, Detective Horn."

"How did you come up with me as your assignment?" Horn asked as he moved his right arm up and rested it on a section of chrome railing behind his seat. He noticed Trower's sly eyes take in every move.

"They give me a name, they pay me, and I do a job. It's a living. I don't complain about it." Harry touched his chest with the fingertips of his left hand as though he were apologizing for having a boring job.

"Who're they?" Horn asked.

Harry held up his index finger. "Now you're getting personal."

Horn watched as Harry jerked his right hand sideways and shucked off the newspaper. Horn stared into the silenced barrel of an advanced-combat Uzi assault pistol. "I'm sure you read the *Times*, Mr. Horn," Harry said, "but you probably never read what was *under* the *Times*." The hulking figure broke into a soft chuckle that was almost friendly.

"Hey!" Harry suddenly yelled, turning his head toward the other two occupants of the car. Horn felt the train slowing. "Front and center, you two."

The two string heads looked tentatively in Harry's direction, their eyes growing wide as they noticed what he was holding. "Get your worthless asses over to the door. You're getting off at this stop."

The two glanced briefly at each other before jumping up and moving toward the door in a wild thrashing of arms and legs. "That's better," Harry said. But Horn noticed the big man never moved the barrel of the Uzi away from its target—which was the center of his chest.

"He—he—he's got a gun," Wild Hair stuttered and pointed accusingly at Horn as he squeezed Dog Work to one side in order to be the first one out when the doors opened.

"I know that," Harry said in mock irritation as the train jerked to a stop. "Now just go on nicely and forget about me and my friend here."

Harry smiled as the pair practically appeared to be sucked out of the train the instant the doors opened wide enough.

A stout man carrying an olive-drab duffel bag stepped into the train and sat down on the bench just inside the doors. "Not this one, pal," Harry called calmly. Horn watched the man turn and look in their direction, his eyes coming to rest on Harry's weapon. "Take the next car down and make life easy on yourself for a change."

Without the slightest hesitation, the man stood and left the car. The doors closed, and Horn noticed the green bag was still sitting in front of the bench where the man had placed it. "Guns seem to have that effect on people," Harry remarked, turning his attention back to Horn as the train jerked forward. "Fool-makers and witness-takers, that's what they are."

Horn thought about attempting to kick the barrel of the Uzi, but it was too far away. He looked around for something to create a diversion with and give himself an opening. His eyes focused on the railing over which he'd rested his arm.

"Now don't get nervous on me," Harry said.

Horn faced Harry and allowed his hand to grip the rail. He flexed the mod slightly and felt the tube's steel brackets give a little. It wasn't much, but it was more than nothing. Horn only hoped the rail wouldn't break in two when he made his move to rip it from the wall of the train.

"I'm not nervous," he said, hoping that his confidence would break Harry's concentration for a split second.

"That's good," Harry said soothingly. "I've heard if you die while your mind is screwed up that it'll move you to the back of the boat."

"The boat? I don't get it," Horn prompted, wanting to keep Harry talking.

"You know, the boat you gotta take across the Styx River. The river of shit." Harry smiled, his eyes gleaming like living gunmetal.

Horn felt a pang of anxiety as Harry raised the barrel of the Uzi a couple of inches. He sensed his time was running out fast. Harry probably intended to leave him at the next stop. Leave him dead.

"Listen, Harry," Horn said, aware that a craziness was running through his mind like music. "You really should get those boots of your shined." He leaned forward slightly and spat square on the toe of the assassin's black boot. At the same time he ripped the section of railing off the wall and swung it down and across in a blur.

The end of the chrome pipe struck the side of the black silencer just as Harry squeezed the trigger. A ream of 9 mm slugs tore into the seat less than six inches from Horn's left arm, splintering pieces of yellow fiberglass as though it were being drilled with a jackhammer.

"Goddammit!" Harry bellowed as Horn lunged across the aisle and banged into his chest. The Uzi fell to the floor in a smoking clatter as Horn tried to maneuver himself into a position where he could pin Harry's arms.

Suddenly Harry bucked his body upward with a surprising strength and agility. Horn found himself facedown on the cold steel floor of the train and felt a stab of blinding pain sweep through his right side. Horn rolled over just as Harry aimed another kick at his face. The killer's black boot swung through free air as Horn brought his right arm across the floor in a sweeping motion, knocking Harry's legs out from under his massive body. He hit the floor on top of Horn and scrambled across his legs in an effort to reach the Uzi.

"You son of a bitch!" Harry breathed hard as he reached out to grab the handle of the weapon. "Shit!" he screamed as Horn kicked down and sent the black machine pistol clattering across the dimpled steel.

Horn dragged himself to his knees as Harry launched himself in a stumbling sort of crawl toward his weapon. Goddamn, he's fast, Horn thought as he reached inside his jacket. But it was too late. Harry had the Uzi in his hands and sent an arc of screaming lead down the length of the car, shattering windows and ricocheting off the metal walls in showers of sparks.

Horn ducked behind the end of the bench and fired three blind shots in Harry's direction. He heard the Uzi cook off again, followed by a loud bang and the sudden rush of cold air. Horn raised his head and caught a glimpse of Harry's trench coat as it disappeared through the emergency exit at the far end of the car.

Moving in a duck walk, Horn approached the open door. The rattling sound of the train's steel wheels blared through the opening. He heard Harry's Uzi roll off another burst and dived behind the abandoned duffel bag before he realized the shots hadn't been fired in his direction.

Horn scrambled to his feet and moved to the side of the door. He counted to three then swung around in a crouch, holding the 9 mm in both hands. The red beam of the laser cut through the darkness, making crazy patterns as it danced in the gloom. Horn saw that the emergency door on the car behind the one he was on had been broken open. A man's body lay in a pool of blood in the middle of the floor. Horn could see a number of bullet holes stitched across the man's forehead. Pitiful pieces of his skull and brain were splattered across the floor behind him, giving Horn the impression that Harry had shot downward at the guy who'd probably been on his knees.

Horn took a cautious step onto the narrow steel-mesh walkway that crossed over the car couplings, wondering where the killer was.

Something in the back of Horn's mind suddenly made him freeze. The sensation was spooky. Just as suddenly as he stopped, the Uzi erupted from the top of the train car, raining down a stream of bullets in rapid succession of blinding muzzle-flashes. Horn felt his modified arm slam down as though it had been struck with a sledgehammer. He fell back into the car, tripping over the threshold and sprawling on his back.

Horn looked down at his arm, surprised he was still holding the big automatic in his hand. The sleeve of his jacket was smoking and Horn could see titanium skin through the shredded material. Three shallow bullet-sized dents ran across the upper portion of his modified wrist. Without getting up, Horn emptied the clip of his weapon into the roof of the train car where he expected Harry to be standing.

"Goddamn!" Harry screamed in pain. There was a loud thud on the roof as Horn scrambled to his feet. He punched the spent clip out of the 9 mm and pulled a fresh one from his jacket pocket, jamming it into the butt of the weapon.

Horn jacked back the slide as he eased out the door, aiming the weapon upward. The dark ceiling of the tunnel sped by as Horn mounted a set of rusting steel rungs that had been welded next to the doorway. It took him two steps before he could peer over the edge of the roof. Horn could see Harry's bulky form sprawled on its side near the middle of the roof. He thought he could see the Uzi farther down, but wasn't sure. The only light was coming from the inside of the cars. It bounced off the walls of the tunnel, giving the whole scene a strange stroboscopic effect.

Focusing the red beam of the laser sight on Harry's chest, Horn crawled onto the roof of the train. He moved carefully toward the big man, who appeared to be out cold. When he got a little closer, Horn flashed the beam and found he'd been correct. The Uzi was ten feet out of Harry's reach.

Horn noted a large splotch of blood on the assassin's trench coat near one of his legs, but could see no other indication that he'd hit his mark. He crawled closer and reached out toward the man's neck, intending to check for a pulse. The paid killer's right hand suddenly came to life and latched onto the barrel of the 9 mm, pushing it up and away. Out of his peripheral vision, Horn saw Harry's left hand swing up from behind his body, a blade glinting in the irregular light.

"Have a taste of this, cop!" Harry screamed as he drove the blade toward Horn, who twisted sideways just enough to deflect the blade with his right shoulder. Its razor-sharp edge still sliced across a section of Horn's back, cutting through his thick jacket as though it didn't exist. He felt a stinging sensation, which was followed by something warm and wet running down his back.

Horn jerked the pistol away and used it to slap the knife out of Harry's hand. The assassin yowled in pain as the barrel cracked across his knuckles. Horn started to let Harry have one across the temple, but found himself painfully bounced onto his side as the big man managed to bring one of his knees up and drive it into Horn's groin.

It was Horn's turn to let out a yell, and it was the only thing that kept him from throwing up. He rolled away from Harry, who struggled to his knees, a string of spit swinging from his gasping lips. Horn sat up and put the beam of the laser directly between Harry's eyes. The big man froze as though he'd just been cursed with an apocalyptic vision.

"Don't shoot," he yelled above the din of the train noise.

"Why not?" Horn couldn't resist saying. "Don't you want to sit at the back of the boat?"

Harry looked puzzled momentarily and then—Horn could hardly believe it—he smiled his I-am-your-godfather smile. "That's good, Detective Horn. You may have what it takes to be in this dirty business, after all. They said you were tough, but they didn't tell me you had a sense of humor, too."

Horn played the laser beam on the man's face. "Once again," Horn demanded, "who are 'they'?"

"I guess I can tell you now," Harry answered, holding his battered hand in the crook of his right arm. "By the way, you did get me in the leg. I thought I had you, though. What made you stop when you were coming out the door?"

Horn raised the beam of the weapon a couple of inches over the top of Harry's head and squeezed off a round. The big man scrunched down instantly. "Holy shit!" he howled. "All right, all right. I dealt with two people. One guy was a big shot for the NEXUS Corporation and the other guy was his boss, I guess."

Horn felt the pieces snap together in his investigative mind. It happened the way it always did, a sort of clicking when his suspicions were confirmed. "Was he Colombian or South American?" he asked, placing the red dot in the middle of the man's sloping forehead, remembering what Sarah had said.

Harry seemed confused by the question. "What do you mean?"

"Did you ever deal with any South Americans, Mexicans maybe?"

Harry shook his head. "No." Horn sensed he was telling the truth. "These guys are anything but descendants of the browner races. The big guy, the big boss, was fair-skinned."

"What was his name?"

"Steller," Harry answered. "Big blond son of a bitch."

Horn couldn't quite make out what Harry had said. "What?"

"Steller!" the big man yelled.

The name hit Horn like a dark wall. He felt as though someone had just run a spire of ice through his heart. Closing his eyes, he saw it again; it had a dimension of reality, like Zone. Without knowing it, he began rubbing the jagged scar that ran across his right cheek with his free hand. He saw Sharon's body flying backward as the .44-caliber slug slammed into her chest. And Julie...he watched her tiny body, limp and broken, tossed to the floor like a rag. Steller's grinning face appeared in front of Horn like a manifestation of insanity. The index finger of the E-mod reacted, and Horn felt the sharp kick of the 9 mm as it barked out its death message. The sound of the weapon going off was like a switch that turned on the lights, and he watched his dark vision vanish. In the same instant a shock ran down his spine as he saw the top of Harry's head fly off in a spray of blood and tissue. The big man's eyes rolled up into what was left of his head, and he toppled backward over the edge of the train.

When Horn realized what had happened, he felt the shock melt from his mind. He had left Steller for dead on New Pittsburg, then had seen the whole asteroid consumed by nuclear fusion. And the dead weren't supposed to come back.

CHAPTER ELEVEN

"DID YOU HAVE TROUBLE finding the place?" Horn asked as he unhooked the chain from the worn facing and allowed the door to swing open.

"Hell, no," Winger answered. "I just looked for the old folks." The young detective walked into the sparsely furnished apartment and looked around as though he were observing a crime scene. "Well, well," he said, smiling, "we finally glimpse the secret lair of the infamous Shadow Master, Max Horn."

"Shadow Master?" Horn coughed more than he laughed. "You're so full of shit you need a license to carry it."

"Look at this place," Winger said incredulously. "It could pass for a rummage sale at the mission." He waved an arm in the direction of Horn's bed, which consisted of a mattress stuck in one corner of the single room. Rumpled bedclothes were piled haphazardly in its center.

The rest of the apartment was furnished with groupings of various items of furniture and equipment that seemed to go together. A small stereo and flat panel entertainment screen were stacked on shelving made from wooden crates. In front of this mélange of mismatched electronics was an overstuffed armchair covered in green corduroy, worn and frayed. Next to it was a large wooden end table and a reading lamp. The table was covered with books and a yellowing stack of newspapers, as well as several empty

beer cans. A large cardboard box filled with both hard-
and soft-cover books had been pushed under the table.

"This must be the kitchen," Winger said, turning toward a counter next to the door, with a sink in the middle.
There was a refrigerator and a microwave oven, but no
stove. "Do you have any coffee?" he asked, staring at the
pile of dirty dishes that threatened to spill out of the sink's
stained porcelain boundaries.

"Yeah," Horn answered, stomping up to a trunk next
to the bathroom door. "There's plastic cups and instant
coffee over there somewhere. Use the microwave." As he
bent over the trunk that served as his chest of drawers, he
felt a stab of pain in his upper back. He was sure blood was
starting to seep through the crude dressing he'd managed
to apply while looking over his shoulder in the bathroom
mirror. "There it is," he muttered, pulling a flat, plastic
package from among the jumbled clothing.

Horn went over to his partner, who was in the process
of punching in the settings on the microwave. "You want
some?" Winger asked without turning around.

"No, thanks." Horn pulled a folding chair away from
the card table that pretty much made up the dining room.
He pulled off his shirt and sat down with his back to Winger. "I didn't ask you over here to make coffee," he said
over his shoulder. "I need your help."

"What's that . . . ?" Winger became silent for a minute
as he turned and saw Horn's back. "Holy shit, partner,
what the hell happened?" The blood-soaked bandage
looked even more dramatic and bizarre next to Horn's
modified shoulder. The combat-green titanium curved
around just outboard of the shoulder blade, joined to skin
that was crisscrossed with stark white tissue.

"Trower was pretty fast in spite of his size," Horn answered as the bell on the microwave sounded. "It's a knife wound."

"Why the hell didn't you go to the hospital?" Winger's voice carried a degree of frustrated anger. "There wasn't anything in your goddamn report about you taking a knife in the back."

"Couldn't," Horn said simply.

"Why not?" Winger pulled open the door of the microwave and removed the cup. "Afraid someone's going to find out you're not invincible?"

"That doesn't smell bad. Come to think of it, I'll take some."

"Huh? What the hell are you talking about?"

"Coffee," Horn answered. "I'll have a cup, after all."

Winger looked at him blankly for a couple of seconds. "Here, take it." He shoved the cup into Horn's hand. "Now, why the hell didn't you see a doctor?"

Horn held up his modified hand and flexed it once. "In case you've forgotten your training, *this* is a felony. Even for cops."

"Oh," Winger replied sheepishly. "I guess you're right."

Horn picked up the plastic package and held it out to his partner. "Ever use one of these?"

"What is it?" Winger turned it over in his hands.

"It's called an MD-1, Miracle Dressing." Horn took a sip of coffee before setting the cup on the table. "It was developed by the military during that minor war in southern Turkey."

"I suppose you want me to . . ."

"Like I said," Horn responded, grinning, "I didn't ask you over to make coffee, or to critique the decor of my apartment, for that matter."

Winger started to open the package. "Next thing I know you'll be asking me to give you a sponge bath."

"You *could* wash your hands," Horn said wryly.

Winger looked at the sink full of dishes. "Where?"

"Try the bathroom."

"The bathroom," Winger repeated as he placed the dressing on the table. He pulled off his leather coat and tossed it over the back of the armchair as he walked across the room. Two minutes later he returned, drying his hands on a towel that had Hilton stitched across it in brown letters. "You know, if you ever run out of money, you could probably sell that bathtub for a mint." He grinned crookedly. "It ought to be in a goddamn museum."

"It still holds water." Horn picked up the package and tossed it to the young cop.

Winger tucked the towel into the webbed harness stretched across his chest. From it hung the odd but deadly-looking machine pistol, a .44 Magnum with a six-inch barrel, two flat-handled throwing knives and a small egg-shaped metal object with a round pin stuck through a mechanism on one end.

"What the hell's that?" Horn pointed to the object, which was the same color as his E-mod.

"That?" Winger grinned, looking down at his chest. "That's also a felony, even for a cop. It's an old type of concussion grenade. I managed to buy an entire dozen from this Mideastern weapons freak over in Brooklyn." Horn's partner spoke as though he had lucked upon a wining lottery ticket. "If the Barracuda saw that she'd . . . hell, she'd probably shit her pants."

"Sorry I asked," Horn said, shaking his head. "The dressing now, okay, Stu?"

Winger opened the package and pulled out a sheet of flesh-colored putty. "What am I supposed to do with this, seal up your windows?"

"Read the instructions."

"Where are they?"

"On the back of the package."

"Oh." Winger turned the package over. He read for nearly a minute before stating, "I got it." Laying the dressing on top of the plastic wrapping, he began removing the bloodstained bandage.

"How does it look?" Horn asked as Winger dropped the bloody rag into a garbage bag next to the sink.

"Could be worse," his partner answered. "Stand by one." He walked back to the bathroom and returned seconds later with a bottle of rubbing alcohol. "This may sting," he said, dousing the Hilton towel with the clear liquid.

Horn went stiff as Winger cleaned the wound. Sting, he thought, was an understatement. The burning sensation grew so intense that his mods jerked involuntarily.

"There," Winger finally said. He tossed the towel onto the table and picked up the putty. "I think you were lucky. It's not that deep and doesn't seem to be infected." Winger worked the dressing between his hands, flattening it as though it were a hamburger patty. "It says this stuff is laced with antibiotics, so we should be all right in any case." Horn felt as though a block of ice were being laid against the wound as Winger applied the dressing, pushing down with his fingers in the center, working toward the edges in order to seal it. "Done," the young cop finally said.

Horn stood and moved his modified arm in a slow circular motion. "Feels pretty good," he said. "It even stopped hurting."

"It also releases an anesthetic into the wound area," Winger said, admiring his work. "How do you feel?"

"Pretty good." Horn rummaged in the trunk again and fished out a black turtleneck. He pulled it over his head, careful not to raise his right arm too far.

"I was thinking about going down to Kelly's for a couple of beers later on," Winger said. He walked to the green chair and picked up his coat. "Want to go?"

"I'd like to," Horn answered, "but for starters we need to go down to the Village tonight."

"What's up?"

"I've been trying to contact the Weed woman and haven't had much luck. I think we might be able to catch her at the Edge."

"The joint where you'd met her?" Winger asked.

"Yup. So why don't you pick me up around seven?"

"Now that I know how to get here, right?" Winger grinned and strolled to the door, opened it, then turned around. He pointed to a poster tacked in the middle of one of the white walls, the only decorative element in the otherwise drab room. It was a black and white print of a mushroom cloud, below which was scrawled, A Religious Experience? "I like it," the young cop said.

"See you at seven," Horn responded dryly. "I'll be waiting on the curb."

As the door closed, Horn turned around and stared at the poster. A strange feeling came over him as if he were seeing it for the first time. He remembered then that it had been hanging there when he moved in and he'd just never bothered to take it down.

Horn idly drifted over to a box of tools and pulled out a cleaning kit. Then he extracted his 9 mm from beneath the mattress. Sitting down at the card table, he broke the weapon down and began the almost therapeutic ritual of cleaning it.

At exactly five minutes to seven, Horn walked down the steps of his apartment building, pleased to see the Elint waiting at the curb. He crawled into the warm interior of the big vehicle and was promptly greeted with a "Howdy-doody" by Winger.

His partner grinned as he pulled away from the slush-covered curb. "Did you have a nice afternoon?"

"Depends on what you mean by nice," Horn said, but provided no further enlightenment.

Winger drove down a side street before whipping the dirt-covered car onto Broadway, heading south. It had been raining during the day, but the temperature had dropped enough with the onset of night that the rain had turned to snow. Winger turned on the wipers as he pulled into the fast lane. Horn pulled the shoulder harness across his chest and fastened it.

"How's the shoulder?" Winger said, glancing over.

"I can hardly tell the wound's there," Horn answered. "By the way, thanks. I can't remember if I said that earlier or not."

"No problem," Winger said. "What really happened with Trower?" he asked, whipping around a battered yellow cab that had almost come to a stop next to the guardrail. "You asshole!" Winger held up a finger and peered into the rearview mirror. "Those goddamn cabdrivers think they're God's gift to asphalt."

"What about Trower?" Horn asked as Winger slipped the car back into the left-hand lane.

"Well, it just seems to me that maybe more went on than what you reported. You seem different. You know, like someone pissed in your bathtub or something."

"How would you act if someone ran a blade through you?" Winger's question had made Horn feel uncomfortable. The answer Winger had come up with made him feel even more so.

Horn's partner laughed and looked at him with a don't-give-me-that-line-of-crap look on his face. "That scratch? After seeing the scars around your mod, I don't think that nasty little knife wound is going to be the cause of mental trauma for you."

Horn suddenly felt very tired. "It was something Trower told me," he heard himself say. "In a way, he killed *himself* when he told me."

Winger looked puzzled. "Your report said you bounced him off the train with that ancient piece of pot metal you call a weapon."

Horn almost managed a smile. The young cop never missed an opportunity to chide him about the weapon, once stating that it had probably been used by Custer when he was taken down by the Indians, and that it hadn't even worked there. "I did," he finally admitted, deciding at that moment to tell Winger about Steller. He figured his partner had the right to know what he might be up against.

"Then what the hell are you talking about?"

"Steller," Horn said, a scratchy feeling forming in his throat as the name came out. "Trower told me he was hired by Steller to kill me."

Winger glanced over at Horn, who was staring out the windshield as if he were mesmerized by the motion of the wipers.

"Steller is the one who killed my wife and daughter."

Winger nodded slowly, but Horn didn't notice. All the detectives as well as the bluesuiters in the precinct knew he'd lost his family, violently, almost two years before. They were considerate enough not to bring it up, however. Horn was especially appreciative of Winger, who rarely brought up the past, unless Horn opened the subject for him.

"I guess he was the one who gave you your mods," Winger said, his voice even.

"True," Horn answered, snapping out of his morose trance. He felt less tired, almost as if a weight had been lifted off his shoulders. "That's sort of the reason I'm telling you about him now."

"What do you mean?" Winger asked. "I don't understand."

"Except for his crotch area, Steller's entire lower body is made up of enhanced mods." Horn looked over at Winger. "Good ones."

"No shit!" The young cop spoke more to himself than Horn. "I've heard stories about guys like that. They're called KMs or something like that—killing machines."

"I've never heard the term, but it fits," Horn said. "What upset me about Steller, besides the obvious, is that he's supposed to be dead."

"What do you mean?"

"I killed him, at least I sure as hell thought I did." Horn lapsed momentarily into a trancelike state. He saw Steller lying on his face, a smoldering hole the size of a cannonball burned through the titanium plating on his back.

"What does he look like?" Winger asked.

"Tall, six-six or so. Probably two-fifty. His mods have him shaped like a weight lifter," Horn said as Winger made the cut through Times Square, wheeling onto Seventh Avenue. "You'll know him by his face, though. He's got short blond hair, like a military flattop, and a square jaw that looks like it's been carved out of marble with a jackhammer. Scars all over his face." A strange feeling of something that bordered on satisfaction welled up in his chest as he added, ''I put some of them there.''

The two cops rode mostly in silence the rest of the way to Greenwich Village. Winger found a parking place on Carmine Street, and they walked the two blocks to the club through a mixture of snow and sleet.

''What is this place?'' Winger asked, pointing to a small chalkboard on an easel just outside the entrance. It was covered with a sheet of clear plastic, but Horn could still read the handwritten message:

Winton Truax
''THIS FAR-FLUNG MADNESS WRITTEN''
TONITE ONLY
9 P.M.
NO COVER

''It's a place where people come to read their poetry,'' Horn answered, pulling open the door.

''No shit?'' Winger sounded mildly surprised, which surprised Horn. He'd half expected his partner to make some sort of crack about the literary bent of the joint.

''Listen,'' Horn said once they got inside, ''go find us a table. I'm going to try and call Sarah. She lives just a couple of blocks from here.''

Winger looked over the crowd. ''Don't you want to see if she's here first?''

''You check, I'll try calling anyway.'' Horn turned and walked down a hall that led to the telemonitors and the rest rooms. He'd considered going by Sarah's place, but he didn't want to take the chance of leading someone there. Someone like a KM, for instance. Horn stuck a credit wafer into the old telemonitor's slot and punched in her number. Almost immediately a still picture of an impressionist painting flashed onto the screen. Classical music played in the background as Sarah's recorded voice requested the caller to leave a message. At the prompt, Horn looked at his watch and asked Sarah to meet him at the Edge any time within the next hour.

He found Winger at a table near the back of the room, farthest from the stage. He was sipping a beer and there was one on the table for Horn. "Thanks," Horn said as he sat down. "Any sign of Sarah?"

"No," Winger answered calmly, staring over Horn's shoulder. "But you know how weird you feel when something you just talked about happens? Like talking about it *made* it happen?"

Horn was in the process of tilting back the beer and stopped cold. "Where is he?" Horn asked, watching Winger's eyes. He set the glass on the table and resisted the urge to turn around.

"At the far end of the bar, kind of in that shadowy area next to the hallway leading to the heads. You walked right past him when you came out of there." Winger whistled under his breath. "And you were right Max—he is one big son of a bitch."

"Keep your eyes on him." Horn fought to keep his heart from racing. "He tracked us here and intends to kill."

"He knows I've seen him," Winger said, "but he's not moving. I think the bastard actually smiled at me when I first spotted him."

A cold chill ran up Horn's spine, piercing his brain with the image of Steller's hellish grin. "He's waiting for us to make a move. This is like a game to him, a death game."

Winger rubbed a gloved hand across the heavy stubble on his face before picking up his beer. "Whatever move we make," the young cop said, "we better make it out of here.'' He tilted back the glass and swallowed a third of the foaming liquid.

"I've got an idea," Horn said. He automatically squeezed his left arm against his side, feeling the bulk of the 9 mm in its shoulder holster. "I'll move—"

"Wait—" Winger cut him off, scraping back his chair. "He's gone down the hall."

"Goddamn it." Horn swung out of the chair, knocking it over. He headed through the crowd, pulling the automatic from the inside of his jacket. He could hear Winger right behind him. "Police, move!" Horn barked as he slammed into a waitress carrying a tray full of drinks. She screamed and fell across a table, dumping the tray in a shower of liquor, ice and broken glass.

Horn ran down the length of the bar, shoving people out of his way. Someone screamed, "He's got a gun!"

"We're cops! Get the hell out of the way!" Horn could hear Winger yelling directly behind him as people scattered, panicked like chickens with a fox in the coop.

Horn slid to his knees and aimed his 9 mm down the hallway with both hands. The red beam of the laser struck a short, fat woman in the chest as she exited the ladies' room. "Move back into the rest room, lady. We're police officers." The woman's eyes grew about three times their normal size, and she disappeared back into the washroom as though she'd been jerked inside with a chain.

"He must be in the head," Winger said, breathing hard.

Horn glanced up at his partner, who was standing behind him, aiming the machine pistol down the hallway. "I'm pretty sure he's not in here," Horn said, referring to the ladies' room. "The woman who stepped out looked calm enough until she saw us."

"Is there a window in the men's?" Winger asked.

"I don't know, I've never used it," Horn answered. "I'm going to move to the other side of this door. Get that woman and anyone else out of there." He stood and turned toward one of the bartenders, who was peering over the bar's edge. "Clear the place," Horn ordered, even though most of the patrons had already scrambled out the door.

"Any time," Winger said as he thumbed the safety of his weapon off and on, never taking his eyes from the door of the men's room.

"Let's go." Horn moved quickly, sliding past the entrance to the women's rest room. He stood, holding the 9 mm in front of his face, his cheek pressed against the wall of the corridor. Behind him, Winger was herding two women out of the rest room and down the hallway. Seconds later Horn felt his partner's hand on his shoulder.

"Ready," Winger breathed behind his head.

"Stay here," Horn whispered before taking two quick steps and rolling past the doorway to the men's room. He came up in a crouched position next to the door as his heart tried to pound a hole in his chest. Every nerve ending in his body sensed Steller's presence.

Horn raised his hand to motion for Winger to move to the other side of the door, when the entire wall above his head suddenly exploded in a shower of plaster and splintered wood. He thought for a crazy moment that a bomb had gone off on the other side of the wall. Horn heard Winger scream something unintelligible and was knocked over on his side as Steller's body tore through the thin wall like a freight train.

Steller hit the opposite wall and bounced back directly on top of Horn, who had managed to roll onto his back. He brought his right knee up and rammed it as hard as he could into the assassin's side. For a moment Horn thought he'd driven his mod into a slab of concrete. He felt the shock run through his leg like wildfire.

"Goddammit, Max!" Horn could now make out his partner's voice. "I can't get a clear shot!"

Horn felt something like a truck ram into his ribs and knew Steller had delivered his first blow. He tried to scream, but the sound became an agonizing cough instead. Horn could see the top of the killer's head flashing in front of his face like a blond flag and finally realized the man's physical orientation. Steller was lying facedown on top of him, his head on Horn's chest. He watched the huge right hand swing up for another blow and bang into the surviving wall of the narrow corridor. Down came the fist, scraping the plaster in a cloud of white dust, and it rammed into Horn's ribs for the second time. The pain was a red-hot poker, and Horn was surprised he didn't hear cracking. He figured the restricted area was saving his life by keeping Steller from a full windup.

Knowing he had to do something before Steller pounded him into a piece of dead meat, Horn brought his modified arm up through the rubble and slammed the upper portion of it against the side of the blond head. The force of the blow was enough to roll Steller's massive body off his, and he immediately shoved himself backward toward Winger.

I've got you now, you son of a bitch, Horn thought as he raised his hand, intending to put a round straight through the top of Steller's head. But there was nothing in his hand. His eyes immediately flashed to the floor near his feet where the 9 mm lay amid the splintered wood and chunks of plaster.

"Shoot!" Horn yelled, as Steller got to his feet, his hands clasped over his head like an executioner's death hammer. "Dammit Winger, shoot!"

As Steller's hands began their downward motion, Horn heard the welcome sound of Winger's machine pistol erupt behind him, sounding like a chain saw with a stuck throttle. He watched as the supersonic bullets stitched a line across the assassin's modified chest, shredding the front of his jacket in a shower of sparks.

Just as Winger raised his line of fire, Steller crossed his arms and covered his face. The stream of lead ricocheted off the titanium like shrapnel, making Horn shield his face with his modified arm.

Winger's weapon suddenly stopped firing. Horn dropped his arm as Steller turned and headed for the end of the hall, which was filled with blue smoke and the acrid stench of cordite. He heard Winger slam another clip into the machine gun and jerk back the slide just as Steller's form plowed into the wall like a wrecking ball.

Horn scrambled for his 9 mm as Winger opened up again. He managed to fire two quick shots as Steller literally blew outward into the alley, slamming into the side of an abandoned car. Horn watched the big man roll off the dented machine and disappear.

"Come on," Horn said, pulling himself up. He headed for the opening Steller had made, feeling as though his blood had been replaced with pure adrenaline.

"Right behind you," Winger said. "I almost had the son of a bitch. I should have shot for his balls instead of his face."

Horn dived through the jagged hole and rolled in the direction Steller had gone, aiming the red beam of the laser like a death beacon. Nothing. The alley resembled a cross between a junkyard and a bomb crater. Snow-covered trash and overturned Dumpsters were scattered about as though some gigantic animal had recently foraged there. Horn sensed that Winger had also emerged into the alley and caught him in his peripheral vision as he moved around the car in the opposite direction. Straightening to his feet, he swiftly met Winger at the front of the wheel-less hulk.

"Tracks," Winger whispered, pointing to a set of foot-prints in the snow. Horn followed them with his laser sight forty or fifty feet down the alley until they cut ninety degrees to the left, disappearing into a recessed doorway.

Horn stared at the four-story structure. "Is that an apartment building?"

"No," Winger answered immediately. "It's a boarded-up mortuary. I remember seeing the sign: Ginsberg's Discount Funeral Home."

"Are you sure?" Horn asked, impressed with such good recall. "We are in the alley."

"Yeah, it's the shortest building on the block."

"Funeral home," Horn said, moving toward the door-way. "I guess that's fitting."

The two cops covered the door simultaneously and stared into a gaping black hole that seemed to suck in the weird snowy light from the alley. A giant steel door hung cockeyed from its lower hinge as though it had been peeled open.

"Does this fucker carry a weapon?"

"Hell yes," Horn breathed as he snaked the red beam up a short flight of stairs and into a hall that seemed to stretch into infinity. "But he'd rather use his body."

"No shit," Winger said. "Are we going in there?"

Horn detected a slight nervousness in Winger's voice. "You afraid of the dark?"

"No, I'm just afraid of what's *in* the dark." Winger grinned crazily.

"Follow me in," Horn said, letting his partner know by the tone of his voice that the small talk was over. "Lag behind twenty or thirty steps, and if you lose me, whistle once, short. I'll blink the sight."

"What's the mission?"

"I'm going to try and draw him out. If he comes after me, it'll give you the opportunity to move up and nail him."

"What do you want to call this insane strategy, trolling for Steller?"

Ignoring Winger's question, Horn closed his eyes for thirty seconds of intense concentration as sequences of moves flashed into his mind like a giant game plan. "You ready?" He moved up the steps and into the darkness. Behind him Winger sighed audibly and muttered something under his breath.

Horn counted fifteen steps down the ink-black hall before he stopped. He listened as Winger topped the stairs, then flashed the laser sight once and moved cautiously into the funeral home. There was an odor in the place that got stronger as he penetrated the interior of the building. Horn didn't peg it at first, but when his eyes began to water he realized it was the pungent stench of formaldehyde. The place reeked of it. But there was also another smell—the smell of death. Horn knew it wasn't anything Ginsberg had left behind. It was emanating from what was waiting for him somewhere up ahead in the blackness. It was the essence of a man whose soul had been lost in a machine, a killing machine.

After a full five minutes of moving down the hall in the deep creep-pause, deep creep-pause manner, Horn reached a dead end. He felt around and discovered another stairway leading up at a right angle to the hall. Horn waited until he sensed Winger was within spitting distance before flashing the red beam onto the dust-covered floor.

Suddenly an explosion erupted in the stairwell above his head, and Horn felt a rush of air across his face as a thumb-sized chunk of lead tore into the block wall behind him. Pieces of concrete peppered the back of his neck, stinging like crazy. Horn felt Winger grab the sleeve of his jacket and jerk him away from the opening just as another booming shot blossomed violently, filling the stairwell with a blinding blue-white muzzle-flash.

Horn transferred the 9 mm to his left hand, shoved the barrel around the edge of the opening and pulled the trigger three quick times, firing blindly toward the top of the stairs. The shots echoed loudly in the dead building, and as the ringing died out, Horn heard a sound that ran down his spine like a straight razor. It was Steller laughing—a deep, resonant booming laughter like bass drums rolling out the announcement, *You are now insane.*

"Nice try, cop, but no cigar." Steller's voice was a cold wind blowing straight out of a nightmare. Horn thought for a brief moment that he was going to throw up, but the feeling passed as quickly as it came. The bitter taste of bile went unnoticed as the heavy pounding of Steller's footsteps came somewhere above his head.

"Goddammit, Max—" Winger grabbed Horn by the front of the jacket "—I don't think this is such a hot idea...."

Horn raised the barrel of the 9 mm beside his head and activated the laser sight. The beam illuminated their sweating faces in a weird red glow, making Horn think, for some crazy reason that they were underground. The perception blinked away as he answered his partner, "You know the way out."

Horn watched Winger stare into his eyes briefly before swallowing hard. The young cop jerked his head toward the stairwell and Horn immediately spun around, heading up the rickety wooden steps. As Horn mounted the top of the stairs, he heard Steller come to a sudden stop. Horn realized he'd entered a room that seemed as large as a basketball court. Light filtered in around the boards that were nailed across the windows, making the high-ceilinged area a strange mixture of dark shadows and thin shafts of light.

A shock jumped through Horn's nervous system like a jolt of electricity as Winger placed a hand on his shoulder. He felt his partner's breath on the side of his face as Winger whispered, "I don't think there's another way out of here."

Horn wondered how the young cop knew that and was about to ask him when a strange, rattling sound made him turn his head toward the opposite wall of the room. Whatever was generating the noise was headed straight for them, and Horn had the impression it was moving like a guided missile.

Something metallic flashed in front of Horn and slammed into Winger's side, knocking him against the edge of the stairwell's opening. Horn watched the metallic object flip up on its end as Winger grunted loudly. He recognized the rolling weapon as an old ambulance gurney. The tubular-wheeled stretcher bounced several feet back across the floor as Winger crumpled like a wadded sheet of paper. Horn crouched next to his partner's side and palmed his chin, trying to see his face. He was out cold or dead.

Steller's laughter again filled the wide chamber of shadows. "The kid's dead, cop. It's your turn."

Horn half stood and aimed the 9 mm from the hip. He took two steps into the shadows and began tracing the beam from left to right, seeking out the source of the death voice.

"This is just like old times, eh?" Steller continued. "Old times in the pit."

The beam cut through the darkness like a translucent red string roped out from the end of the weapon to the other side of the room. Horn was tracing the laser across several drums stacked against the wall when a blinding flash erupted less than a foot from its sighting point. Even before the rocking blast reached his ears, Horn knew what it was—Steller's Magnum cooking off like a cannon.

In the same microsecond during which he clearly perceived this, Horn felt the slug slam into his modified shoulder. The force of the blow spun him 360 degrees, as though he were a top with an off-center axis. Horn pulled the trigger on his weapon, and blue-white light bathed the room as though a bolt of lightning had erupted from the barrel of the 9 mm. The flash seemed to get hung up in its tenth-of-a-second passage through time, and Horn could see Steller on the other side of the room, his gleaming titanium chest shining through the shredded jacket. The assassin aimed a long-barreled SuperMag from the side of his hip. Horn raised his eyes to the square-jawed face just as time caught up and the strobe blinked out. He could have sworn Steller was smiling.

Something on the border of his subconscious told Horn to move sideways and he did, just as Steller's Magnum burned another round straight through the space that still held his aura. Before the muzzle-flash from Steller's shot had faded, Horn squeezed the trigger on his weapon, sending another lead meteor streaking across the room. Then both men began firing as fast as they could pull the triggers, their big weapons pounding the darkness.

Horn suddenly found himself on the floor and wondered if he'd been hit. The firing had stopped, but he realized his finger was still squeezing the trigger of the empty

9 mm. "You stupid son of a bitch," Winger barked into his ear, "this ain't the Old West." Horn realized Steller must have spent the rounds of his Mag, too, and reached into his jacket. "Move toward the stairs," Winger growled urgently and pushed his partner toward the stairwell.

"What the hell—" Horn's words were cut off by the exploding flash of Steller's weapon. Dirt and chunks of the wall above their heads rained down on the two cops. "Shoot the bastard!" he yelled, fumbling for a fresh clip. Horn wondered why Winger wasn't unloading with the machine pistol and turned his head just as Steller fired again. The bullet drove into the floor, splintering the wood as it plowed a supersonic furrow through its rotting grain.

"Get to the stairs!" Winger croaked, sliding sideways.

Horn pulled a clip out of his jacket and promptly dropped it. He swore in frustration. Steller cooked off another round, and Horn cringed, waiting for the bullet to blow the top half of his head off. It didn't happen. Instead, in the lightning flash of the gunfire, he watched Winger pulling the pin of the little concussion grenade he'd shown earlier in Horn's apartment.

"Merry Christmas, asshole!" Winger yelled crazily as he sidearmed the death egg across the floor.

Horn heard Steller's weapon fire one last time just as the grenade went off, shocking the entire building as though a formation of F-32s has just gone supersonic directly overhead. He felt Winger slam into his back, and the two men rolled six steps down the stairs before coming to a stop in a heap.

"Come on!" Horn said, disentangling himself. Followed by Winger, he crawled back up the stairs and peered into the smoke-filled room.

"Did I get him?" Winger asked.

"Don't know," Horn answered. He traced the beam of the laser through the haze, then suddenly remembered the weapon was without a clip. This time he managed to extract the last one he was carrying and was about to insert it into the butt of the big automatic when the pounding of boots on the wood floor caused him to jerk his head up. Horn watched in amazement as Steller's huge figure flew like an ominous shadow straight for the stairwell. "Shit!" he gasped, forcing himself to concentrate and ram the clip home. Just as he pulled the slide back, Steller veered to his right and dived straight through one of the boarded-up windows in a shower of splintered wood and broken glass.

Horn scrambled up and sprinted to the window. He watched Steller pull himself up from the snow-covered pavement two stories below and head down the street in a measured, machine-driven stride. Forcing himself to concentrate, Horn activated the beam and pinned it on the assassin's bouncing back. He took a deep breath, moved the beam to the back of Steller's head and squeezed the trigger. The weapon kicked up in his hand, and he saw sparks fly off the running man's shoulder.

"Let me try." Winger shoved Horn to one side with his hips. The young cop held his Magnum in both hands and aimed steadily. Just as he fired, Steller changed direction and dodged between two cars parked at the side of the street. The bullet shattered the rear window of a car, and the huge killer disappeared around the corner.

"Son of a bitch," Winger spit. "The fucker's got eyes in the back of his head."

Horn looked over at his partner's sweat-bathed face. For some crazy reason it made him aware that his own body was soaked. He watched Winger turn toward him, that mad, crooked grin forming on his stubble-covered face.

"I guess we better get silver bullets," the young cop said, the energy of battle still dancing madly in his eyes.

"So far," Horn answered, wondering what his own eyes looked like, "I haven't heard a better idea."

CHAPTER TWELVE

THE NUMBER 1 NEXUS LIMOUSINE sped across the George Washington Bridge at more than seventy-five miles per hour, its proximity sensor beeping almost constantly in the driver's headphones as he weaved in and out of the traffic. Serving as a backdrop to the rusting steel of the ancient bridge was the greenish-brown Hudson. Smokelike vapor was rising from its oil-slick surface and wafting above in clouds. The river curved off toward Englewood and disappeared into a mixed horizon of crumbling factories and gray winter sky.

Inside the quiet comfort of the limo, Steller watched Ashley cross her legs, exposing her black-stockinged, lithe thighs. He figured it was Ashley's way of greeting him and was conscious that he felt nothing: no stirring, no interest, no desire. Since he had known the woman, she had given him several opportunities to become intimately acquainted with her. Steller had always declined in a manner in which an alcoholic might decline the offer of a drink. Sex had been displaced by the near euphoria he experienced when he used his E-mods, the design of which had only one purpose—invincibility. He could kill with immunity.

"Why didn't you take the helicopter?" Steller questioned, folding his black-gloved hands in his lap. He watched Ashley take a cup from a tray between the two seats and sip her coffee.

"Want some?" she offered. Steller shook his head. "The helo's down and unavailable. Anyway, I thought a small excursion in the car would give us a chance to talk."

Steller looked out the window for a couple of seconds and watched the run-down factories and warehouses speed by as the Mercedes left the bridge. They were heading for Fairlawn, where Ashley was to sign papers executing the sale of a small NEXUS division that handled the data processing for the New Jersey State Welfare Department. He turned toward his boss. "So talk."

"You're a little touchy, aren't you?" Ashley asked, and the hint of a smile passed across her face like a shadow.

Steller ignored her question and realized he was rubbing his neck. He remembered being blown headfirst into the stack of drums when the cop's grenade cooked off. Steller cursed himself, but didn't change his facial expression. He quit rubbing his neck and returned the hand to his lap as an irritation arising out of his subconscious made his mods jerk imperceptibly.

"What happened?" Ashley dipped her red lips into the coffee again. "And I'm not asking just to get on your nerves. I need to know how much of a threat Horn is to the project now that he's, well, still alive."

"His partner had a goddamn concussion grenade. Fortunately it was one of the old ones, or I probably wouldn't be here," Steller said. The fact that he'd survived the blast merely perpetuated his belief that he was incapable of being destroyed, that he was invincible when it came to being matched against a mere human body. Still, the fact that his mission had been to destroy Horn, and yet Horn had survived, stuck in his throat like a poison-tipped *shuriken*.

"This isn't the first time Horn has deflected your attempt to..." Ashley's voice trailed off, and she appeared to be traveling through a bad memory. Anxiety was reflected in her eyes like the tips of two icebergs,

"This won't be another New Pittsburgh, I guarantee it."

Ashley seemed to step out of her contemplative moment. "You guarantee it?" she asked, sarcasm dripping from her words. "Come on, Mr. Steller. This running death match has resulted in negative returns for NEXUS. It's got to end."

"All right," Steller said acceptingly. "How do you want to work it?"

"We work it by not working it, at least for now. Right now I'm giving the execution of Hoke's project priority over anything else, including your obsession with Horn."

"No problem." Steller flexed his gloved hands a little. He had no intention of giving up his quest to kill Horn. He felt he'd been programmed for nothing else.

"*Your* priority is to ensure that Anderson Hoke carries out his part of the plan. I don't want anyone or anything to interfere with what he's got to do."

Steller raised his eyebrows slightly. "Including the cop?"

"Only if he physically interferes," Ashley said, lowering her voice as if to emphasize the seriousness of what she was saying. "Otherwise, avoid him like the plague. The Super Bowl is the day after tomorrow. I doubt if Mr. Horn has time to extend his investigation to the point where he could pose a real threat to the operation." Ashley paused for a couple of seconds. "However, after the transfers are validated, you have license to go after him with whatever it takes."

"Is Project Green Mole that critical?" Steller asked, wondering where Ashley got off telling him that he had license to go after anyone.

Ashley's expression sagged as though all her mental energy had suddenly been replaced by weariness. Her true age fleetingly started to manifest itself across her face, hinting at lines and hollow shadows. "It's *that* critical," she answered. "Our debt-to-equity ratio has slid off the face of the earth. If we don't pull off this scheme, NEXUS will be in receivership by the Fourth of July."

Steller half shrugged. "I didn't realize things were that unstable."

"You never really needed to know," Ashley answered. "But that's okay. I only tell you now so you'll understand the importance of ensuring Mr. Hoke lives up to his end of the bargain."

"I understand," Steller said.

"To that end, I want you to spend the next two days with Hoke. You can sleep in the lounge at the site."

"How?" Steller asked. "I'm not accessed."

"Once we get back to the city, call Dave Coulie." The weariness, and along with it the marks of age, suddenly left Ashley's face. She had returned to her all-business demeanor. "I've already made arrangements for you to have unrestricted access to the CYNSYS facility. Don't let Hoke out of your sight before or after the Super Bowl."

"What do you mean?" Steller asked.

"I mean, Mr. Hoke will be running more funds through that little hole in the back of his head than the government wastes in a year." Ashley spoke patiently, as though she were teaching a slow learner. Steller noticed, but let it slide off his back.

"I'm aware of the figures," he said, letting Ashley know by the tone of his voice that he was growing tired of her attitude. "What's the point?"

"Hoke, after all, may have aspirations of becoming wealthier than the present arrangement affords. I don't want to give him the opportunity to disappear."

"Well," Steller said as an idea crawled out of the darkness somewhere in his mind, "I think we do want him to disappear—afterward, that is."

At Ashley's irritated, puzzled look, Steller smiled benevolently. "Here's the crux. After we ensure *all* the funds are in NEXUS-controlled accounts, Mr. Hoke takes off. Permanently." Steller allowed his smile to expand across his face. "After all, he *is* an embezzler."

"I see," Ashley remarked after several seconds of silence. "That's similar to what I have in mind, but we can discuss the details in a while. First, I wanted to ask you if you'd found out anything regarding Gorman's murder."

Steller laughed to himself. He could tell Ashley hadn't thought of anything with respect to covering their tracks after tapping such an enormous amount of electrocash. While it was true that he hadn't known NEXUS was in such dire financial straits, Steller was keenly aware that his boss almost always underestimated his ability to come up with creative solutions for difficult problems. She hadn't even considered how they would avoid the attention of the WCC after they finally figured out that over a billion dollars of their betting line had been diverted right under their noses. Then—Steller caught himself just before he shook his head in pitiful amazement—she had the cods to say it was similar to the setup she'd thought of. It was funny, funnier than hell, but all Steller said was, "Nah. Been real busy lately."

Ashley looked at Steller steadily. "Doesn't it bother you that Gorman's murder is so coincidental to our 'necessary business steps'?"

"His murder could have been totally unrelated to what we initiated. I understand the guy had more than his share of hang-ups." Steller knew Ashley had a point, but he didn't feel like conceding anything to her. He figured it was too late to do anything more than up his awareness as the deal came down. Besides, he was used to operating on the margin.

"Let's talk about the postexecution scenario," Ashley said, pulling off the jacket of her suit. She placed it on the seat next to her. "I will arrange to have the helicopter at the helipad as soon as the game is over. You bring Mr. Hoke and we'll proceed straight to La Guardia. I've been scheduled for a trip to Germany for more than a month now, so one of the Lears has been reserved. We'll take Hoke, and you can dispose of him over there. He's not going to be on the manifest so there won't be any record of him leaving the country." Ashley smiled. "NEXUS always gets VIP treatment from La Guardia customs. Also, I've already informed Mr. Hoke that he'd be leaving by helicopter directly after the game, so that first part, at least, won't be a surprise."

"Why Germany?" Steller couldn't help but think that Ashley might have had a plan after all. He was mildly impressed.

"We've got people there who can unravel Mr. Hoke's maze for routing the electrocash. He's too smart to settle for such a low percentage. I want to make sure we get everything he manages to slip under the rug."

"I see," Steller said, unconsciously flexing the mod of his right hand as he ran the plan through his mind. "Getting us away right after the game is a good plan. And your remark about Hoke taking a higher percentage gives me an idea." Steller had to admit to himself again that the woman was making a number of good points as well as displaying some pretty acute forethought.

"What's that?" Ashley asked, lazily pouring herself more coffee.

"Maybe Hoke knows something about Gorman's murder."

"I hadn't thought of that," Ashley admitted, and Steller was surprised that she did. "It would seem likely that he might. But we can't do anything until we get to Germany. You can question him over there. Also, we can't ask him a thing about it until we close all the loops on the cash transfers. I don't want to jeopardize the operation by spooking him in the middle of it."

"Makes sense," Steller said. "I'll just be his shadow for now."

"Exactly," Ashley's voice lilted as a pleased glint lit her eyes.

Steller looked thoughtful before he continued. "There is one more requirement before I commit to executing the plan."

Ashley raised her eyebrows, obviously surprised that Steller had a stipulation. "What is it? Would you like a larger cut of the earnings? I'd be glad to give you Hoke's original share. I'm sure he—"

"No," Steller said, waving a hand. "It's not that. I couldn't care less about the money."

"Then what is it?"

"I want some insurance in case the cop does show."

"Go on," Ashley said, "what kind of insurance?"

"Horn spent the better part of a night with a woman in the Village. And his actions in the past have shown..." His words trailed off as a pain, like the sharp stab of a migraine, crossed between his temples. Then he said, "He's not really the type for one-night stands."

"How do you know about this woman?"

"I followed Trower the night he was tracking Horn. He made his move after the cop had left her apartment."

Ashley looked at him curiously. "So what are you proposing?"

"I'm going to snatch the woman," Steller stated matter-of-factly.

Ashley managed a minuscule shrug. As far as she was concerned, the vital details were all settled. "Go on," she said.

"You haven't forgotten about the NEXUS guest house out on Long Island, I'm sure," Steller said, knowing Ashley spent nearly every weekend at the luxurious beach house, each time with a tanned, fit, handsome young man in the prime of life.

"Yes," she said, a degree of annoyance creeping into her voice. "The one on Smithtown Bay. I use it on occasion myself, but what's that got to do with the woman?"

"I want to hold her there," Steller said, "after I pick her up tomorrow night."

Ashley heaved a little sigh. "Oh, is that all? For a minute there, I didn't know what you were talking about."

"Then you don't have a problem with it?"

"No," Ashley answered. "If it makes you feel better, go ahead. Just spare me the details."

Steller realized the limo had come to a stop and watched Ashley slip into her jacket. "You want me to come with you?" he asked, as the driver opened the door for her.

"No. This will take less than ten minutes."

Alone in the back of the limousine, Steller thought of Horn. A gut feeling told him the cop would show up just when the handle was being pulled. The blond killer felt a strange sensation, almost a quiver, race down the titanium tube that encased his spine. For a brief moment he thought the sensation might actually be fear, fear because there was an unknown quality about Horn, an unpredictable spark beyond brute cunning and strength.

RUBEN ZAMORA LEANED BACK in the padded leather seat of the Beech Aerospace Black Star as it climbed effortlessly to eighty-nine thousand feet. He looked on as Eloy, the man he liked to refer to as his auxiliary brain, punched data into the keyboard of a flat-black PC. It was set up on a table that folded out from the walls of the plush cabin. Leonard sat forward of the two men, staring out a round window through his goggle-like sunglasses.

"Would you like Leonard to get you a drink, Eloy?" Zamora suggested. "It might settle your nerves." He smiled to himself as he watched his brain look up from the keyboard briefly, his dark eyes darting about without making contact with Zamora's. The Colombian often wondered if his skinny, mustached *compadre* was a closet amphetamine freak. The man seemed to vibrate with a nervous energy.

"No thanks," Eloy answered, returning his attention to the computer. "Maybe later. I'll take a smoke, though."

Zamora picked up a pack from the tray on his armrest and tossed it and a lighter on the table. Then he turned to Leonard. "How about a Scotch on the rocks?" He held up one finger.

"I'm calculating the GPS window now," Eloy said, leaning back in his chair and lighting a cigarette. "Thanks." He leaned sideways, handing the package and lighter back to Zamora. "It looks like our original estimate was pretty damn close."

"That's good," The Colombian said as he took a short glass of amber liquid and ice from Leonard. He placed it on the armrest and lit a cigarette, inhaling deeply before blowing the smoke toward the ceiling. "How close?"

"I'll be able to tell you in about five minutes," Eloy said, staring at the backlit LCD. "It's running the algorithms now, but this machine is slower than my grand-mother's heartbeat.''

"Sure you won't have a drink?" Zamora took a healthy swallow of Scotch, then blew through his clenched teeth, making a whistling sound.

"Why not," Eloy answered as he stood, bending slightly to keep his head from the molded composite ceiling. He unbuttoned his vest and loosened his tie before taking the seat opposite the Colombian.

"One of these for Mr. Sanchez, also." Speaking to Leonard, Zamora held up his glass.

"Where the hell are you taking me, Ruben?" Eloy asked, his voice carrying a lightness that bordered on laughter.

"You'll like this place," Zamora answered, lighting a new cigarette from the butt of his old one. "It's a small island about two hundred miles off the eastern coast of Australia. I like to call it my *escondite*. One of my uncles bought it many, many years ago. It's nice, you'll like it."

"I'm sure I will." Eloy took the glass Leonard was holding out and glanced at the computer, which suddenly made a series of clicks before lapsing back into its normal hum. He laughed. "Listen to that son of a bitch. It sounds like it's ready to roll over and die." Eloy took a large drink of his Scotch. "I really should get a new one, but old Jorge there has sentimental value." He nodded toward the computer.

"Sentimental value?" Zamora smiled, thinking that Eloy's laughter sounded strangely similar to the click the computer had just made.

"Yeah," Eloy said. "Remember, I used Jorge to make the weight estimates when we cut the Lompoc deal."

"Oh, yeah." Zamora chuckled softly.

Eloy looked at Zamora with a blank, noncommittal expression on his face. "You really intend to go through with this?"

"Yes," Zamora answered after several seconds of silence. "Does it trouble you?"

"Not really," Eloy answered. "If it weren't for you, I'd still be hustling skin on some border somewhere. I trust your judgment, Ruben."

Zamora raised his glass, and Eloy returned the gesture. Both men tossed down their drinks. "Even if they don't release our people, it will prove to the Americans that we're more than the common thugs they think we are. They'll have to acknowledge we're a power."

"What about the gringo?"

"Hoke?" The Colombian nodded. "To tell you the truth, we're going to pull the little beggar out. We need the money." He asked for another Scotch, then went on. "By the way, did you manage to set up a program to trace the transfers?"

Eloy shook his head. "Yeah, Ruben. As a matter of fact, I tried several programs, but the son of a bitch is smart. He has some complicated way of tagging onto the microwave burst transmissions that's damn near impossible to filter. We could nail ten percent or so if I worked on it for five or ten years."

Zamora waved a hand lazily. "I get the message."

"Wait, there he goes." Eloy got to his feet as the computer made a sound like the quick shuffling of new cards. He slipped into the chair in front of the computer and stared at the screen.

Zamora took his glasses out of his shirt pocket and put them on before pulling himself out of the seat. He stepped behind Eloy and gazed at the screen, rubbing his temples with the tips of his fingers. An elaborate matrix was spread across the LCD that time-phased the positions of six different GPS satellites with the transmission cone of the commo center on top of the Superplex.

"Now watch this." Eloy punched in a set of numbers. "Halftime is guaranteed to the advertisers. Big bucks, you know." He glanced over his shoulder at Zamora and grinned. "So we know the third quarter will start on time." Eloy turned back to the screen and punched in another series of numbers. "If we use worst and best case-scenarios for the length of the third quarter, that should give us a window of forty-eight consecutive minutes to extract the gringo before number three here—" he pointed a finger to one of the column headers on the screen "—relays down the destruct commands and they can turn out the lights."

"Forty-eight minutes, huh?" Zamora rubbed his chin.

Eloy suddenly sat up straight in his chair. "When *did* you tell him to effect the lockdown?"

"At the end of the third quarter, friend," Zamora chuckled and patted Eloy on the shoulders. "Now calm down. You have it right." The Colombian turned his head. "Leonard, bring my friend here another Scotch. Make it a double."

CHAPTER THIRTEEN

"To what do I owe this honor?" Winger asked as he opened the door of his apartment.

"I was in the neighborhood," Horn answered as Winger closed the door behind him. "Anyway, I thought I'd return the favor."

"What favor?" The young cop turned and walked across the carpeted floor to a table in the center of the room, which was covered with several firearms, many of which Horn didn't recognize. He figured he'd caught Winger in the middle of cleaning the weapons. A wooden box containing solvents, oils and rags was on the floor next to the table.

"Yeah," Horn answered, "I came over to inspect this dump, you know, like you did mine the other day."

Actually, the apartment was anything but a dump, Horn realized. While sparsely furnished, it was orderly and clean, consisting of a small kitchen to one side of the living area and a single bedroom, which he could see through a door on the opposite wall. The bed was neatly made in military fashion.

"You're full of shit, partner." Winger laughed. He was wearing a gray New York City Giants T-shirt that had the lower portion ripped away, faded jeans and rubber shower thongs. "You want a beer?"

"No thanks," Horn declined. "I can't stay long."

Winger picked up a half-empty bottle of Budweiser from the table and walked to a large screen video that was running a sports program. He punched a button on the top of the console, and the screen went blank. "Sit down," Winger said, turning. He motioned to an upholstered love seat that obviously served as the living room couch.

"Thanks." Horn took off his jacket before sitting down. He watched Winger pull a chair away from the table and turn it toward him. The young cop plopped into the chair, crossed his legs and took a sip of beer.

"What do you mean you don't have time?" Winger grinned. "I'm familiar with your social calendar. It isn't exactly something you'd publish in the *New Yorker*."

"Screw you!" Horn laughed. "Actually, I'm working tonight."

"At least you didn't disappoint me. What's up? Do you need me?"

"No," Horn answered. "But I wanted to let you know what's going on for tomorrow."

"I know what's going on for tomorrow," Winger cut in. "I'm going to be sitting in front of the old wide screen here, sucking down a bunch of these—" he held up the beer bottle "—and watching the Super Bowl."

"Sorry to disappoint you, partner, but it looks like we'll be working." Horn saw a look spread across Winger's face that was a mixture of shock and gloom. It was as though he'd just watched his pet dog get run down by a truck. "You can tape it," Horn offered as a weak consolation.

"It's not the same." Winger shook his head slowly. "Fuck."

"What can I say?" Horn couldn't keep from smiling. He hadn't expected his partner to take the news so hard, and it seemed funny that not being able to watch a football game could cause such a reaction. "Are you still there?'' Horn waved a hand at his partner, who was staring blankly at a spot on the floor.

''Some partner you are,'' Winger said suddenly, standing. He abruptly tossed his empty beer bottle into Horn's lap and walked across the room into the kitchen.

Horn set the bottle on the table and followed him into the small, brightly lit area. He watched Winger open the refrigerator and pull out another beer and a couple of white paper-wrapped packages and a large jar of mustard, which he placed on the counter next to the sink.

''Okay, so tell me what the hell is going on.'' Winger twisted the cap off the long-necked bottle and turned toward Horn. ''What's so damned important that we have to work on Super Bowl Sunday, for chrissake?'' He tilted back the bottle and swallowed a quarter of it.

''It looks like we're going to pick up Hoke right after the game is over,'' Horn answered.

''What do you mean 'it looks like'?'' Winger opened a cabinet over the sink and took out half a loaf of dark rye bread.

''Those are Kelso's words,'' Horn said. ''I'm supposed to meet Christina Service later tonight to get the details.''

''Since when did the Barracuda start giving cops their work assignments?'' Winger seemed to be coming out of his funk over not getting to watch the Super Bowl. He spread a thick coating of mustard across two slices of bread. ''You want a sandwich?''

''No, but I'll take a beer now.'' Horn opened the refrigerator and pulled out one of the brown bottles. ''To answer your first question, Kelso says this is a special case. The assistant D.A. claims to have some new information. We're supposed to work directly with her.''

''Lucky us,'' Winger scoffed as he piled corned beef from one of the packages onto the bread. He opened the other package, removed several slices of small-hole Swiss cheese and placed the pale cheese on top of the mound of corned beef. "Sure you don't want one?" he asked.

"No thanks," Horn answered as he watched Winger take a huge bite.

"So, we're supposed to pick up Hoke," Winger said from behind his sandwich.

"Yeah. Why don't you come for me tomorrow around noon? I'll fill you in on whatever direction I get tonight, and we can head on out to the Superplex."

"The goddamn game doesn't start until two-thirty. Why are we going out there so early?"

"We'll stop and get something to eat on the way," Horn suggested. "I don't want to get hung up somewhere in traffic."

Winger nodded as he leaned against the edge of the counter. "By the way, did you ever get hold of that woman you were trying to call the other night?"

"Sarah Weed?" Horn asked.

"Yeah," Winger said. "Weed."

"Yeah, I finally reached her. As a matter of fact, I'm supposed to see her tomorrow after we get off work."

"You may not need to," Winger said.

"What do you mean?"

"If we pick up Hoke and he spills his guts, well, you may not need to run her through another one of your charming interviews."

"I'll probably see her anyway," Horn said, sipping his beer.

"What?" Winger's face lit up and his jaw dropped slightly as he grinned. "Another woman?"

"What do you mean 'another woman'?" Horn knew he was about to get a ration of shit from his young partner and immediately regretted asking the question.

"Well," Winger said, holding up the index finger of his right hand, "first there's this Sarah Weed chick, who doesn't know whether she should spend her time biting the cuffs of corporate America or reciting poetry. And then—" he held up a second finger "—there's the Barracuda!" The young cop laughed wildly then choked. He grabbed his beer and pulled back a quick swallow. "I can only guess," Winger said as he wiped his mouth with the back of his hand, "that you're not meeting her at her office."

Horn couldn't help smiling. "Are you done yet? I think I'll go down to the zoo or some place that offers a more intelligent level of conversation."

Winger seemed to suddenly downshift to a more sober gear. "Hey, I almost forgot. Shit. I've got something for you."

"Okay," Horn said cautiously, wondering what his partner had up his sleeve.

"No shit, it's a present." Winger set his beer on the counter. "Wait here, I'll be right back."

He disappeared into the bedroom and returned moments later with a flat oval-shaped object that looked like a canvas patch or some type of bandage. He held it out and Horn noticed a dull green handle sticking out of a slot in the porous material. "What is it?" he asked, holding the item, which fitted into his hand.

"It's a genuine Diamond Edge throwing knife. I had to order it from that outdated mercenary place in Colorado. I'm surprised they had it." Winger was beaming. "Go ahead, take it out of its sheath. It's made of composites so you can walk right through a metal detector and it won't even cause a hiccup."

"That's a comforting thought," Horn said, pulling the heavy blade out of the thin scabbard. He placed it in his left hand to get a better feel for the weight and admired its clean lines. The knife was shaped almost like the handle, its point and double edges gleaming in contrast to the dull green of the composite material, which reminded Horn of the combat titanium covering his mods. "Is this stuff really some kind of diamond material?" he asked, holding the blade up to the light.

"Yeah," Winger said. "That's why they call it a Diamond Edge. You don't see too many of them these days. Go ahead, try it out."

"What do you mean?" Horn was a little puzzled by his partner's suggestion. "Try it out where?"

"Against the wall over there." Winger pointed to what looked like a tabletop butcher block that had been hung on the wall next to the bedroom door. "It's my practice board."

"You go ahead," Horn said, handing the blade to Winger. "I haven't thrown a knife since I was a kid."

"Well, watch. It's easy." Winger took the handle between his thumb and forefinger. "All you do is bring it over your shoulder, right next to your ear and point your index finger at your target." The young cop slowly made a couple of the motions he'd described before snapping his arm as though he were cracking a whip. The blade slammed into the center of the wood with a dull bang and hung there, its point driven a good inch into the scarred-up grain.

"Why did you get me something like that?" Horn asked, impressed with Winger's mastery of the weapon.

"I'm just trying to cover your ass, that's all," the young cop answered as he walked across the room to retrieve the knife. "After Trower almost nailed your butt, I figured you needed some kind of extra protection for when I'm not around."

Horn smiled to himself as Winger handed him the blade. His younger partner had nagged him almost constantly to trade in his old 9 mm laser-sighted automatic for something with more "put-down power," as he'd put it. Now he wanted to force a knife into Horn's arsenal as though it were an offering of his benevolence.

"I don't think it's really my—" Horn started to protest, but he was cut off in midsentence.

"I don't want to hear one goddamn word about it, Max." Winger was adamant. "When you see where you wear the damn thing, you won't even care. As a matter of fact, you won't even know you're wearing it. Now throw the son of a bitch!"

Horn allowed a look of surprise to manifest itself on his face before he brought up the knife in his gloved right hand and whipped it toward the practice board in a blur.

"Holy shit!" Winger cried out as the blade hit the wood, sounding like a rifle shot. The young cop crouched as though a jet had just broken the sound barrier directly over their heads. He straightened up and walked toward the wooden target. "I forgot about your freaking arm, for chrissake. Look at this shit!" Winger gestured to the blade, which was buried to the handle. "I'm sure as hell glad you didn't miss. I can just see poor old Mrs. Thompson next door sitting down with her cat to have some tea and getting a blade run through the heart like a stray missile."

Horn couldn't help but laugh. "Let me help," he said, walking across the room. Horn grabbed the handle with his right and slowly rocked the blade back and forth until it was loose enough to pull out. He had to admit the dull green knife made a formidable weapon, especially when it was propelled by his E-mod.

"How about wearing it on a trial basis?" Winger asked. "At least until this thing with Steller blows over."

Blows over? Horn wondered about his partner's choice of words. More like blows up, he thought. "If it'll make you feel better, I'll try it for a week or two."

"Shit hot," Winger said, suddenly grabbing Horn by the shoulders and kissing him on the side of the head.

"You crazy son of a bitch." Horn shoved Winger away and walked back to the kitchen.

"Take your shirt off," Winger said, picking up the flat scabbard from the counter.

"Screw you, partner," Horn replied as he picked up his beer and took a long drink. "First you kiss me and now you want me to take off my shirt. I think your genes are confused."

"No, no." Winger laughed crazily. "I'm going to apply this hummer, don't worry." He waved the scabbard in front of Horn's face.

"Apply it?" Horn asked.

"Yeah, it goes right here." He reached around and tapped the center of Horn's upper back, between the shoulder blades. "If I remember correctly, old Harry's blade didn't reach that area."

"No, it didn't," Horn answered, taking off his shoulder holster before pulling the turtleneck over his head. "Anyway, it's as good as healed. I took the MD off yesterday."

"Let me see," Winger said as he moved behind Horn. "Jesus, the wound's almost a scar already."

"Go ahead, put the scabbard on."

Winger peeled a protective backing from the clothlike material and centered it carefully before sticking it to Horn's skin. He smoothed it out with the heel of his right hand. "Let me have the knife." Winger reached his arm around Horn's side and took the blade. "There," he said, placing the blade in the slot. "How does that feel?"

Horn flexed and rotated his shoulders. "I can't even feel it," he said honestly. "How do I take it off?"

"You don't have to," Winger answered. "That's why they used to call it an advanced body weapon. You can shower with it, sleep with it, you'll probably forget about it. If it bothers you at night, take the blade out. The scabbard is supposed to integrate with your skin, or something like that. I'll take it off for you when you're ready." Winger grinned. "It's kind of like removing a tattoo—very painful and it leaves a hell of a scar."

"You're so full of shit you must have a cork up your ass," Horn said as he pulled on his shirt. Winger attacked the remains of his sandwich as Horn brushed his hands through his short hair. "I gotta go," Horn said, glancing at his watch.

"You driving anything?" Winger asked as he pulled a fresh bottle of beer from the refrigerator.

"No, I caught a ride over here in a black-and-white."

"Well, take the Elint." Winger reached in his pocket and tossed Horn a set of keys. "You can pick me up tomorrow."

"Thanks," Horn said. "And thanks for this, too." He pointed a thumb over his shoulder.

"No sweat, partner. No sweat."

Twenty minutes later Horn pulled into a no-parking zone in front of a club called Domino's that was just off Fifth Avenue, near Rockefeller Center. He took the plastic placard that had the New York City police emblem over the words Official Police Business, and placed it on the dash.

Horn found Christina sitting at the padded mahogany bar reading a folded copy of the *Times*. "Am I late?" he asked, even though he knew he wasn't.

"No," she answered, placing the newspaper on the bar. "I just got here. You want to find a table or a booth?"

Horn watched the assistant D.A. slip off the high bar stool, her conservative black skirt slipping tantalizingly up on her thighs. She looked good, Horn thought as her cool blue eyes locked on to his like a weapons radar. He started to tell her, but held back, remembering the meetings in her office where he was the grass and she the proverbial lawn mower. Instead, he said, "There's a booth over there," and led the way across the quiet room whose hardwood tables were accented by red leather chairs and brass railings.

Taking the coat she was carrying, Horn hung it on a rack that was bolted to the end of the booth. He slipped into the booth without taking off his jacket, which made Christina smile slightly.

"Do you think this is going to be a short visit or are you cold?" she asked, nodding toward his chest.

Horn looked down, then realized what she was talking about. "Oh," he said. "No on both counts. I'm wearing this, that's all." Horn pulled the jacket open slightly, revealing the 9 mm slung in its black leather holster. She nodded without saying anything and continued to stare into his eyes.

"Drink?" he asked, raising his hand to signal a short-skirted waitress. Horn had noticed Christina hadn't been drinking anything at the bar.

"Scotch and soda, with a twist," she said.

Horn ordered her drink and a beer for himself before turning back toward the assistant D.A. "This is a lot nicer than meeting in your office," he ventured.

"I read the report on Trower," she said, ignoring his comment. "That was a pretty messy job, at least according to your description."

The way this is going, it may as well *be* your goddamn office, Horn thought. "Messy? I'm afraid I don't follow," he said.

"All your cases seem to be subject to EF review," she answered, referring to an Internal Affairs review of cases where so-called excessive force was used.

"I can't help that," Horn said, checking the irritation that flashed through his brain. "If you know they've all been reviewed for EF, then you also know it's been justified each time. I'm sure the Trower case will fall out the same way. After all, the bastard was trying to off me. If you recall, you were the one who told me he was in the city."

"Don't be so sensitive, Detective," Christina said as Horn handed a credit wafer to the waitress, who had returned with their drinks. "I wasn't implying it wasn't justified. Let's just say your propensity for attracting violence is well above the average for NYPD detectives."

Horn shrugged and took a sip of his beer. He sensed the woman wasn't really out to indict him and was mostly just wary of him. "You this spooky around all cops?"

"Spooky?" Christina looked a little taken aback by his question. "I'm afraid it's my turn not to follow."

"Exactly," Horn said. "Spooky is sort of like messy."

"I see your point," the woman said. She smiled openly, but not too openly. Horn figured she was one who would never let her guard down totally.

"Captain Kelso said you had some information that might help my case," Horn continued conversationally as Christina sipped her drink. "He also said you anticipated obtaining a warrant for Anderson Hoke's arrest and would give me direction on the specifics about picking him up.''

"That's correct," she confirmed, stirring her drink. "The warrant's been cut, and we want you to pick him up right after the game tomorrow. Our guess is that he's going to tap the green line and head for higher ground as soon as the winner is decided.''

"The green line?" Horn ran the term through his memory. "Where have I heard that before?"

"Excuse me," Christina said. "I don't know where you may have heard it before, but in this case it's the entire betting line for the Super Bowl. We think Mr. Hoke plans to tap it, so to speak, electronically, and net himself, or someone else, almost a billion dollars in electrocash that can't be traced.''

"It jibes with what my sources have said." Horn took a sip of his beer. "And, as I understand it, he designed the computer system that controls all the betting."

"That's correct, and the guy has been in trouble before.''

Horn nodded, recalling what Sarah had told him. "But you implied he might be working for someone else. Care to elaborate?''

"Well," Christina said, setting down her drink, "we believe he's had sponsorship from inside his own company.''

"I don't have any conclusive evidence, but I tend to agree with what you say." Horn had decided against saying anything about Steller; he didn't want to open up a discussion that would lead Christina down the dark twisting road to his past.

"We're pretty sure that Trower was hired to eliminate you because of the trail you were taking.''

"Yes," Horn agreed and made an encouraging gesture for Christina to explain what she was saying. Instead he was caught flat-footed by what she said next.

"Why do you wear gloves all the time?" she asked, crossing her arms and leaning across the table. Horn watched her stare at the black leather concealing the titanium mod that had become his right hand. "I noted it the first time I met you."

Horn gazed at her in silence for several seconds before answering, "Trauma injury to my right arm. I wear gloves on both hands to make it look . . . normal." He knew he'd chosen the wrong word as soon as he'd said it. Horn felt odd and was glad that his slacks provided coverage for both knees. At least he wouldn't have to explain how his knee had been completely destroyed. Disintegrated. Bigtime trauma injury.

"The state gave me an electromechanical replacement. It works pretty good." Horn flexed his hand a couple of times.

"I thought officers were dropped off the line when they took one of those," Christina said as something between sympathy and pain flashed briefly in her eyes. She nodded at his hand.

"Usually," Horn said. "I passed all the physical tests, however, and they gave me a permanent waiver to work the streets. It's in my records."

"I'm sure it is," Christina replied, her eyes shifting from Horn's hand to his face.

Something in her look told him she saw more than his words had revealed, and the same strange chill he'd felt when they first sat down came over him. The woman puzzled him. At times he got the impression she almost approved of his tactics; however, this perception was fleeting, consistently blown away by her discourses regarding police ethics and operational excesses. Still, Horn couldn't help wondering why she'd wanted to meet him off her normal turf. Maybe it was to put them on neutral ground, he thought.

Horn ordered them both another drink, glad of the interruption. He was afraid she would attempt to probe further into his past, though something in her eyes told him she wouldn't. Still, Horn found it convenient when the waitress made her rounds; it gave him an opportunity to change the subject.

"What I was about to say before," Horn said, his voice businesslike, devoid of emotion, "was that someone tried to take out my partner and me the night before last. You probably haven't seen the report yet."

Christina raised her eyebrows. "Obviously they didn't succeed. Is your partner okay?"

"Yes. Thanks for asking." Horn meant what he said. He was surprised she'd asked about Winger's welfare before jumping right into the who, where and why.

"Where did the assault happen?" she asked.

"At a club down in the Village. We'd gone down to try and locate an information source, and the guy tried to take us down right inside the place. Fortunately, none of the patrons got hurt, but unfortunately, the guy who was trying to kill us didn't get hurt, either." Horn smiled and Christina chuckled in a restrained, pleasant manner.

"Did you know the man? Did you get a good look at him?" After she asked the questions, her gaze latched onto Horn's eyes, waiting to see the truth in them.

"No," Horn said smoothly. "We followed him into an abandoned building and it was too dark to see anything but muzzle-flashes. He got away." He waited for the assistant D.A. to lean across the table and say, "You're full of shit.'' Horn was certain she was reading him like a comic book.

''That doesn't happen to you very often, does it?'' Christina asked after several long seconds of silence.

''What?'' Horn was confused as well as surprised by her question. ''What doesn't happen very often?''

''That one gets away.''

''Not very often,'' he admitted, and managed to keep from stuttering. Horn had the sensation that he'd just run a red light. He looked at the elegant blond woman and wondered why she hadn't broadsided him in the intersection.

''Think it was connected with the Franklin case?''

''Probably.'' He took a drink of beer to wet his throat, which had suddenly become dry.

''You want to elaborate?''

''We were in the area where Trower tried to take me out. This guy was probably trying to pick up where Harry left off.''

''Harry?'' Christina shook her head, indicating Horn had lost her.

''Trower,'' he explained. ''Harry Trower.''

The assistant D.A. nodded her head. ''Good old Harry,'' she said.

Horn was surprised at her mildly sarcastic remark. It was as though she'd crossed over into his world, at least for a moment, and was joking. It was his world in that she was looking at the light side about someone who had tried to blow his brains somewhere west of New Jersey. Horn looked at her drink and wondered if it was the Scotch talking. He hoped it wasn't.

''Yeah,'' Horn answered, ''he was a real charmer.''

''You must have hit a hot button somewhere to make them come after you.'' Christina took a leisurely sip of her drink. "The question is, who is Mr. Hoke working for? And if this operation is being sponsored by NEXUS management, how far up the line does it go?"

Horn hesitated before offering his opinion. "I imagine it goes up about as far as you can get. It's doubtful that a murder sanction would come from, say, the janitor."

Christina smiled dryly. "You better stick to being a cop. As a comedian you'd die."

"Hell," Horn replied, laughing, "I guess you're telling me it's safer being a cop, correct?"

"I guess I used the wrong word." She colored slightly.

Christina assumed her business demeanor again, but Horn sensed there was something different about her. She seemed more relaxed. "I have a feeling Mr. Hoke will cooperate once we explain his situation regarding the murder charges."

"What happened to the old innocent-until-proved-guilty scenario?" Horn asked. "Anyway, unless you've got some evidence I haven't seen, what real proof do you have that Hoke was tied in with the Franklin killing?"

"We'll have the motivation," she answered. "That's why we're having you pick him up *after* the Super Bowl. We hit him over the head with the fact that he murdered Franklin and his girlfriend, or had them murdered, so he'd be in a position to tap the green line. He'll roll over and do tricks once we do that. I guarantee it."

Once again, Horn's mind tripped slightly over the term *green line*. "Probably," he said.

"It'll be most instructive to find out who's really the power behind all of this."

"I have one piece of information about Hoke that doesn't quite fit the scheme of NEXUS corporate involvement."

"What's that?" Christina asked, her interest evident.

"My sources have spotted Hoke in the company of some people who aren't limited to white-collar crime and murders of convenience. He was in the company of South Americans, Colombians maybe."

"Recently?" A look of concern flashed across Christina's face.

"Yes. As I understand it, and admittedly part of this is my inference, these guys' style pegged them as part of the old Mexican Mafia or remnants of the Medellin cartel. Machine guns, drugs and money being their forte."

"Is this for real?" Christina asked.

"As far as I know," he answered. "Why?"

Horn saw her size him up mentally as though trying to decide whether to tell him something. "It's probably just a coincidence," she finally said, "but I saw a pretty strange bulletin yesterday from the Mountain States division of the FBI."

"Go on," Horn encouraged her.

"You understand this information has an AG classification," she said, more as a statement than a question. Horn nodded.

"Apparently the FBI turned over what looked to be a makeshift bomb manufacturing plant in a place just west of Boulder, Colorado. It was being run by three or four people who had worked at the old Rocky Flats weapons plant before the Department of Energy shut it down." Christina paused and moistened her lips with her drink. "Anyway," she continued, "they did a black probe on one of the guys—"

"Black probe?" Horn interrupted.

Christina cringed slightly, and Horn realized she must have inadvertently disclosed the strange-sounding term. "A black probe," the assistant D.A. explained, lowering her voice, "is a chemical and physical procedure used to make someone talk. It can only be authorized by the President and only in cases where there's a national emergency, or at least one threatened."

"You've got to be kidding me," Horn said skeptically. "I've never heard of such a thing."

"Do me a favor." Her look told Horn she was doing anything but kidding him. "Forget you ever heard the term."

"Forgotten," Horn acknowledged. "However, I'm curious as to why they had to take such an extreme approach. At least I assume it was extreme."

"You use the proper adjective." Christina stared blankly for a few moments giving Horn the impression she was recalling something with the magnitude of a plane crash. She suddenly snapped out of the near-trance and once again locked onto Horn's eyes. "The FBI used the somewhat archaic method to extract the information because they found plutonium on the premises. They also found the conventional explosive C-72."

"What is C-72?" Horn asked, even though he was beginning to see what she was leading to.

"It's a relatively old explosive that can be shape-charged to compress a fissionable material to critical mass."

"Like plutonium," Horn offered.

"Correct."

"So these guys were making nuclear weapons in one of their garages?"

"They made *one*," Christina answered, "and it wasn't exactly in a garage. As I understand it, they purchased most of their equipment at an auction the government held when they scrapped the very plant they'd worked in. Pretty amazing, huh?"

Horn had to admit it was amazing but not particularly surprising. "What does it have to do with the fact that

Hoke was seen with a number of suspect South Americans?''

"According to the person they did the number on, the one bomb they made was sold to a group of Colombians who are loosely based right here in the city. That's why we got the bulletin.''

"Shit," Horn said, drawing in his breath. "Pardon my language, but does this group of Colombians go by any particular name?''

"They're called the Seven Families. I don't really know where they get the seven, because there's really only one man who appears to head the group. His name is Ruben Zamora.''

"I've heard of the Seven Families," Horn said, folding his arms and leaning across the table. "Weren't they a continuation of one of the last drug cartels from down there?''

"Sort of," Christina answered. "Zamora's father and several of his uncles had a sizable family operation going right around the turn of the century. They were called the Invisible Cartel because they had survived so long in spite of the drug wars of the nineties.''

"It's my understanding that the Seven Families are into a lot more than drugs," Horn said.

"That's correct. The FBI considers them a borderline terrorist faction, and that's why they've put out a worldwide alert. They ran Ruben Zamora's profile through their behavior simulator to define the probability of his detonating the weapon." Christina smiled in a manner that reflected no humor. "Using it for extortion, by the way, is a foregone conclusion.''

"What was the conclusion?''

"Well over ninety percent.''

Without reacting, Horn asked, "You think Hoke is somehow involved in this?"

"It's probably coincidental," Christina answered, "but I can assure you the subject will be on the agenda when we interrogate him. Did your source give you a description of the people he was seen with? The FBI no doubt have photographs of Zamora and his usual entourage."

"No," Horn answered, "I got the information through the usual indirect route. I can work back, but it may take some time. What are they doing in the meantime?"

"Excuse me," Christina said, "what do you mean?"

"Is there any effort directed at locating the weapon as opposed to tracking down the people who bought the damn thing?"

"As a matter of fact," Christina stated, "they're doing exactly that. Since Zamora and his people seem to call New York home more than any other place, the mayor has gotten the military to fly over certain areas of the city with an aircraft that's basically a sensor package. According to the FBI's analysis, the weapon probably leaks enough radiation that they should be able to pinpoint its location within a couple of yards. That is, if it's here."

Horn was impressed with the woman's technical knowledge. At least she had the vocabulary for what she was talking about. "When are they going to do the overflights?" he asked.

"They started today. I was told it would take a while since they have to fly low and do a slow sweep. I think they use a helicopter as the platform."

"Is the Superplex included in any of the overflight areas?" Horn asked. He was aware of an almost imperceptible sinking feeling hanging somewhere on the edge of his consciousness.

Christina had the doom-seeing look on her face once more. "I don't know, and I won't be able to find out until first thing in the morning, either. Damn."

"Winger and I will head out to the Superplex about the same time the game starts," he said. "It's pretty much a long shot that the bomb and Hoke are connected. I don't want to get into any kind of a panic mode, especially since there's supposed to be more than two hundred thousand bodies at this place tomorrow."

The sinking feeling came off the fringes of Horn's consciousness and jumped straight into the pit of his stomach with both feet. *Bodies,* he'd said. He focused on Christina, who seemed to be fighting the same feeling. There was something bad lurking in the shadows. Horn could sense it now as though he were watching the first thin plume of smoke from a match dropped on a bed of pine needles. He was glad when she spoke.

"If you're thinking what I'm thinking, there's not much we can do about the game tomorrow." Christina's voice carried an edge that Horn hadn't heard before. It wasn't exactly fear; it was more a loss of total control, no doubt stemming from the lack of a plan. "The fact that Hoke was seen with some people who may have looked like the Colombians wouldn't elicit anything from a judge except a hard line." She paused and stared at Horn for several seconds, her icy blue gaze fixing his in a way that suspended him momentarily. He had the feeling he and she were up on some crazy tightrope stretched across a bottomless pit. Her eyes were saying, *Don't look down.* "In any case," she continued, never taking her eyes from his, "I don't think there's much we can do about the situation other than play out the hand we've been dealt."

Horn was glad she hadn't verbalized what they were both thinking the threat might be. "I don't think we have much choice," he said. They would play out the hand, all right, Horn thought, but who had been dealt the joker? Poker with death as the stakes.

"What I will do," Christina said, "is pull as many strings as I can to get the Superplex and the surrounding area overflown as early as possible tomorrow."

"If it hasn't been done already," Horn added. "And if it has been, we've got nothing to worry about."

"True," Christina said. "If they'd found something, we would have heard about it. What I'll do is call you first thing in the morning and then arrange a way to keep in touch the rest of the day. What's your home number?"

Horn pulled a pen from his inside jacket pocket and scribbled the telemonitor number on a cocktail napkin. He handed it to her. "I put our call sign on there, too."

"Charlie Sierra Uniform Niner," Christina read. "Sounds like a janitorial code," she pointed out with a smile.

"Usually it is," Horn told her good-humoredly. He knew their meeting was over and couldn't help feeling she'd called it to glean information from him, rather than provide it. Horn hardly blamed her; she was just doing her job.

"Talk to you tomorrow, first thing," Christina said, getting up from the table.

Horn walked her outside. "Can I give you a lift?"

"No thanks. They give me a driver. It's embarrassing sometime, but the D.A. and his assistants aren't the most popular people in New York, especially among the criminal element."

"I understand," Horn said. "I have that same problem myself." He turned up his collar against the cold damp air. He watched her walk across the sidewalk and get into a black sedan that had double-parked next to the Elint.

As Horn fished for the keys in the pocket of his jacket, he remembered where he'd the term *green line*. It was recited by Chesterfield on the stage at the Edge: "...inside the green line, by the steel tombstone..."

Horn had the horrible thought chill his mind that if the bomb turned up at the Super Bowl, the Superplex would become a giant marker for a mass graveyard.

CHAPTER FOURTEEN

SUPER BOWL SUNDAY DAWNED amid blowing snow and a stiff winter wind that swept in across the Hudson like a giant squall. Dark gray clouds roiled in the bleak sky, flashing lightning occasionally as the storm was sucked on toward the Atlantic by a massive low pressure zone, promising the city bad weather for the next several days. For the old heads, it was near-perfect weather for football: temperature in the upper teens, snow and a forecast that called for the storm to get worse during the course of the game.

Horn had been awake for more than two hours when Christina Service called at six that morning. "Bad news," she'd said, then given him the rundown. Apparently the helicopter had been scheduled to overfly the Superplex and its surrounding area the day before, but a mechanical problem as well as the weather had grounded it. A special crew had been assigned to bring the aircraft up and an overfly was scheduled before noon. However, Christina had added, a more realistic estimate would have them airborne sometime in the afternoon—if they were lucky and the weather allowed it.

Horn had decided not to brief Winger on the possibility that a nuclear weapon might have somehow plugged itself into the already insane equation they were trying to solve. He figured the young cop didn't need to know about it unless it came true.

"Looks like there won't be a blimp today," Winger remarked as the two of them drove slowly up the Henry Hudson toward the Superplex.

Horn looked over at his partner in the passenger seat of the Elint, dunking half a doughnut into steaming coffee. He shoved it dripping into his mouth and made a hearty slurping sound as he devoured it almost instantly.

"Hand me my coffee," Horn said as he slowed to steer around an old station wagon that had apparently spun out on the slick, snow-packed expressway.

"Look at this shit," Winger growled as he pulled a plastic cup out of a white paper sack on the floor. He peeled off the lid and handed the cup to Horn. "It ain't fit for man nor beast out here."

"I agree." Horn took a sip of coffee before bumping up the defroster in a futile effort to keep the windshield from frosting over.

"I was watching Kenny Ahern's *Sports World* last night," Winger said as he absorbed another half doughnut. "He's got Denver by six points, but with this weather, I think the Giants have a hell of a chance of blowing them away."

"What are the odds running now?" Horn asked out of curiosity.

"Apparently the odds makers don't think it's going to be as close as Ahern does. However, if the Giants pull it off, someone is going to make a shitload." Winger grinned as he fished around in the bag for another doughnut.

Traffic only crawled along the jinked-up freeway. After more than two hours, Horn pulled off onto the Riverside exit and joined a long line of cars obviously heading for the same place he was. Looking at his watch, he muttered, "Hell, the goddamn game has started by now. Look at this traffic—people are still waiting to get into the parking lot."

In the distance he could see the huge black shape of the Superplex hunkering in the blowing snow like an evil castle.

"Want me to hang out the light?" Winger asked. He already had his hand on the magnetic flashing light used for emergencies.

"Go ahead," Horn said, "this shit is ridiculous."

Winger pulled the light from under the seat and rolled down the window. "Son of a bitch!" he yelled as cold air washed into the car's interior. "There, it's on. You can roll if you're able." Winger cranked the window shut as though something evil were trying to get into the car. "Damn, it's cold out there."

Horn flashed his headlights several times until the car in front of him pulled up enough to let him get onto the snow-covered shoulder. He gunned the engine and spun sideways onto the narrow strip between the line of cars and the guardrail. The rear end of the unmarked cruiser nicked the galvanized metal. Winger emitted a groaning sound.

"What's wrong with you?" Horn asked, even though he knew what his partner was thinking.

"Goddammit, Max," he began. Horn had to work to keep from smiling. "You should have seen all the paperwork I had to fill out the last time you got antsy behind the wheel. Please try not to hit anything else. This is, after all, a slightly different situation than when you took me into the Bronx the other night."

"Don't worry. I'm sure it's nothing more than a scratch," Horn assured his partner as he pulled away from the off ramp and onto the surface street. "And you're right, the situation is different. There's no one shooting at us this time."

"At least not yet they aren't." Winger chuckled and rubbed the stubble on his face.

In spite of the light flashing on the top of the car and Horn's aggressive driving, it took another hour to reach the entrance to the huge parking lot that circled the Superplex. It was jammed with an almost endless sea of parked cars and buses that surrounded the massive structure like a herd of strange metallic beasts, their humped backs covered with snow.

Horn rolled down the window and flashed his badge as Winger removed the light. "So what?" the guard at the gate said through the fur edging of his parka.

"We're on official business," Horn barked, hoping the guy would hurry up before he lost his patience. "Call your supervisor if you have to, but make it quick."

"You gotta be shitting me!" The man's laughter barked out from the fur in a cloud of vapor. "Look at this crap!" He motioned to the line of vehicles stacked up behind the Elint. "It's been like this since eight in the morning, and the goddamn second half of the game has already started!" The man leaned down toward the open window as if to emphasize what he was going to say next. "I don't need some rent-a-cop rolling in here like a goddamn hot monkey telling me to make—"

The man's diatribe was suddenly cut short as Horn grabbed him by the front of his coat and jerked his head into the car. The fur-trimmed hood was knocked back as his head bounced against the top of the window opening, revealing a fat red face and bulging green eyes.

Horn latched onto the balding man's face with his right hand and squeezed until the fat lips puckered together. He had to resist the urge to flex his mod and crush the man's jaw. "You've got five seconds from the time I release you to open the gate. You understand?" Horn felt the man trying to nod and helped him do so by pushing his head up and down a couple of times. "Then go do it," he said, shoving the man's head out of the car.

The force of the shove made the man fly backward and land on his butt in the snow. He immediately scrambled to his knees and crawled to a control box mounted on a pipe sticking out of the median between the in and out lanes. Horn watched the orange barrier blocking their entrance rise and he drove into the parking lot.

"What an asshole," Winger said.

"I must be one. I shouldn't have been so rough."

"Don't worry about it," the young cop said. "I would have punched his lights out. Rent-a-cop! But you're right about one thing."

"What's that?" Horn asked as he backed into one of the few remaining spaces in an area marked with yellow signs reading Emergency Vehicles Only.

"You are an asshole," Winger answered, laughing.

"You're probably right."

Horn looked toward the huge structure, where long lines of people were still pouring into the large garage-door-like entryways. Looking back toward the gates, he noticed that the line of cars had dwindled. He figured it was going to be a real mess once the game was over and everyone who had been dumb enough to drive to the stadium got in their machines and hit the road.

Horn's attention was drawn to the sky above the Superplex by the familiar whomping sound of a helicopter. The bright blue lights inside the stadium were funneled like the single beam from a giant flashlight up into snow-filled sky. It created a weird effect as though the Superplex were emitting a massive wand of offbeat energy into the winter storm that churned overhead. Into this strange zone of light and snow flew a radically modified HH-80 fly. It reminded Horn of a moth flying into the blue light of a backyard bug-zapper. He stared, fascinated, and almost expected the insectlike machine to disappear in a smoking flash.

"Look at that son of a bitch!" Winger gasped, pointing to the chopper. The pilot obviously had his hands full trying to control the machine. It was bouncing around and swinging wildly as though it had been hung from a loose spring. "I don't know how the hell he can keep it under control in this wind. Look at those goddamn flags." The young cop pointed to a row of multicolored flags that stuck up from the curved end of the horseshoe-shaped Superplex. They were being whipped around violently in the gale.

As the metal-skinned bird struggled to maintain controlled flight, Horn wondered if the pilot would be able to complete his scanning of the complex. Fixed to the belly of the Sikorsky-made aircraft, he could see a large panel covered with what appeared to be glass circles, and knew it was looking into the metal and steel maze for something only it could see.

Horn's gaze drifted down to the flat black sides of the stadium, which were covered with thin blotches of snow. Uncomprehendingly he saw the steel overhead doors of the Superplex suddenly roll down and slam shut with a bang that could be heard inside the Elint in spite of the windows being rolled up.

At first what he'd seen didn't register in Horn's mind. Somewhere on the periphery of his consciousness he heard Winger say, "What the hell was that?" It suddenly dawned on Horn what had happened, when he realized people's arms and legs were sticking out from under each door's cold steel edge. The entire Superplex, at least from what Horn could see, had been sealed off.

"Try to bring up someone on the FM and find out what the hell is going on," Horn said. "Something's coming down, and I don't like the looks of it." He heard the chopper pass directly overhead before its distinct sound faded in the howling wind.

Winger punched two buttons on the Elint's commo panel and asked for a pickup by any other police officer in the vicinity of the Superplex. After several seconds a black-and-white that happened to be patrolling near Isham Park came up. Horn listened to one of the officers state that they weren't aware of anything out of the ordinary.

"Try reaching someone inside the place," Horn ordered as he watched people begin to collect around the sealed entrances, waving their arms and milling around in anguished confusion. An old-style paramedic vehicle fired up and pulled out of a slot a few cars down from the Elint and headed toward the stadium.

"Nothing," Winger said.

"Then patch through on a goddamn telemonitor feed. Surely they have business lines." Horn noticed his heart was beating like a hollow drum.

"All right, here's the one we need," Winger rattled excitedly, his fingers moving over the tiny keyboard in a blur. "Superplex Security Department." He punched the enter button.

Horn listened to a recording come up after the audio had run through two synthesized rings: "Thank you for calling the Superplex Security Department. We are currently experiencing technical difficulties with our electronic systems and cannot respond to your call at this time. If you are calling about an emergency, you may contact the corporate offices of Piper Security at 555-6606. Thank you."

As soon as Winger punched off, the incoming light came on and a series of short beeps bounced out of the speaker.

The young cop punched the receive button. "Charlie Sierra Uniform Niner," he said.

"This is UW dispatch." A woman's voice could be heard over the static cracking in the background. "I'm patching through a priority-one call. Please go to red."

Winger punched in a six-digit number. "I think this is the first time I've ever used the secure channel. I'm surprised I remember the goddamn code."

Horn felt his stomach pick up momentum in a downward direction. Even before Christina spoke, he knew it would be her voice that came from the speaker.

"Detective Horn?" the assistant D.A. said, the urgency in her voice sounding strange and distant.

"Go ahead," Horn answered. "Detective Winger is with me."

"The helicopter got a positive read from inside the stadium," Christina said as though she'd just told someone they had terminal cancer. "The location has been pinpointed, and I've got someone working with the Building Authority, trying to pull up the actual construction overlays so I can tell you how to find it. We need you to get it out of there as soon as possible. They think it's probably armed."

"What the hell is she—"

Horn cut Winger off by holding up a hand and shaking his head. The young cop's face was thick with confusion. "I'm afraid there's a problem on this end," Horn said, surprised that he sounded so calm.

There was silence on the other end of the link that lasted nearly twenty seconds. "Come again," Christina said weakly as though she really didn't want to hear what Horn was going to say.

"The Superplex has commenced a shutdown," Horn informed her. "As far as we can tell, all the entrances have been sealed off."

"What?" Christina's voice held a mixture of amazement and fear.

"We can't raise anyone inside the place, either. Apparently they've lost their ability to communicate." Horn noticed Winger was staring at him with a look on his face that said, I'm beginning to get the picture. He could tell his partner wasn't liking what he saw.

"Stand by," Christina ordered tersely. Horn could hear muffled voices in the background. After nearly a minute she came back on the line. "Can you penetrate the place?"

"Forget it," Winger piped up, surprising Horn. "I've read about the security system it's got. The only way in is over the top."

"Get us a helicopter," Horn said. Then he added, "How much time do we have?"

"Hold on," Christina responded, and once again Horn could hear garbled voices in the background. "Sorry," she finally answered. "The weather has shut down flying."

"What about the bird that was just here?" Winger broke in, his voice cracking slightly.

"It had to make an emergency landing less than a mile south of you. We're pulling the data off its computers over a secure link. Another one might be airborne in an hour or so, but I don't think we have that long. Listen—" Christina's voice dropped "—here's the bottom line. The FBI thinks whoever set this up intends to... Wait a minute..." There was a pause of several seconds before the assistant D.A. resumed speaking. "This may be a break. The FBI got a ransom demand."

"Shoot," Horn said grimly.

"The release of several individuals currently in prison…
We were correct, at least partially correct."

"What do you mean?" Horn asked.

"We're dealing with the Seven Families. Zamora."

"Shit." Horn made the comment more to himself than
anyone. He felt his skin crawl.

"You've got to get in there, Max." Christina's voice
resumed its urgency. "The FBI says they can guide you in
disarming the device. The guy they BPed laid it out for
them, and supposedly it's fairly straightforward."

It struck Horn odd that the woman had chosen that
particular moment to call him by his first name. As far as
he could remember it was the first time she had done so.

"BPed?" Winger looked at Horn, confused.

"I'll explain it later," Horn said out of the corner of his
mouth before directing his speech toward the built-in microphone. "As a possibility, we can try to go through a
wall."

"Forget it," Winger answered. "I told you I read about
the place. The lower part of the structure is built like a
nuclear reactor. It's got concrete and steel walls a foot
thick."

"There has to be a way," Christina prompted. "I've got
a feeling it doesn't matter one way or the other if the de-
mands are met and they release the prisoners."

"I have to agree," Horn said, his stomach falling away
into space. "We'll try something. You get whoever it is
ready to brief me if we do get in. Have you got its location
pinpointed yet?"

Before the assistant D.A. could answer, Winger shouted
hoarsely, "I got it!" He snapped his fingers. "It's a long
shot, but not that long."

"What are you talking about?" Horn demanded.

"Lenny," Winger said, his voice cracking with excitement. "He told me he and his buddies used to sneak into the goddamn place while they were building it...said they went through the sewers! If we can find the little bastard, I know he can get us in the place."

Horn flashed back on the conversation they'd had when he took Winger with him to meet Dr. August. "He lives near here, doesn't he?"

"Lives might be the wrong word, but yeah. Highbridge Park, north end. Let's go!" Winger looked at his watch and punched a button on its side. "How much time do we have?" The young cop directed his question to the microphone as the Elint fishtailed out of the parking space.

"What the hell are you two talking about? Who's this Lenny?" Christina asked.

"We'll explain later," Horn answered. "Any guess at all on how much time we might have?"

"I don't know. The ransom message just called for 'immediate release.' It didn't give an 'or else' time they'd detonate the weapon. I'm guessing you have maybe an hour, tops. And I'm only basing it on the supposition that they are involved in tapping the green line, and that they'll hold off until then."

"Put the light on," Horn said, as he took them toward the same gate through which they'd entered.

When they sped through the gate, they found little traffic on the outbound as Horn ran the Elint down snow-packed Academy Street. He flipped a switch on the dash as they neared the Broadway intersection, and an obnoxious siren blared out from behind the grill.

"Watch it!" Winger suddenly rose up in his seat as Horn blew through a red light straight toward the side of a dirt-encrusted bus.

Horn cranked the wheel hard to the right, but it had little effect. The Elint shot forward like an arrow aimed at some invisible target on the side of the lumbering gray machine. Out of instinct, Horn jammed down on the accelerator as the bus loomed and filled the windshield. The spinning wheels grabbed just enough to cause the cop car to drift to the right a couple of feet. The car's left side slammed into the left rear corner of the bus and spun around as though it were a top.

"What the—" Winger yelled as the machine spun diagonally across the intersection, jumping the curb and taking out a traffic light.

The radio crackled, and Christina's voice floated into the car, asking what was going on just as the Elint kissed the side of an abandoned hotel.

"I swear to God, Max, sometimes I think you're trying to get us both killed," Winger said, his voice suddenly calm.

Horn looked over at his partner, who had taken out his big .44 and was in the process of checking the cylinder. "That's quite a switch," he said, flipping off the siren before burning onto Sherman Avenue. "One minute you're about to jump out of your skin and the next you're acting like we're on our way to watch the dedication of a new water tower."

Winger eyed Horn, his patented grin causing his jaw to cock slightly to one side. There was a glint of near-madness in his eyes as he said, "We've got a job to do, and it's a tough one. I figure we'll make it or we won't." The young cop shrugged slightly as he stuck the big Magnum back in its holster. Horn couldn't tell if he was serious or leading up to some kind of punch line.

"Will one of you answer me?" Christina's voice cracked out of the speaker like dry ice. "What is going on?"

"Just a minor traffic problem, for now," Horn answered as he flipped the siren on again and slid the straining machine onto Dyckman Street.

"Wouldn't you know it?" Winger said nonchalantly as the cop car swung sideways and headed for yet another collision. The two men were jerked violently as the passenger side of the Elint slammed into the side of another bus.

"Go down St. Nicholas and take the first left," Winger directed.

Horn started to turn the siren on again but decided against it. He figured it hadn't done them much good so far. "Christina, are you still there?" he asked, raising his voice.

"Yes, we're still running the sensor data through the big computer."

"We're going to be pretty busy here," Horn said as he turned onto St. Nicholas and floored the Elint. "I'm signing off until we make it into the place."

"Roger," Christina answered. "Good luck."

Winger punched the commo panel to stand by. "Before I forget," he muttered, pulling a small hand-held radio from a fixture beneath the dash and sticking it in one of the jacket pockets.

"Before you forget what?"

"This." Winger patted the lump under his jacket. "The radio, fool." He grinned crazily at Horn, then turned and stared out the window, which was cracked like a spiderweb from their impact with the bus.

"You all right?" Horn asked, glancing at his partner.

"I'm okay." Then Winger pointed to the left. "Turn here."

Horn wheeled onto Audubon Avenue as Winger put his fingerless gloved hands on the dash and peered out the windshield. "Is this it?" Horn asked impatiently.

"Yeah. Slow down. Pull into that parking lot next to the Big T." He pointed to a run-down convenience store.

Horn parked next to an overflowing garbage bin, whose contents were being whipped out and blown down the street by the violent winter wind. The entire area appeared to be deserted, and the sinking, useless feeling in Horn's gut returned.

"There's nobody here," Horn complained. "Look at this goddamn place. It's like a cryogenic warehouse, for chrissake. Think we're really going to find your pal in this deep-freeze?" He looked at Winger, who already had his hand on the door handle.

"Five minutes," the young cop said, looking at his watch. "If we don't pick him up in five minutes we better head for higher ground."

"It's your ticket," Horn said. "Let's dance."

The two cops got out of the car and Winger led the way down the alley behind the Big T. Horn was surprised when Winger stopped him after they'd walked less than half a block.

"Wait here," Winger said. "I want to talk to these folks over here."

Horn watched his partner nod his head toward a pile of cardboard boxes and trash piled next to the boarded-up and dirty brick backside of someone's forgotten business dream.

"What the hell are you talking about?" Horn questioned in bewilderment, scanning the heap of landlocked flotsam.

"There are people over there," the young cop almost whispered, genuine concern in his voice. "Don't talk so goddamn loud, they'll hear you."

Horn couldn't think of anything to say as Winger turned and walked to the snow-covered heap.

Winger bent over and appeared to be speaking into a black crack in the mound of waste. Snow swirled in the bleak alley, and for a moment Horn was sucked into a timeless sort of warp zone. He viewed the scene in strange fascination, unconsciously raising his hand to his head, feeling for something. Horn jerked his hand down and shivered violently when he realized he'd been checking to see if he was wearing the VR helmet.

"Shit," Horn murmured, wiping the sweat from his brow, in spite of the subzero temperatures. He swallowed hard and waited for his mind to crash-land somewhere between reality and what he was in the process of watching.

"Okay," Winger said as he walked back to Horn. "The little beggar is right around the corner."

Horn followed his partner into a dead-end, blind T off the main alley. "There he is." Winger pointed to what looked like a spread-out stack of newspapers on top of a grate. A dirty brick was set in the center of the yellowing newsprint and steam rose around the strange heap like white smoke.

"Where?" Horn asked. "I don't see anyone."

"Here," Winger answered. He walked over and picked up the brick, then dropped it back on the pile of newspapers. "Yo, Lenny!"

Horn heard a loud grunt followed by a stream of cursing that sounded like a machine gun firing four-letter words. A small man in an old, grease-stained fatigue jacket crawled from beneath the papers. He held a tape-handled butcher knife in one hand and raised it over his head.

"Lenny! It's me, Winger!" Winger backed away quickly, holding up his hands. The knife froze in midair as Lenny blinked his wide eyes behind thick, black-framed glasses that had a chain of mismatched rubber bands connecting the earpieces.

The wizened, homeless man appeared to be not much older than his late thirties and was less than average height. He was wrapped in an assortment of clothing, all joined together by safety pins in the crucial places. His mismatched boots looked sturdy enough, but as Horn took in the sight, he realized that something about the man didn't quite fit. Horn realized what it was when Lenny slowly smiled and slipped the knife into one of his boots. He reached into a pocket of his jacket and pulled out a cordless electric shaver. Flipping a switch on the side of the hand-held razor, Lenny began stroking his already clean-shaven cheeks.

"Winger, you son of a bitch," Lenny croaked, smiling madly while he ran the shaver over his face. "You almost tasted steel, the hard way."

"Sure, Lenny," Winger said, putting one of his hands on the little man's shoulders. "This is my partner, Max Horn." He nodded toward Horn.

"You keep pretty low company if you hang around this asshole," Lenny said, looking into Horn's eyes. He flipped off the shaver, stuffed it into a pocket and directed his attention back to Winger. "You got a smoke?"

"You know I don't smoke," Winger answered as Lenny pulled a half-consumed butt from one of his breast pockets and lit it with an ancient-looking Zippo.

"I thought maybe you'd started." Lenny took a deep drag and blew the smoke through his nose, the wind whipping it sideways in front of his smooth face. "What brings you to the other side of life?"

"We've got a rush job for you," Winger said. "But we'll make it worth your while."

"What is it?" Lenny ran a hand through the matted brown hair on his head. "I'm kinda busy, you know."

"Yeah, I know," Winger said, slapping Lenny on the side of his arm. "I'm talking about big-time compensation, though. What do you say?"

"What do you want me to do, ice somebody?" Lenny had smoked the cigarette down to where he was having to hold the butt with the tips of his dirty fingernails.

"Max here, and I need you to get us into the Superplex, like mucho pronto."

"You guys are cops...why don't you go through one of the gates?"

"They're all shut down," Winger answered. "But I don't really have time to explain it. You want the job or not?"

Lenny's dark eyes shifted behind the glasses as though he were calculating something in his mind. "Yeah," he answered, "I can get you in, but it ain't gonna be cheap."

"Name your price." Winger said. He took Lenny by the arm and began leading him out of the alley. Horn followed, turning up his collar in an effort to keep the cold wind off his neck.

"What're you offering?" Lenny asked, pulling his arm out of Winger's grasp.

Winger shook his head and held out his hands, palms up. He appeared to be searching for something that would satisfy the little access artist. "How about a goddamn car?" Winger grinned and slapped Lenny on the back, as though it was one of the best ideas he'd ever had.

"Huh?" Lenny looked momentarily confused. "A car? You gotta be shittin' me."

"No," Winger said enthusiastically. "You can live in it. There it is." He pointed to the battered Elint parked next to the convenience store. It looked like something that had been dragged behind a tank through three or four war zones.

Lenny stopped ten feet from the scarred machine and stared at it as though he'd just been insulted. "Fuck," he said, "this ain't no car, it's a goddamn dog turd."

"Get in," Winger said, opening the back door. "We'll negotiate on the way."

"All right, but you're going to have to come up with something better than this metal slice of road kill." Lenny crawled into the back seat as Horn fired up the engine. "Get over to where West 207th dead-ends. I can have you in, or at least under, the place in less than ten minutes."

Horn backed out of the parking lot and headed toward St. Nicholas with a roostertail of snow blowing up behind the battered machine. "You got the light?" he asked, glancing at Winger.

Winger laughed. "Your freakin' light is smashed against the side of that bus you ran into. It didn't do much good anyway."

Horn ignored his partner's comment and reached down to flip on the siren. Nothing happened. He jiggled the switch several times, but no warbling scream erupted from the front of the car.

"And you want to give me this useless junk as payment?" Lenny chuckled as he leaned over the seat.

"What can I say?" Winger held on to the dash as Horn slid the speeding machine onto Nagle Avenue. The vehicle really started to repay the rough treatment as the engine made a strange grinding sound. "I must have lost my head.

See if you can find room in your sterling heart to forgive me."

"You're lucky I like you, Winger," Lenny said. "Or you and your buddy here would still be back in that alley with the rest of the garbage."

Winger burst into laughter. "So, Lenny, what've you been doing since the last time I saw you—going to ninja school?"

"Like I said, you're lucky I like you."

Horn pulled up to a tall chain link fence that was stretched across the dead-end street. In the near distance he could see the Superplex hunkered down in the blowing snow.

"Let's get this over with," Lenny remarked huffily, climbing out of the car. "I ain't got all day to screw with you guys."

Horn and Winger followed their guide to a steel mesh gate, secured with a chain and rusted padlock. "Gimme a boost," Lenny said, hooking his fingers into the mesh and raising one of his boots.

"No need for that," Horn told him. He grabbed the chain with his right hand and jerked it off the steel gate as though it were a piece of string.

Lenny whistled, his eyes growing wide. He looked at Winger, who merely shrugged his shoulders.

"Where to, Lenny?" Horn asked, pulling open the gate.

"Follow me," he answered and led them through a snow-covered maze of broken asphalt and piles of dirt. "Here we go," he said, stopping over a manhole cover set into a mount of concrete.

Lenny leaned over and brushed away the snow from the round steel slab. He looked at Horn, raised his eyebrows, then nodded at the cover. Horn reached down and hooked a finger into the keyhole and flipped the heavy lid into the snow.

"After you." Horn gestured toward the hole and Lenny slipped into it as though it were the most natural thing he'd ever done in his life. Winger followed and Horn dropped in behind him, nearly gagging as the stench of raw sewage filled his nostrils.

Winger coughed and swore under his breath. He pulled a small penlight from inside his jacket and shone it into the darkness.

"You got it." Lenny laughed, apparently unaffected by the odor. "If a building's got a bathroom, I can get into it."

"Let's go," Horn ordered. He gazed into the slime-covered concrete tunnel and wondered what was waiting at the other end. Horn had the feeling they had dropped into the bowels of a hideous monster.

"You got the light," Lenny said, giving Winger a shove. "Go on, I'll give you directions."

Lenny kept one hand on the young cop's back as they moved into the darkness. Horn followed, aware that his Gore-Tex boots were sticking to the floor of the sewer as though he were wearing suction cups. He didn't have to look down to know why.

The three men wound through the stinking tube for several minutes, Lenny barking directions whenever they came to an intersection or fork. Horn noticed that the farther they went, the smaller the tunnel was getting. He could see Winger up ahead, walking bent over, the beam from the penlight casting weird shadows on the blackish-green walls.

"Hold it." Winger held up his hand as a loud beeping erupted from his jacket pocket. He crouched into a half squat and pulled out the radio. "Here." He handed it to Horn, who punched it on.

"Horn?" Christina's static-laced voice echoed strangely in the sewer.

"Go," he said into the tiny mouthpiece.

"We've got it pinpointed and I have an agent standing by to brief you on how to disarm the thing."

"Disarm, what the hell is she talking about?" Lenny asked.

"Shut up." Winger tried to put a hand over his mouth, but Lenny knocked it away.

"Let's get in the place first," Horn said. "I'll contact you as soon as we do."

"Are you close?" Christina's anxiety could be heard in spite of the static.

"Probably," Horn answered. "I'll call." He punched off the radio and handed it back to Winger. "What the hell's that sound?" A strange buzzing filled the tunnel. Horn looked toward what he thought to be the source of the sound and nearly fell over. Lenny was running the shaver up and down his neck as though he were painting a pole.

"What the hell is this disarm shit?" Lenny shoved the razor back in his pocket. "I got a right to know."

"Come on, ninja man." Winger grabbed Lenny by the sleeve, dragging him along as he moved down the tunnel. "The only right you've got is on the wrong side of your brain."

After moving for another hundred yards, Winger pulled up, their progress blocked by a steel grate that had been welded into reinforced concrete sticking out from the sides of the tunnel. "What the hell is this?" Winger grabbed Lenny and pulled him up next to his side. He shone the light around the circular grating, which had a yellow sign hanging from one of the steel straps. "Use tunnel sixteen for access to main system," he read aloud. "You know about this, Lenny?"

"How the hell should I know?" Lenny held up his hands. "It wasn't there three weeks ago, honest. Look at the goddamn welds, they're new."

"You're right," Winger said as he directed the light onto the fresh burn marks.

"Listen," Horn said as a rumbling sound came from somewhere on the other side of the grating.

"Well, I'll be goddamned," Winger said, cocking his head. "It's cheering...they're still playing the game for chrissake! We must be close."

"That's correct," Lenny piped in. "If I remember right there's a steel ladder about ten yards on the other side." He tapped the grate with his knuckles. "It takes you up through a steel sort of a manhole into a room that's got all kinds of pipes and other shit in it."

"You know a way around this?" Winger asked, playing the flashlight around the sign.

Before Lenny could answer, Horn stepped around Winger and grabbed the top of the grate with his right hand. "Take off, Lenny. We'll catch up with you later and settle up."

"You got it," Lenny said with evident relief as he disappeared down the dark tube.

Horn could hear their guide's sucking footsteps echo strangely as he flexed his mod and felt the metal grating tear away like tissue.

CHAPTER FIFTEEN

JIM OLIVER WAS SWEATING. He felt as though he'd spent the past hour and a half in a steam bath instead of standing, running and falling on the rock-hard artificial surface of the Superplex. The field was a sheet of glare ice, and the windchill was well below zero. In spite of this, Oliver was sweating bullets and anything else he could squeeze through the pores of his skin. He'd just watched the Giants score fourteen unanswered points to tie his team for the lead at twenty-four all.

"Slant-six, out and back," the Denver offensive coordinator's voice poured into Oliver's right ear through a tiny speaker built into his helmet. He bent over and barked the play to the rest of the players in the huddle before they broke and headed for the line of scrimmage. As soon as they set up in a modified shotgun, Oliver began the count. The spun aluminum ball sailed back from between the center's legs like a lazy bullet and the big quarterback's mind switched into the fast lane. He picked up on a blitz by the Giants' outside linebackers and stepped into the pocket while the linemen collided like two herds of human bulls. Oliver sidestepped one of the attacking linebackers, pumped once to the left side of the field, then turned and fired the gyro-stabilized ball down the right sideline toward Henry Swayne, who was just making his comeback hook. Suddenly out of nowhere, the Giants' free safety, Mike Dunne, came flying across Swayne's line of sight and knocked the ball away, then collided with the tight end's upper body. The momentum carried both players out-of-bounds, and they knocked over a photographer before landing in a snowbank.

But Oliver didn't see any of it, for just as he released the ball, the blitzing linebacker from the left managed to shake the blocking tailback and blind-sided him, knocking his already bruised and battered body to the artificial surface, which was the consistency of cured concrete. He pulled himself up in time to see the field judge giving the signal for an incomplete pass.

Oliver shouted in frustration and ran over to the umpire when he saw it was Dunne who had broken up the play to his favorite receiver. "Listen," he screamed, to be heard over the roar of the crowd as well as from anger, "that son of a bitch has been all over my guy all goddamn day! When are you guys gonna do your job and nail his ass?"

The umpire was wearing a stretch white face protector in an effort to fight the weather. The stockinglike headgear had holes for his eyes and mouth, nothing more. It made him look like a burn patient. He motioned for Oliver, who stood six-six, to lean over. When he did, the man in the black-and-white-striped-jacket grabbed the quarterback by the front of his orange and blue jersey and hissed, "Get your ass outta my face or you're outta the goddamn game!"

Oliver muttered angrily to himself as he stepped backward and gave the signal for a time-out. He turned and jogged to the sidelines, unsnapping his helmet and shoving it back so it rested halfway off his head. The restless crowd booed loudly.

The Broncos' quarterback stopped in front of John Huddleston, the gray-haired heavyset coach of the team. He was wearing an orange Broncos parka and had his arms crossed over his chest. A remote camera drone hovered ten feet above and directly behind him, swaying in the wind as it real-timed the sideline meeting.

Oliver was breathing hard and spoke between gasps. "That goddamn Dunne is eating Swayne alive. If we don't score on this drive, we may be in deep shit."

Huddleston turned his head slightly and spit in the same direction the wind was blowing. "I know it," he said, turning back to face Oliver. "The Giants are on a roll. Why don't you try baiting Dunne away with Swayne and hitting Lawton?"

"Lawton's hands are frozen," Oliver said, shaking his head. "He's missed four already. Swayne can catch it if we could get Dunne off his ass. They've got the little fucker working our guy one-on-one. To hell with their free safety position, they know Swayne's the only threat we've got."

"Well," Huddleston said, his face never changing from its perpetual deadpan, "we gotta do something. It'll cost fifteen yards, so make it worthwhile." The coach turned his head and glanced at the scoreboard. "It's second down, so go ahead and do it."

Oliver pulled his helmet down and fastened his chin strap. He nodded and turned to head back onto the field, but Huddleston grabbed him by the sleeve and pulled the earpiece of his helmet toward his face. "I don't want to see Dunne back in the game, understand?" Oliver nodded again and felt the coach release his grip. He ran back to his waiting players just as the referee blew his whistle, indicating the time-out was over.

"This is a long out on a short snap," Oliver had to yell over the din of the crowd and the howling wind, both of which seemed to be amplified by the shape of the Super-plex. He turned toward Swayne, who looked like a wet rag that had been beaten against a rock. "I'm coming to you, but don't turn, just keep going." At first the speedster from Arkansas looked confused, but that expression was quickly replaced by an understanding smile. His green eyes flashed behind the scarred face mask like emerald neon.

Oliver did a quick count from the shotgun and back-pedaled with the ball. He watched Swayne hit Dunne five yards off the line of scrimmage then take off like a meteor down the sidelines. Dunne was right on the receiver's heels as Oliver ran sideways to his right until he was in line with the fleet-footed duo. He planted his right foot and brought the aluminum bullet directly past his ear, grunting loudly when it left his hand as though it had been shot from a rifle.

The football tracked like a rope from his hand straight to the back of Dunne's helmet. There was a loud sound like a massive slab of ice cracking. The point of the aluminum ball slammed into the painted Kevlar helmet, knocking it completely off the free safety's head. Dunne's arms spread out as though he were flaring out to land, which is what he did, slamming facefirst into the rock-hard artificial turf and sliding for twenty feet before coming to a stop. He didn't move. The ball landed two feet from his sweat-covered head, which was steaming in the cold air.

The crowd immediately erupted into another chorus of disapproval, only louder. The back judge took two steps toward Oliver and threw his yellow flag directly into the quarterback's chest. Oliver smiled to himself as they stepped off the fifteen-yard personal-injury-with-the-ball penalty and carried the unconscious Dunne off the field on a stretcher.

On the very next play, third down and twenty-five, Oliver watched Swayne pull away from the rookie who replaced Dunne and hit him on a crossing pattern. Swayne did the high step all the way into the end zone, and the

Broncos celebrated amid a shower of snowballs and boos that rained down from the crowd.

While the majority of the more than two hundred thousand fans tried to help the Giants regain control of the game by screaming and stomping their feet, the electro-cash betting lines were going crazy with the flurry of bets swarming in before game's end.

THE ROAR OF THE CROWD sounded like distant thunder to Hoke Anderson. He was in the CYNSYS Control Center, engrossed by the green line. He was halfway through the tapping operations, and his head was ringing with the cracked bells of a massive headache caused by a bus overload when he'd scrammed the security system. He had to jerk the HI connector out of the back of his neck to keep from passing out and falling facefirst into the console. The pain had been exquisite and clean like a burning bolt of blue lightning shoved down his hollow spine. For more than ten seconds he felt it lase at more than eighty megahertz between his brain and every nerve ending in his body before he was able to control his body enough to reach a quivering hand back and snatch the death plug out of its mental socket. Hoke would gladly have exchanged those ten seconds for a year or more of his life.

One of the negative side effects of the lockdown was that it was taking Hoke longer than planned to access the green line and effect the actual tapping. He had reluctantly shoved the gold-plated plug back into his brain rope and cringed when the buses came up, floating there, waiting for his hook to drag them into his conscious control. Hoke had held his breath, half expecting a replay of what had happened earlier when he'd back-doored the physical security system and, in effect, hijacked control of the system's buses. He almost passed out from relief when it didn't happen.

As the snowstorm of electrocash blew across the screen like the white squall raging outside, Hoke felt the headache fade like cheap paint in the Mojave. Mesmerized momentarily by the immense activity, he allowed the bus-controlling impulses of his brain to drift in and out of the flow several times. For him it was like swimming in the mythical fountain of youth.

Hoke felt refreshed and all but forgot that he'd nearly flushed his mind into an electronic sewer just minutes earlier. The HI felt good plugged into his spine. Instead of the conduit for the electric impulses generated in his head, the fiber optic ribbon was like a high-pressure hose pumping pure adrenaline into his nervous system.

Resisting the urge to languish in the soft white fire that burned across the screen, Hoke began his mass manipulation of the flow. He activated his flash-paper-protected program and attendant subroutines that would step the embezzled cash through a series of complex transfers.

Hoke initiated a couple of noninterfering BIT routines, which immediately flashed Zero Defect status symbols. He moved back a couple of steps and watched his coded brainchild do its stuff. His admiration was short-lived, however, as Alexa Burton tapped him on the shoulder.

"What do you want?" Hoke growled as he whipped around and faced the petite woman, who cowered noticeably.

"Nothing," Alexa blurted out, then apparently remembered what she'd intended to say. "I mean, there seems to be a problem with the security—"

"There's no goddamn problem!" Hoke moved toward the woman. "Now, get the hell out of here."

Alexa immediately hurried out the door, her face flushed. Hoke turned back to the screen and allowed himself to be drawn into its soothing river once again. The green line seemed to absorb his concentration, focusing it for him as though it had become a natural part of his mind. He wondered, without the slightest degree of anxiety, who was controlling whom. The HI had made the machine as much a part of him as he was a part of the machine.

Hoke's comfortable link with CYNSYS was once again broken as another set of fingers tapped him on the shoulder. He could see in the reflection of the screen that it wasn't Alexa and turned around to face the tall form of Dave Coulie, chief of security for the entire Superplex.

Coulie's face was gaunt, his skin stretched in a mask of worry. Hoke noticed that an automatic weapon was hanging inside the security chief's blue blazer and recalled that Coulie didn't normally carry a gun.

"What's up?" Hoke forced his voice to sound casual.

"We've got a pretty serious problem," Coulie answered, his green eyes searching Hoke's rapidly.

"I really don't have any idea what you're talking about." Hoke gestured to the console behind him, which was lit up like the control panel of a fighter jet. "And I'm kind of busy now—" he allowed a degree of irritation to mix with his words "—so why don't you let me do my job."

Coulie seemed determined to go on. "Well, the problem is that the physical security system has been scrammed. We did a tie-in from down in the basement and traced the command straight up here. I've got about twenty-two casualties from the doors alone."

Hoke watched Coulie's eyes search his for a reaction. "Maybe it was a glitch in the system," he said, his vocal cords suddenly feeling like worn-out rubber bands.

"I don't think so," Coulie answered. "We did a complete..."

The security chief's voice seemed to fade and float away. Hoke could still see the man's thin lips moving, but felt his eyes drawn to a point over Coulie's shoulder. A chill settled over him as Steller moved out of the shadows next to a row of auxiliary processors along one wall. It was as though the huge man had materialized from one of the machines.

"...shakedown of the entire data link yesterday." Coulie's voice snapped Hoke out of his brief vision. "The overriding lockdown command came from here, I'm sure."

"Problem here?" Steller said as he moved directly behind the security chief.

"What the hell—" Coulie jerked around at the sound of Steller's voice and immediately reached for the big automatic.

"Not so fast," Steller instructed calmly as he clapped his hands over Coulie's arms pincer style and squeezed.

A shrill, warbling scream erupted from Coulie's throat as Steller applied pressure. The huge assassin slipped his left hand down and clasped it over the bulge under Coulie's blazer where the security chief fumbled with his holstered weapon. Hoke watched Steller's gloved hand flex and heard the sound of bones cracking and metal crunching.

Coulie screamed again and his face went white as Steller gave a final twisting squeeze, then released his viselike grip and allowed his victim to drop to his knees. Coulie lapsed into choked sobbing, his broken arms hanging limply from his slumped shoulder.

"Get back to work," Steller said calmly to Hoke as he half straddled Coulie's kneeling form. "You do your job and I'll do mine."

Right, Hoke thought as he turned back to the console. He could taste bile rising in the back of his throat. You do your job and I'll do mine.

With grim fascination he watched Steller's reflection in the monitor as the black-leather-clad killer grabbed Coulie by the back of the neck with one hand. Steller took several steps backward, twisting Coulie's body over so it was facedown. The security chief tried to raise himself, but Steller forced him down easily, as though he were holding a small puppy.

"You'll never get away with it," Coulie gasped in pain.

Hoke knew he was listening to the words of a dead man and a chill went up his spine as Steller laughed. The green line blinked several times as Hoke's reaction apparently disrupted the HI.

"That's funny." Steller spoke in a normal tone, but it seemed to boom inside Hoke's head. "Whether or not we get away with it can't be a concern of yours."

Hoke was unaware that his mouth had dropped open as he watched Steller, almost effortlessly, whip Coulie's body into the air. There was a loud snap mixed in with the thudding of the security chief's legs as they were jerked up and slammed against the floor. Hoke knew the snap was Coulie's neck breaking like a piece of dead wood.

Steller dragged Coulie's lifeless body next to the row of processors and dropped it there unceremoniously. He appeared to forget about the limp form as soon as it left his hand. Hoke cringed as he watched the blond killer walk toward him and felt the hair on the back of his neck bristle as Steller stared at the reflection in the monitor.

Steller's voice was hard. "The lockdown—it wasn't in the plan."

Hoke tried to swallow but his mouth was dry. He glanced across the console in a weak attempt to pretend he didn't hear the square-jawed death bearer.

"The lockdown," Steller said again, grabbing Hoke by the arm and spinning him around. "Don't make me ask you again."

Hoke stared at Steller. "It's a part of the plan now," he heard himself say.

Steller raised his eyebrows as though he were mildly surprised by Hoke's answer. "Explain," he ordered.

"I have another client," Hoke said. "They paid me to shut the place down. Don't worry—" he held up his hands "—it won't interfere with our plans."

Steller's expression didn't change. He stared at Hoke as though he were looking at a piece of furniture.

When it was clear that Steller wasn't going to say anything, Hoke felt he didn't have a choice but to elaborate. "They're using it as leverage to get a couple of guys released from prison. They have a bomb planted in the Superplex."

"Who's 'they'?" Steller asked.

Hoke tried to work up enough spit to swallow, but only managed to hang a halfhearted effort somewhere in the middle of his throat. "Friends of mine," he lied. Hoke knew Steller was smart enough to figure out he was screwing NEXUS if money were his motivation for lunching the security system. "My brother's one of the guys we're getting released."

Steller gazed at Hoke with an I-know-you're-lying look jammed into his eyes like the strip chart from a failed polygraph. "You better hope your little sidebar doesn't screw this operation up."

"We might have one problem," Hoke told him quickly, his nervousness causing his voice to crack slightly. "The last report I had was that all flight operations were grounded." Hoke pointed toward the windows that looked out over the playing field. Snow was blowing and swirling inside the stadium, making crazy patterns through the banks of blue-tinted lights.

While he waited for Steller's reaction, Hoke thought about the World Network Sports helicopter Zamora had arranged for the getaway. It was planned to take him to JFK, then to the Azores on a transatmospheric jet. If all went well. . . .

Steller didn't look out the windows, but continued staring at Hoke's face. "You should have thought of that before tripping the switch," he said. "You may have a lot of brains when it comes to computers, but for common sense, you don't have shit." The scarred jaw dropped a fraction of an inch and he grinned. At least Hoke thought it looked like one.

But Hoke was also worried about Zamora. In an earlier meeting with the Colombian, it had become clear that the man had found out who all the participants were—including Horn, a detective with the New York police who was sniffing around. Zamora had warned Hoke that he had only two choices: he could be rich or he could be dead.

The man hadn't been joking, Hoke reflected fearfully. Because, no matter what, he'd been determined to blow the Superplex away—fans and all. For credibility, he'd said, so they'd know he was a power to be reckoned with.

As his eyes swung back toward the blond killer in black, Hoke admitted he'd put himself between a rock and a hard place.

CHAPTER SIXTEEN

PUTTING HIS E-MODS to good use, Horn broke open the steel trapdoor that led them into a combination storage room and switching station for the stadium's water and sewer systems. The room was huge, stocked with drums and plastic cans amid a maze of pipes and electronic monitoring devices that blinked green in the dim light. Horn figured they were somewhere below the riverside section of the stands. He could hear the distant roar of the crowd above, like a strange choir rolling their voices through a conduit of concrete and steel.

"They must be having a hell of a game up there," Winger said as he stepped off the top rung of the ladder and followed Horn into the room. "I bet the—"

"Get Service on the radio," Horn interrupted. "Let's find out where the goddamn thing is—now that we're in." As Winger pulled the radio out of his pocket, Horn suddenly felt an odd sensation sweep over him. There was a strong sense of déjà vu, but there was more than the normal moment of queerness followed by several seconds of wonder. Something ominous was running through Horn's consciousness, a sustained stream of darkness. "He's here," Horn said as he realized what he was sensing.

"What?" Winger asked as he fumbled with the handheld. "Who's here?"

"Steller," Horn answered, coming out of his blind stare.

Winger stopped working the controls of the radio and looked up at his partner. "How the hell do you know that?" The young cop's face grew pale. "What do you do, smell the son of a bitch?" He resumed punching the flat buttons of the radio.

"Something like that," Horn answered, taking the radio as it came to life with a blare of static. "Get ready to take notes."

"Charlie Sierra Uniform Niner," Horn managed to say before being interrupted by Christina.

"Where are you?" she demanded.

"We're inside the complex," Horn answered, "but I'm not sure where yet. Give us the bomb's location."

Horn heard the assistant D.A. sigh with what sounded like a cautious measure of relief.

"We've made it over one hurdle at least," she said. "The bomb's in what's called the tongue. We did an overlay of the blueprints with the sensor coordinates, and the bomb is in a utility room down a hall that connects the CYNSYS control room with a lounge area."

Horn watched Winger scribbling on a worn notepad and asked, "It's in a utility room, but *where* in the room?"

"It appears to be beneath something like a sink. The facilities A and E guy who did part of the analysis said there could be a grating. Their schematics didn't go down to that level of detail."

"What about the bomb?" Horn questioned. "How do we disarm it?"

"Let us tell you what it looks like first," Christina said. "We don't know how it's hidden, so let me give you a description just so you'll recognize it."

"Hopefully it wasn't slipped into a concrete pour," Winger whispered.

Horn held up a hand and frowned. He had to admit, however, that his partner had a good point. "Go on," he said.

"I'm going to put Agent Topping on," Christina said. "He's the one who actually BPed the guy in Colorado."

"Okay," Horn said as he watched Winger mouth the BP term. He shook his head and the young cop gave him the finger. Horn couldn't help but smile in spite of the circumstances.

A pleasant-sounding male voice came over the radio. "Agent Topping here. The weapon is in a machined stainless-steel-over-lead case approximately three feet long and ten inches in diameter. It's shaped like a bullet—rounded on one end, flat on the other. They may have painted it or done something to cut the shine, so don't just look for a silver bullet, if you know what I mean."

"Understood," Horn said. "Go on."

"Once you find the thing," Topping continued, "you're going to have to unscrew the head." The FBI agent paused momentarily as though he were figuring out how to verbalize the description. "It's the rounded end with a short stub of an antenna sticking out from its center. You just unscrew the whole thing like a cap. Inside you'll find one of the old press-and-twist connectors linking the head, which is the RF trigger, to the rest of the bomb. Just disconnect it and you're home free."

Winger leaned over to the radio. "Are there explosives in this RF mechanism?"

"No," Topping answered. "The conventional HE is shaped around the fissionable material in the larger portion of the case. They must have found the design for this weapon drawn on the wall of a cave."

Winger laughed briefly at Topping's remark and shook his head. "Is there any restriction or limitation on when the command to torch the thing off is transmitted?"

"I'm afraid I don't follow," Topping replied.

"Can they transmit the detonation signal at any time, or are they limited to a particular window?" Winger clarified his question.

"As far as we can tell," the agent said soberly, "they've got satellite coverage. Theoretically they can blow it whenever the mood strikes."

"What are we waiting for?" Horn said, tossing the radio to winger. "Let's go."

Horn led Winger up a set of metal stairs to a landing and a single steel door. As he reached for the handle, the gray metal slab swung open and a stocky dark-haired man wearing a blue windbreaker with Security stitched over the left breast stepped through the doorway. He was holding an automatic weapon in his right hand and raised it suddenly when he saw the two cops.

"Who the hell are you?" he asked, backing against the door, which had closed behind him.

"Take it easy," Winger said, holding up one hand. "Police officers." He started to reach into the inside of his jacket.

"Hold it, goddammit," the guard yelped nervously and Horn cringed as he watched the man's finger jerk back on the trigger. At the same instant he saw a blur out of the corner of his eye and watched Winger's right boot slap the side of the weapon just as it discharged. The explosion echoed in the room and Horn heard the bullet ricochet off the pipes behind him. The automatic bounced off the wall next to the door and clattered down the stairs.

"You dipshit." Winger grabbed the guard by the front of the jacket. "I ought to—"

Horn put a hand on his partner's shoulder as Winger slammed the guy against the pipe railing and appeared to be on the verge of shoving him over the edge. "Take it easy," he said, pulling Winger back a step. Then he turned his attention toward the man who was cowering next to the railing. "We really are police. Tell us how to get to the tongue."

Horn noticed a small microphone clipped to the collar of the guard's jacket. He reached out and plucked it off, and a small radio pulled out of a side pocket and hung from the microphone's wire. Horn crushed the microphone between his thumb and forefinger before tossing the thing over the railing. "Well?" he said.

"Just follow the stairs up to ground level. There's a set of moving stairs that'll take you up to the second floor." The guard spoke quickly, watching Winger out of the corner of one eye. "Once you get there, there's a set of double glass doors that lead into a secure area that accesses all the upper level area."

"The CYNSYS Control Center?" Horn asked.

"Yeah, as well as the VIP areas and the helipad." The guard managed a full-blown glance at Winger. "But don't count on making it that far, even if you are cops."

"What the hell is that supposed to mean?" Winger piped in, taking a half step toward the guard.

"They've got the tube jammed up like a backed-up drain," the man answered. His eyes darted back and forth like a trapped animal's.

"What the hell's the tube?" Winger asked impatiently.

"It's a security choke point. You gotta go through it to get to the tongue."

"That's our problem," Winger said, grabbing the guard by the sleeve of the jacket and pulling him out of the way so he could open the door.

The young cop stepped through the doorway into a wide stairwell and pulled the guard after him. Horn wondered what he was up to and was mildly surprised when Winger swung his right hand up behind the man's back and smacked him with the edge of his palm just behind the left ear. The guard's head jerked forward as though it had been stamped with a punch press. He crumpled to the floor as though his bones had suddenly disappeared.

"Don't worry," Winger said, grinning at Horn. "I didn't kill him."

Horn stepped over the unconscious form and followed his partner up the stairs. They found the moving stairs just as the guard had said and made their way up through a mass of people who seemed oblivious of the fact they were prisoners inside the stadium. Horn figured it was probably fortunate that the crowd didn't realize there had been a lockdown. He didn't want to imagine what would happen when that many people got into a collective panic. Through the huge tunnels that led to the actual arena, he could hear the crowd roaring and intermittent announcements blaring over the loudspeakers as the game continued.

"It's probably just as well they don't know what the hell is going on," Winger yelled over the din, apparently thinking the same thing.

Horn nodded as they stepped off the stairs and then pointed to a set of doors marked Restricted Access. A cipher lock was fixed to one of the doors.

"What do we do?" Winger asked. "Knock?"

"Something like that," Horn answered as he walked to the doors. He pulled the 9 mm out of its holster and passed it to his left hand. "I don't think being cops is going to buy us much in terms of getting the doors open." Horn watched Winger follow his lead and pull out the hybrid machine pistol. Several people in the hallway saw the two men's weapons and started an exodus from the area amid scared mutterings.

"Ready?" Horn asked as he drew his right arm back, sideways. At that moment a blue-jacketed security guard rounded a corner in the hallway, holding what looked like a 12-gauge autoloader across his chest.

Horn immediately raised the automatic and fired a round over the man's head into a recessed light fixture, which exploded in a shower of sparks and blue smoke. The guard jerked backward and fell as his feet slipped out from under him. The shotgun went off and blew the tip of his shoe away as though it had been instantly erased. He screamed in pain as the shot ricocheted down the hallway, then dragged himself backward around the corner, a trail of blood smearing across the concrete floor behind his mangled foot.

"Go." Winger pulled back a lever on his weapon and nodded toward the double doors.

Horn recocked his arm and swung it against the steel facing. He heard a loud popping sound as the locking mechanism broke away. One side of the double doors swung open, which was followed by the high-pitched wail of an alarm going off. Horn stepped through the door and headed straight down a tunnellike hallway bathed in red light. He heard a single shot go off behind him, and a bullet whistled next to his head before it slammed into the door at the end of the hall. Winger's machine pistol barked out a short burst, which was followed immediately by a moaning scream.

Without slowing, Horn drove his right foot into the door next to a chrome plate where the handle should have been. He consciously flexed his modified knee and felt pain shoot through his ankle and lower leg as the door blew open as though it had been pressurized. Horn felt Winger run into his back as he stumbled into a brightly lit hallway that curved gradually until it disappeared in either direction. Directly in front of his face Horn stared at double glass doors across which was etched: CYNSYS Control Center—Authorized Personnel Only.

"Think you can find the bomb?" Horn asked as he turned and swung the door shut, bending the edge of the metal with his right hand so it was jammed tight against the steel facing.

"Yeah," Winger answered, "but what the hell are you going to do?"

"*He's* in here." Horn nodded over his shoulder toward the glass doors.

"Who, Hoke? Forget about him—"

"No," Horn cut his partner off. "Steller. He's waiting for me."

"You have to be full of shit," Winger said, a degree of exasperation ringing in his voice.

"Find the bomb, take it apart. You don't need me," Horn said calmly. "Call Service and the agent if you get hung up. Now move it."

Winger gave his partner a look of mixed anger and helplessness. "You're an asshole," he said, "but I'm going to let you buy me a beer tonight." He grinned, then took off down the hall.

Horn heard tentative banging on the steel door behind him as he grabbed the handle of one of the glass doors leading into the CYNSYS Control Center and jerked hard. The steel bar that served as the locking bolt snapped off and fell to the carpet with a dull thud. He walked into the room and stared at Steller, who was half sitting on a waist-level shelf that ran around the edge of the horseshoe-shaped room, just below the huge windows that looked out over the playing field. The snow swirled behind Steller, whose black leather coat hung open revealing his huge SuperMag still hanging in its shoulder holster. The big assassin had his hands clasped across one of his thighs as though he were bored. Horn raised the 9 mm and activated the laser sight, placing the red dot of the beam directly in the middle of Steller's scarred forehead.

"What took you so long, cop?" the huge man said conversationally. "I was beginning to worry about you."

Horn glanced about the room and noticed Coulie's crumpled body lying next to the processors. He looked over at Hoke, who stared at him blankly, as though he'd experienced some sort of sensory overload. Turning back toward Steller, he heard himself say, "I thought you were dead."

Steller tilted his head back and laughed strangely, his deep voice echoing in the electronics-filled room. "You can't kill *death*," he answered, dropping his square jaw into a morbid grin.

Horn felt his finger automatically pulling on the trigger but consciously forced it to stop as Steller held up a hand. "I wouldn't do that, at least not yet."

Something in the assassin's voice told Horn that an unexpected card was about to fall out of the deck. "Explain," he said, realizing that it was taking more than a minimal mental effort to keep from pulling the trigger and blowing away the top of the blond man's head.

"I've got your girlfriend," Steller said, dropping his hand. "What's her name?" He leaned back and pointed to Hoke. "You know, she used to be his girlfriend, too."

"Sarah Weed." Horn supplied the name as an empty feeling spread through his chest and into his stomach. He thought it strange, but he wasn't surprised.

"Yeah," Steller said, raising his eyebrows. "Good old Sarah the Weed. A little screwy, but all in all, not a bad chick. Now drop that goddamn popgun before you piss me off." He slipped off the ledge and stood, rolling his head around as though his neck were stiff. Horn hesitated a moment then let the 9 mm slip from his fingers. "Here's what I'm going to do." Steller pulled a slip of paper out of one of his coat pockets and held it up. "This tells you where to find the woman." At the same time he spoke Steller pulled out the SuperMag and aimed it at Horn's midsection. He walked over and handed the folded paper to Hoke. "All you have to do to get your hands on it is finish what we started—" Steller paused for a moment "—I guess it was more than a year ago. You have handcuffs?"

Horn wasn't sure if he'd heard Steller correctly. "What?"

"Handcuffs," Steller said. "Toss them over here, I want to make sure Mr. Hoke doesn't run down a hole or something."

Horn surprised himself when he reached into one of his jacket pockets and pulled out a self-locking reinforced nylon strap that functioned as disposable handcuffs. He tossed it to Steller, who grabbed one of Hoke's hands. "Wait," Horn said. "Look at the note." He directed his speech to Hoke, who seemed to snap out of his dullard state.

"Me?" Hoke asked, drawing his head back slightly.

"Go ahead," Steller said, obviously knowing Horn's intention. He released his grip on Hoke's wrist. "Just read it, don't speak."

"Does it say where the woman is?" Horn asked. Hoke looked at the piece of paper and then up at Horn, finally nodding affirmatively. "If you're lying, you're a dead man," Horn heard himself say.

Steller grabbed Hoke's wrist and pulled it down, looping the engineer's arm around one of the legs of the console. "Other hand," he said.

Horn watched Hoke clasp his hands together around the stainless steel leg as Steller laid the strap across the man's wrists. The assassin glanced at Horn then laid down the SuperMag in order to use both hands to pull the strap through the ratchet loop on one of its ends. Horn didn't hesitate and dived straight for the 9 mm. He heard Hoke yelp in pain as Steller jerked the strap tight.

Rolling as he landed, Horn grabbed the big automatic and swung toward Steller. The red beam tracked across Hoke's forehead and glinted off the edge of the console. He heard Steller laugh the same instant he picked up the man's hulking form in his peripheral vision. Horn squeezed off three rounds as he whipped the weapon around and watched the huge window behind the killer explode in a shower of glass.

Snow swirled in through the window as Horn tracked the beam up to Steller's head and fired twice more. The killer's arms shot up in front of his face and both bullets ricocheted off into the main CYNSYS console. Sparks filled the air, and the steady hum of the electronics changed into a grinding warble. Hoke screamed as the green line flashed crazily on the monitor, and out of the corner of one eye Horn could see the kneeling man try to pull the HI plug out of the back of his neck.

"You son of a bitch!" Steller's voice boomed in spite of the wind and crowd noise that roared through the broken window.

Horn dropped his aim to Steller's crotch, but the big man turned sideways as though performing a crazy dance. Something shiny flashed next to the assassin's head, and Horn watched the killer bring his arm around in a blur and launch the SuperMag straight for him, throwing it by its long barrel. He jerked his right arm over his face an instant before the weapon struck, knocking the 9 mm from his hand and sending him sprawling on his back. The metallic taste of blood washed over his tongue and the right side of his face felt strangely numb.

The sound of Steller's boots running across the carpet toward him prompted Horn to roll to one side. He felt the assassin's knee glance off his back, followed by a loud grunt as he pulled himself up. Horn rolled once more then sprung to his feet. He turned and faced Steller, who stripped off his coat and tossed it to one side.

"Just like old times," the assassin said, his polished titanium skin gleaming through the rips in his black turtleneck where the 9 mm slugs had struck. Horn noticed Steller's eyes seemed to gleam the same way—hard and cold, built to kill. "This time you won't make it out alive."

Horn glanced around, his eyes searching for an object he could use as a weapon. A sense of desperation crept out of a dark corner of his mind and he tried to force it back, wondering for the briefest moment if it was his turn to die. He looked at Steller and saw what he thought might be his death reflected in the assassin's eyes.

"You can't die without a fight," Steller said, his words making Horn's flesh crawl with disgust.

"I don't intend to," Horn said, spinning around, bringing up his foot like the ball of a mace. It struck Steller across the jaw with a whacking sound. The blond head snapped sideways, and Steller staggered backward several steps before gaining his balance.

"Keep it up, cop," Steller slurred his words, his jaw hanging at an odd angle. "Your death becomes more meaningful by the second."

Horn moved in and faked another kick. He brought his right arm around in an attempt to clothesline the side of Steller's head. The assassin saw the blow coming and jammed his left forearm up in its path. Horn felt the shock run down his back, as if he'd tried to clothesline the front of a speeding freight train. "Goddamn!" he gasped, backing away, his teeth chattering.

"Your turn," Steller breathed and took two steps toward Horn. He swung his right arm sideways as though it were a sickle. Horn tried to duck, but the massive forearm drove into his shoulder before glancing off and striking the side of his head.

Horn saw stars and had a weird sensation that he was floating; as the moment unhung, he realized that he actually was flying. He landed in a heap against the side of the CYNSYS console where Hoke was tied. Horn looked at the cuffed engineer, who was less than two feet away, and watched the man's lips moving in slow motion. He was saying something, but Horn couldn't hear what it was. There was a ringing in his head, and everything seemed to be functioning at the wrong speed. He was in the border zone where every one of his senses was hallucinating in some manner. Suddenly he realized what Hoke was saying as the man's voice broke through his veil of pain in one long scream: "Look out!"

Horn rolled to one side and caught a glimpse of Steller's boot swinging toward his face like a death pendulum. He felt the rush of air on his ear as the assassin buried the black leather missile six inches into the side of the console exactly where Horn's head had been resting a tenth of a second earlier.

Sparks and smoke erupted from the hole as Steller jerked his booted foot out, cursing furiously. Horn staggered to his feet and backed way, holding on to the side of the console for balance. His head cleared slightly as he watched Steller turn toward him.

Horn took two steps and took a flying leap, aiming a roundhouse right fist for the side of Steller's face. The big man ducked and Horn felt his modified hand barely scrape the top of his head. He tried to step back, but Steller's arms shot out and gripped his waist in a death lock. Horn blew a painful whistle involuntarily from between his clenched teeth as Steller squeezed. Horn felt something ripping apart inside his body and heard the whistle change into a full-blown scream.

Steller lifted Horn into the air and shook him like a rag doll, and strange laughing curses gurgled from his throat.

Horn forced himself to concentrate and covered Steller's right ear with the palm of his left hand. He jerked his right hand back and slapped the killer's left ear as hard as he could. Steller looked up momentarily just before his eyes rolled back in his head. He released his grip on Horn and moaned loudly, dropping to his knees. Steller cradled his head in his hands as Horn staggered backward.

Leaning against the console, Horn tried to regulate his breathing in order to control the pain that threatened to run away with his mind. He was somewhat relieved to see that Steller seemed to have a similar problem. The assassin was shaking his head as a trickle of blood ran out of one nostril into his gasping mouth.

Horn sensed something moving behind him and swung around. He stared into the single round eye of a remote camera drone that hovered just outside the broken window, its antenna hanging from the rear of the teardrop-shaped craft like a long thin tail. Horn figured someone, somewhere was getting more of a show than just the game.

There was a blinding flash of light, and Horn thought for a moment that lightning had struck the tongue. He found himself jammed against the wall just below the RCD, which weaved and bobbed in the wind. Horn turned his head toward Steller, who towered above him like a living tombstone. The assassin's jaw hung open and spit drooled down his chin.

"Now you die," Steller slurred. He grabbed the back of his shirt and ripped it off, exposing the polished titanium covering his upper body like armor. The hard metal was molded nearly perfectly. The pectoral and other muscles were powerfully defined, making Steller look like a freakish machine turned weight lifter.

Horn struggled to his feet, sliding his back up the wall until he felt the glass-strewn ledge digging in at kidney level. He watched Steller hesitate a moment before making his move, lunging at him like a bull going after the red cape. Horn waited until the last second, then sidestepped. At the same instant, he brought his right knee up and rammed it into the assassin's crotch like a pile driver. Gagging loudly, Steller fell across the ledge, and Horn was immediately on the killer's back, swinging down with his right hand. He aimed for the back of the blond head. Horn's fist rammed into the backs of Steller's hands, which had suddenly whipped up and locked their titanium fingers behind his head.

"You can't kill me!" Steller's words, mingled with grim laughter, blew back through the window on the howling wind. "I'm already dead!"

Horn pounded even harder, which seemed to intensify the assassin's insane laughing. A sharp gust of wind suddenly blew the RCD halfway through the window, its buzzing filling the room before it began backing out. Horn grabbed the cablelike antenna and wrapped it around Steller's neck several times before the drone took up the slack, its buzz reaching a strained pitch as its progress was halted.

Steller began choking as the RCD continued trying to pull itself away from the window. Horn moved away a couple of steps as the big killer leaned backward, fighting with the whining drone. There was a loud snap as the antenna broke, and Steller did a stumbling cartwheel across the floor, rolling to a stop near the glass doors. Horn watched the RCD fly off, uncontrolled, into the snow-filled light.

"Look out, cop!" The hoarse sound of Hoke's voice brought Horn's head around and he stared at Steller, who had pulled himself to his feet, a grin spread across his twisted face like an abstract painting. In his shredded gloved hand was the big SuperMag.

"Well, I have to admit one thing," Steller slurred, his cracked jaw lagging his lips by a tenth of a second or more, "that was a pretty good move with the RCD. I'm surprised you thought of it."

Horn saw his 9 mm lying next to the assassin's boot. He wondered how long Steller would talk before he touched off the big cannon and turned out the lights forever. Horn thought his earlier feelings were now confirmed; it was his time to die.

"Spare me the eulogy, Steller," he said, forcing his eyes from the end of the gun barrel. "Get it over with."

Horn's mind blinked into a sort of hyperspace, and a myriad of strange thoughts flashed through his head in fast forward. It didn't take long. He managed to keep the door closed on his family, and after that there wasn't a whole hell of a lot. Some pretty, interesting women... And Winger. Winger was young. Horn hoped he would live... the crazy kid...

Horn blinked several times and felt something akin to his VR experience sweep through his senses like a warm wind. "Winger, you crazy bastard," he muttered aloud, and felt adrenaline dump into his system like mercury. Horn rubbed his blood-smeared neck, then slipped his hand beneath the collar of his turtleneck. He reached between his shoulder blades and grasped the flat handle of the throwing knife Winger had affixed to his back.

Horn whipped the knife out from it scabbard with such force that it ripped the collar of his shirt. He brought it up and over, right next to his ear, just as Winger had instructed, and released it, pointing his finger straight at Steller's head.

The thin flat blade struck the huge assassin directly between the eyes, just above the bridge of his scarred and bent nose. The knife had been hurled with such force that it buried itself four inches into Steller's brain, splitting the hemispheres. The huge man's eyes crossed and stared up at the death handle, and a look of utter disbelief blinked across his face like a dying star. The AutoMag slipped out of his hand and he tipped backward like a felled tree. His head smacked against the floor with a sickening thud.

As he walked over to the spread-eagled form, Horn knew Steller was dead. He kicked the handgun away, then wondered if he'd done it out of habit or subconscious doubt that the assassin was really dead.

"Jesus Christ!" Hoke's voice interrupted Horn's thoughts. "You killed the son of a bitch. I can't believe it."

Horn ignored the man and placed his foot on Steller's face, then unceremoniously reached down and worked the blade out of the assassin's skull. A gush of blood erupted from the death wound as Horn finally tugged the knife free. He wiped the blade on the side of Steller's face before straightening up and putting it back in its secreted scabbard.

Horn took two steps before leaning over and picking up his 9 mm. He then turned and walked to Hoke, jerking out the folded piece of paper that was till jammed between the engineer's slick fingers.

"What the hell is this?" Horn said as he stared at the white slip on which was scrawled: The Fine bitch can lead you to the Weed woman. He pulled the hammer of the 9 mm back and aimed the red beam of the laser sight straight into Hoke's left eye. "Talk."

"No, it's true!" Hoke literally chirped. "Ashley Fine . . . she knows where Steller stashed Sarah. Honest to God." The engineer tried to hold his hands up, but the cuffs stopped them at chest level. "She's supposed to meet us upstairs in one of the choppers.

"You sound like you're selling encyclopedias," Horn said as he reached down and snapped the nylon cuffs free. "You better be telling me the goddamn truth."

"I am." Hoke rubbed his wrists, then glanced at his watch. "She should be there now. You ready to go?"

Horn picked up Steller's black leather coat, then grabbed Hoke by the arm. "Not just yet," he said, shoving the engineer toward the glass doors.

CHAPTER SEVENTEEN

HORN STEPPED through a door marked Custodian Station, shoving Hoke ahead of him, and watched as Winger swung around, aiming the machine pistol toward them.

"Goddammit," the young cop snapped. "Don't you ever knock?"

Winger was on his knees in the center of the garage-sized room, which looked as if it had been turned upside down and shaken. Broken mop handles, rolls of paper and cleaning supplies were scattered everywhere. Horn could see a hole beneath the wide utility sink that appeared to have been kicked into the wall.

In a small cleared-out area in front of Horn's sweating partner lay the bomb. The weapon's sleek, stainless-steel form was aesthetically pleasing in an eerie sort of way. Its bullet shape and polished casing made it look like a round waiting to be loaded into the chamber of a giant gun. "I can't get the son of a bitch off," Winger breathed, his voice revealing his fatigue and frustration. Sweat was running down his face in rivulets. He had tossed his jacket to one side and the shirt beneath his webgear was soaked.

Horn looked at the smooth head of the weapon around which Winger had wrapped his belt as a makeshift wrench. He crouched and ran the tips of his gloved hand across the seam that girdled the circumference of the bomb six inches or so below the rounded head. There were nicks and scratches along the thin line where Winger had tried to loosen the head.

"Go stand in the corner, goddammit and don't make me repeat it."

Winger's voice caused Horn to look up. He turned his head and watched Hoke move from the door and walk to the back of the small room. "It is supposed to unscrew, isn't it?" Horn asked, turning his attention back to the bomb.

"It is supposed to unscrew, isn't it?" Winger repeated his partner's words.

For a moment Horn thought the young cop was mocking him. He looked up and saw Winger speak into the hand-held radio, which was resting on an overturned bucket.

"Yes, counterclockwise," a static-laden voice came back. Horn recognized it as Topping's. "Try running hot water over the seam."

Winger laughed crazily and looked up at Horn. "Listen to this asshole. He thinks we're trying to open a goddamn jar of peanut butter."

Horn peeled the glove off his right hand and lifted the weapon, resting it across one thigh. He was surprised at how heavy it was and figured Winger must have had a hell of a time extracting it from the wall. Horn wrapped his titanium fingers around the head, over the belt and twisted hard. A squeaking noise was emitted from beneath his modified hand, as flattened strips of shredded leather squeezed out between the fingers like pulp.

Horn released his grip and wiped away the remains of Winger's belt. He rubbed the palm of his E-mod on his pants. "Hold the bottom," he ordered, nodding toward the lower half of the weapon.

Winger wrapped his hands around the base of the bomb as Horn placed his hand over the smooth head as though he were palming a ball. A creaking, pneumatic squelch came from Horn's titanium-covered arm as he flexed, tightening his grip until the electromechanical joint threatened to rip itself from what was left of his natural shoulder. He felt the head give slightly, then break free, causing him to pitch forward against his partner.

"Hot damn!" Winger said, almost gleefully. "You did it." He slapped Horn on the shoulder and helped him set the bomb upright, resting on its flat end. Horn quickly unscrewed the fine threaded cap while Winger spoke into the radio. "Did you hear that, Topping? We got the cap off, no thanks to you."

Instead of Topping's voice, they heard Christina Service speak. "That's good. Are you there, Max? I'm a little confused."

"Yeah, he's here," Winger answered for him, "but he's kind of busy right now."

Horn pulled off the cap and a foot-long bundle of multicolored wire stretched between it and the body of the weapon. He grabbed the wire with his left hand and was just about to jerk down when Winger screamed, causing him to freeze.

"Holy shit!" the young cop yelled, and there was a look of disbelief and fear slapped on his face. "What the hell are you doing?" Winger grabbed Horn's fingers and pried them from around the bundle. "No offense, partner, but I think you've been breathing dumb air."

Horn watched Winger gently tug the bundle up from a honeycomb material that lined the inside of the weapon, revealing an olive-green cannon plug. Winger grasped either side of the connector and twisted delicately until it

popped apart. "There," he said, breathing a sigh of relief.

At almost the same instant, Horn heard a loud series of
clicks coming from the cap of the weapon. He tossed it in
the corner next to Hoke and looked at Winger.

"Jesus." The young cop whistled. "Are you thinking
what I'm thinking?"

"I hope not," Horn answered, rising to his feet.

"Who's on the other end of this thing?" Winger
grabbed the radio and spoke as Horn helped him up.

"Service. Is it disarmed."

"Yeah, it's disarmed," Winger answered, hesitating a
moment before adding, "but maybe I should say I *think*
it's disarmed."

Horn grabbed the radio away from Winger and couldn't
help smiling. The young cop grinned sheepishly and
shrugged his shoulders.

"This is Horn."

"Good," Christina said. "Let me tell you, there are
some people down here breathing a hell of a lot easier."

"I've got Hoke," Horn said, glancing toward the engineer, who had slumped against the wall like a bag of sand.
"I need to use him to open one more door."

"What do you mean?" Christina asked. "I don't understand. We've already got black-and-whites outside the
complex. As soon as they figure out how to release
the—"

"They've got one of my sources stashed somewhere,"
Horn answered.

"Why do you need Hoke?" Christina's voice carried an
edge of irritation.

"He's my key," Horn said, resisting the temptation to
toss the radio into the sink.

"I hope you're not thinking about pulling some sort of cowboy crap on this case, Max."

Horn held out the radio to Winger, who shook his head and mouthed the words, No Way. "I'm having trouble hearing you, Ms. Service," he said. "I think we have a problem with the commo link."

"Okay, goddammit," Christina said. There was more in her voice than true acquiescence. "Have it your way, but you and I are going to have a serious talk when this thing is over."

Horn ignored the threat. "I hear you," he said. "Is that all?"

"Yes. No—wait." Horn could hear Christina talking with someone on her end of the link. "Here, Topping has some information you need to know."

Winger rolled his eyes as the FBI agent's voice came over the radio like a commercial. "Listen, boys, I didn't tell you this before, but I'm afraid you're getting one hell of a dose of rads. First, you need to screw that cap back on, but don't reconnect the wiring." Horn heard Topping laugh.

"I'm telling you," Winger said, "the guy's an asshole. I thought he was okay at first, but he's really a bona fide asshole."

Horn held up a hand as the agent continued. "Second, you need to keep anyone and everyone away from the thing until we can get a lead-suited crew in there to retrieve it. You guys can plan on spending the better part of a week in detox once things are wrapped up. By the way," Topping added, "who the hell is winning the Super Bowl? I haven't heard."

Horn tossed the radio into the sink. "That means you stay," he said, looking at Winger.

"Bullshit," the young cop said halfheartedly, obviously aware that his arguments would be useless. "Why me?"

Horn held up a hand. "Who else is there?"

Winger's face lapsed into a tired, disgusted expression as he walked over to the sink from where Topping's voice echoed up asking what was going on. Winger turned on the water.

Horn peeled off his jacket and pulled on Steller's thigh-length black leather coat and turned up the collar. It was too large by a long shot, but he figured it would get him through the first wicket.

"Let's go," he said, giving Hoke the come-on with his index finger.

Horn led Hoke by the arm to a roped-off stairwell that had an arrow-shaped sign painted on the wall reading Helipad—Authorized Personnel Only. A nervous-looking guard stood behind the velvet-covered rope holding a small telecommunications device. Horn noticed a rubber-gripped revolver hanging in a buttoned-down holster from the man's belt.

"Hold it, chief," the guard said as Horn reached down to unhook the rope. "What the hell are you doing? Can't you read the goddamn sign?" He pointed toward the arrow.

Horn reached into his back pocket and pulled out his leather badge holder. He made sure the coat swung open enough that the guard could see the 9 mm hanging from his side, recalling the old adage that a loaded gun will get more than a kind word. "NYPD," he said, flipping the badge open and holding it in front of the guard's face.

"No sweat, chief," the guard said, reaching down himself to release the brass hook. "But you better put some lead boots on that boy." He nodded to Hoke. "It's blowing a shit storm up there."

Horn didn't say anything and dragged Hoke past the guard and up the stairs. He leaned hard against a smoked-glass door and shoved it open into the wind and blowing snow. The scene on the huge concrete slab was a mixture of confusion and chaos set against the backdrop of blinking lights and swirling white snow. There were five helicopters on the pad, and Horn watched that number diminish to four as a sleek blue and white Douglas 680 with the Presidential seal emblazoned on its rotorless tail boom lifted off. The machine banked right and shot down over the Hudson like a rocket, its twin turbines screaming like banshees as the pilot tried to compensate for the uncertain wind conditions with more speed. The flashing red strobe disappeared in the darkness as the helicopter burned down the river, jinking violently in the wind.

"Where's our bird?" Horn yelled, pulling Hoke toward him.

"Over there," Hoke answered, pointing to a jet-black Aerospatiale with NEXUS INTERNATIONAL painted across its smooth nose in gold letters. The helicopter appeared ready to launch. Its turbine was whining and it bounced slightly as the pilot reversed the pitch of the rotor blades in order to keep the sleek machine pressed to the concrete.

"Let's go," Horn said, pulling the engineer after him. He turned his head away as he slid open the passenger door and shoved Hoke into the warm cabin of the aircraft. As Horn backed in and pulled the door shut, he heard Ashley order the pilot to take off. The sound of her voice made his mods twitch involuntarily.

"Listen, Steller," Ashley said as Horn fell back against the padded bench seat while the aircraft lurched up and away from the helipad. "Two more minutes and you would've been—"

Horn watched the woman's mouth drop open in disbelief as she stared at his face. Her expression blossomed with a blend of fear and shock. She looked as though someone had just doused her unexpectedly with ice water.

"Hello, Ashley," Horn said, holding on to the back of the seat as the helicopter banked suddenly and dropped away from the top of the Superplex. He stared at the silver-haired woman who was sitting across from him and felt a strange sense of enjoyment course through his chest. He smiled. "Long time no see."

"Where's..." Ashley's lips hardly moved as her question trailed off after one word.

"Steller?" Horn finished it for her, then answered. "He's back at the Superplex. I don't think he wanted to miss the end of the game."

"He's dead," Hoke interjected, surprising Horn.

Ashley turned her head toward Hoke, who had slumped in the seat next to her, his head bouncing as the helicopter flew through the turbulence. "Dead?" she repeated more than asked. Her expression of shock heightened momentarily, then seemed to melt away as though she'd suddenly resigned herself to the situation.

"Dead," Hoke repeated.

"Now that we've established that fact," Horn said, "tell your pilot to head for where you've got the woman stashed."

"I don t need to tell him," Ashley answered, pulling her hand from beneath a fold in her coat. "That's where we were going anyway."

Horn looked down at her hand, which was holding a slim plastic device no bigger than a package of cigarettes. Two stainless-steel needles stuck out of a slot in the end of the smooth black case, which he recognized as a Mini-Mark Electroweapon. The little hand-held stun gun was capable of administering a lethal jolt of electricity, and Horn knew he was well within the thirty-foot range of its thin wired probes. He tried to see what the shock level setting read, but Ashley's gloved hand covered the controls.

"You've got some problems, Ashley," Horn said calmly, wondering with a strange curiosity how his mods would react if she hit them with the weapon. "Frankly, I don't know if you've got any real solutions, either."

"You two know each other?" Hoke asked, once again surprising Horn by interrupting.

"He's one of your problems." Horn ignored Hoke's question but nodded toward the disheveled engineer, who was trying to comb his thin strands of hair back across his bald spot with the tips of his fingers.

"We know about Mr. Hoke's underestimation of the revenue from the operation," Ashley said. "Why do you think I had Steller turn into his shadow?"

"I'm not talking about something as mundane as him embezzling stolen money right out from under your nose," Horn said, almost enjoying the conversation. He figured he would have been enjoying it except for the primed set of shock points aimed at his stomach. "Weren't you aware of his liaison with the Colombians?"

Ashley looked over at Hoke for a few seconds. "What the hell are you talking about?" she asked, turning back toward Horn.

"Who do you think locked the place down? Mr. Hoke here cut a deal with Ruben Zamora to sabotage the security system so they could hostage out—"

"He's lying," Hoke broke in, his voice nervous and high-pitched. "There was a malfunction in the system, nothing more."

"So that's what the panic was all about," Ashley said to herself.

"Instead of him cheating you out of fifteen or twenty percent of your revenue," Horn said, ignoring Hoke completely, "he was going for broke. Like they say, 'take an inch, take a yard, take it all.'"

"I'm telling you, the son of a bitch is lying!" Hoke's voice squeaked with a desperate blend of anger and fear.

Horn held his palms up, and turned toward Hoke. "She'll find out soon enough when the accounts you were supposed to funnel the cash into ring up empty."

Hoke appeared on the verge of saying something, but he clamped his mouth shut and slumped back in the seat.

"You're my immediate problem," Ashley said, addressing Horn. "You, as well as the woman, have become excess baggage. As long as I've got Mr. Hoke's body, I've got the electrocash."

Horn felt the helicopter descending and glanced out the window. He recognized Eaton's Neck Point and figured they were going to land somewhere on Long Island. As he turned back to face Ashley, Horn automatically squeezed his left arm against the bulk of the 9 mm beneath the coat and wondered if he would get a chance to use it.

The aircraft bounced several times as it touched down, spinning half around before it came to a stop. Horn heard switches being flipped in the cockpit and the engine went into its shutdown mode. He half turned toward the door but froze as Ashley spoke. "Not so fast," she said before turning her head toward the flight deck and yelling out, "Williamson, get back here right away!"

Almost immediately a baldheaded man wearing a blue flight suit and yellow aviators stepped through the small opening that led to the cockpit. "What is it?" he asked.

"Both these men need an armed escort into the house," Ashley said, holding up the Mini-Mark.

Williamson glanced at the weapon, which was still trained on Horn, and pulled an ugly snub-nosed revolver from a shoulder holster hanging under his left arm. Horn heard the hammer cock as the pilot said, "My pleasure, Ms. Fine."

Ashley led the mismatched entourage across a small compound to a large house set on the edge of what Horn figured was Smithtown Bay. It almost had to be since they'd landed shortly after crossing Eaton's Neck. Horn could see waves breaking on Long Island Sound, their whitecaps dancing wildly in the strange winter light.

Horn figured they were expected, for a large man carrying a 9 mm automatic, not unlike his own, opened a set of carved wooden doors that served as the main entrance to the shake-shingled house. Williamson ushered them in and the doorman, who was built like a prizefighter, shut the door.

"Bring them to the great room," Ashley said, dropping her coat on a bench in the entryway. Horn and the rest of the group followed her up a short flight of steps into a huge carpeted area with a high-beamed ceiling and a round freestanding fireplace in its center. An entire wall consisted of floor-to-ceiling windows that looked out across Long Island Sound. The rich brown carpet accented the red leather furniture scattered about the room, giving the place the air of a country club. A small bar was built into one wall, which was covered with paintings of sailing ships and seascapes.

"Where's the woman?" Horn asked, turning to Ashley, who walked behind the bar. He noticed she still carried the Mini-Mark and watched her place it on the marble top of the bar before pouring herself two fingers of amber liquid from a cut-glass decanter.

"Mr. Stanton, get the woman," Ashley said to the man who had met them at the door. Then she downed the liquor in a single swallow.

Horn watched the hulking form of Stanton disappear down a wide hallway before he walked slowly to the bar. Ashley immediately dropped her hand to the shock weapon. "Take it easy," he said, holding up his hands. "I want conversation, not trouble."

"Set the brainchild down," Ashley said over Horn's shoulder.

Horn turned and watched Williamson motion for Hoke to take a seat in an armchair next to the fireplace. Horn turned back to Ashley. "Let Sarah go. She's not a part of this."

"You two are going to be buried together," Ashley said coldly, her eyes drilling into Horn. "Payback's a bastard, isn't it, Detective?"

"What the—?"

Horn turned toward the sound of Hoke's voice and watched as Sarah walked into the room, followed by Stanton. He wondered how many more bodyguards were in the house.

Hoke let his arms drop over the sides of the chair as he stared at Sarah. "What the hell are you doing here?"

Horn watched Sarah turn toward him and noticed she looked scared, but otherwise okay. He turned back toward Ashley and said, "Can't you shut him up?"

Ashley stared at Horn for several seconds with an almost puzzled expression on her face. "I just told you I'm going to bury you with your girlfriend and you're worried about the tone of his voice?" Ashley nodded in Hoke's direction.

Horn shrugged and Ashley laughed. "This man's got a gun, Mr. Stanton." She again spoke over his shoulder, the humor draining from her voice as quickly as it had come. "It might be a good idea if you took it."

Stanton pointed his automatic at Horn's head and lumbered toward him with all the grace of a stalking rhino.

"Just go ahead and shoot the son of a bitch." Hoke tilted his head back and yelled the death message toward the ceiling.

"Shut the fuck up," Stanton said, slapping the side of the 9 mm against Hoke's head. He walked up to Horn and jammed the barrel of the weapon into the center of his chest. "Gimme the piece," he ordered.

Horn pulled open the coat, exposing his weapon. Stanton reached in cautiously and extracted it, then backed away cautiously. Horn watched the big man place the weapon on the edge of the fireplace.

"Wait a minute," Ashley said as Stanton started to move away. She motioned him over to the bar. "We need to dispose of Detective Horn here, and his girlfriend, soon. Any suggestions?"

Horn figured Ashley might as well have been asking Stanton if he knew where to get her car washed instead of how to execute a double murder. Her eyes looked like balls of ice, cold and unforgiving.

"Yeah, I've got an idea," Stanton said, resting his gun hand on the bar, keeping the barrel of the automatic pointed at Horn's chest. "All we have to do is have Williamson fly them out over the Sound and let them out." Wilson smiled and Horn watched the light glint off several gold teeth.

Ashley nodded slowly as she poured more of the liquor in the glass. "That should work," she said.

Horn knew she was serious and figured he'd better make his move soon. He took a sidestep toward the end of the bar where Stanton was standing. ''That's not so hot an idea,'' Horn said, wondering what he was going to do next. He felt his mods tense strangely, as though they knew something was getting ready to come down. The clean sensation of adrenaline washed through his body causing him to feel light-headed, nearly giddy.

''Just stay the hell where you are,'' Stanton said, his eyes focusing on Horn's face.

Horn wasn't aware of having made a decision, but suddenly his right arm was moving up and sweeping across the surface of the bar. He was startled for a split second, for he hadn't willed his mod to move. At least he didn't think he had. The blur of his forearm struck the heavy decanter in front of Ashley so hard that it shot down the length of the bar as though it had been fired from a gun. The glass projectile slammed into the end of Stanton's 9 mm, then bounced into his chest, knocking him backward several steps.

''You son of a bitch!'' Stanton screamed and grunted simultaneously as he tried to recover the automatic into a firing position.

Horn moved toward Stanton as though he were on a rail. On the way he took a swipe at Ashley, knocking her backward against the wall. She screamed loudly. He saw the deadly Mini-Mark shoot across the carpeted floor like a bug. A loud pop erupted behind him and a glass mirror behind the bar shattered. Horn knew Williamson had been aiming for his back and shuddered as he swung his hand down on Stanton's wrist, knocking the 9 mm to the floor.

''Move, Stanton, you jerk! I can't get a clear shot!'' Horn heard Williamson screeching in the background as he wrapped his arm around the big man's head and twisted him violently downward. He screwed Stanton's barrel chest in the direction of Williamson just as the pilot's snub-nose barked again. The thumb-sized chunk of lead tracked across the room and slammed into Stanton's heaving stomach like a hot spike. The man screamed at the top of his lungs as blood gurgled through the bullet hole in his gut.

Williamson fired again, this time hitting Horn's human shield in the head, splattering blood and pieces of sticky brain tissue across his shoulder and against the wall behind them. Horn ducked quickly and latched on to Stanton's 9 mm. He brought it up around the limp form draped across his arm and fired five quick times before the weapon jammed open, its slide hanging behind the automatic as smoke floated from the exposed chamber. He watched Williamson stagger backward, one hand on his neck, which was spurting blood like a fountain. The pilot hit the back of an overstuffed couch near the windows and flipped over it, his booted feet following his body in a wild arc.

Horn dropped Stanton's heavy form and rose shakily. He heard, "Your turn, cop." Horn turned his head to the left, and he stared at the probe end of the Mini-Mark, which was aimed straight at his chest. Instinctively Horn drew his right arm across his upper body and stepped back straight into Ashley, who was struggling to her feet. He quickly grabbed her by the arm and jerked her in front of him, wrapping his modified arm around her neck in a sloppy half nelson.

"Shoot!" Ashley yelled, kicking her spike-heeled boots back into Horn's shins.

Horn felt her long nails dig into the side of his face as he watched Hoke move toward them, doing a stuttering little dance in an attempt to get a clear shot. He was holding the flat pack of the shock weapon out in front of his hunkering form like a flashlight.

"Shoot, goddammit!" Ashley frantically screamed and twisted her body to one side.

Horn's mind went into slow motion as he watched the Mini-Mark jump in Hoke's hand. The silver forked probes lunged toward him, trailing two hair-thin strands of wire like miniature versions of the old wire-guided missiles. He saw Hoke's eyes grow wide and his left arm rise slowly into the air as he stopped his maneuvering dance. The world suddenly snapped back into real time as a blinding blue-white light exploded in Horn's head. He felt the needle-like probes embed themselves in his side, sending almost eleven milliamps coursing through his body like a bolt of lightning. His right knee kicked up involuntarily, raising Ashley's body up and back slightly. At the same instant, his right arm went south, glitching down with such force that Horn thought it would rip itself from his shoulder. He heard Ashley's neck break like a dry twig.

The probes jerked out of his ribs as Ashley's lifeless body fell out of his grasp and across the death wires. He dropped to his side, shaking uncontrollably as his mods ran amok, their electromechanical linkages squealing like pigs in a slaughterhouse.

The effect subsided in less than five seconds, but Horn had lost track of time. He felt as though he'd just been swung by his spine on a joyride through hell's worst back-street.

The rocking sound of a single gunshot brought Horn the rest of the way out of his shocked stupor, and he looked up just in time to see the front of Hoke's chest explode out-ward, spraying pieces of his body across the room like shrapnel. A dazed, almost surprised expression passed across Hoke's face as he fell forward stiffly. Behind him stood Sarah, holding Horn's 9 mm in both hands.

Horn pulled himself up just as Sarah collapsed to the floor, her eyelids fluttering crazily. He walked over and pulled the automatic from her sweat-slick hands, uncocking the hammer before sliding it under his arm. Bending down, Horn picked her up and took her over to the leather couch. He placed her on the cushions, then peeled off his left glove, pressing his index and middle fingers against her neck.

Her pulse seemed okay. Horn figured she'd just fainted. He straightened, walked over to the windows and stared out at the stormy, wind-whipped Sound. Weird flashes of lightning danced through the blowing snow.

Horn didn't know how long he gazed into the storm before his focus shifted to the room's reflection in the glass and the carnage that was spread across the brown carpet. Something was wrong with the entire scene and Horn realized with mild shock what it was. The blood, the death...they were nothing. He felt nothing. He looked down at his E-mod and flexed its grip slowly, the feedback running through his spine, telling his brain that the machine was on-line, charged with an energy that was light-years beyond flesh and bone. A shudder ran up the back of his neck, and he felt a sweeping white light flash through him.

What he'd done that day hadn't been for himself. He thought of the two hundred thousand whose lives had been spared. But he was free of the past himself. He'd paid all his debts.

DON PENDLETON's
MACK BOLAN.

SIEGE

One by one, Japanese-held businesses in the U.S. are being
destroyed, leaving innocent people dead and compromising a
sensitive CIA-Justice Department investigation in Tokyo.

The enemy has the ultimate weapons—power and money—and the
bloody trail of greed and murder leads Mack Bolan to a conspiracy
that could crumble America's financial structure.

ABLE TEAM® DICK STIVERS

Check out the action in two ABLE TEAM books you won't find in stores anywhere!

Don't miss out on these two riveting adventures of ABLE TEAM, the relentless three-man power squad:

DEATH HUNT—Able Team #50 $2.95 ☐
The lives of 20 million people are at stake as Able Team plays hide-and-seek with a warped games master.

SKINWALKER—Able Team #51 $2.95 ☐
A legendary Alaskan werewolf has an appetite for local Eskimos fighting a proposed offshore drilling operation.

Total Amount	$ _____
Plus 75¢ Postage	.75
Payment enclosed	$ _____

Please send a check or money order payable to Gold Eagle Books.

In the U.S.	In Canada
901 Fuhrmann Blvd.	P.O. Box 609
P.O. Box 1325	Fort Erie, Ontario
Buffalo, NY 14269-1325	L2A 5X3

Please Print

Name: _____

Address: _____

City: _____

State/Province: _____

Zip/Postal Code: _____

GOLD EAGLE®

ATD-1

PHOENIX FORCE

Don't miss the action in two PHOENIX FORCE books you won't find in stores anywhere!

Check out these two high-voltage PHOENIX FORCE adventures:

SALVADOR ASSAULT—Phoenix Force #49	$2.95 ☐
Phoenix Force put their lives on the line as they fight for peace in El Salvador.	
EXTREME PREJUDICE—Phoenix Force #50	$2.95 ☐
The streets of Marseilles become a battleground as Phoenix Force uncover a sinister KGB conspiracy.	

Total Amount	$ _____
Plus 75¢ Postage	.75
Payment Enclosed	$ _____

Please Print
Name: _____
Address: _____
City: _____
State/Province: _____
Zip/Postal Code: _____

GOLD EAGLE ®

PFD-1